MEN
in
UNIFORM

Courteous, courageous and commanding—
these heroes lay it all on the line for the
people they love in more than fifty stories about
loyalty, bravery and romance.
Don't miss a single one!

AVAILABLE FEBRUARY 2010
A Vow to Love by Sherryl Woods
Serious Risks by Rachel Lee
Who Do You Love? by Maggie Shayne and Marilyn Pappano
Dear Maggie by Brenda Novak
A Randall Returns by Judy Christenberry
Informed Risk by Robyn Carr
Five-Alarm Affair by Marie Ferrarella

AVAILABLE MARCH 2010
The Man from Texas by Rebecca York
Mistaken Identity by Merline Lovelace
Bad Moon Rising by Kathleen Eagle
Moriah's Mutiny by Elizabeth Bevarly
Have Gown, Need Groom by Rita Herron
Heart of the Tiger by Lindsay McKenna

AVAILABLE APRIL 2010
Landry's Law by Kelsey Roberts
Love at First Sight by B.J. Daniels
The Sheriff of Shelter Valley by Tara Taylor Quinn
A Match for Celia by Gina Wilkins
That's Our Baby! by Pamela Browning
Baby, Our Baby! by Patricia Thayer

MEN
in
UNIFORM

USA TODAY Bestselling Author

LINDSAY McKENNA

HEART OF THE TIGER

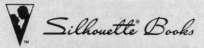

Silhouette Books

Published by Silhouette Books
America's Publisher of Contemporary Romance

 SILHOUETTE BOOKS

Recycling programs
for this product may
not exist in your area.

ISBN-13: 978-0-373-36259-2

HEART OF THE TIGER

Copyright © 1988 by Lindsay McKenna

This edition published by arrangement with Harlequin Books S.A.

For questions and comments about the quality of this book please contact us
at Customer_eCare@Harlequin.ca.

® and TM are trademarks of Harlequin Books S.A., used under license.
Trademarks indicated with ® are registered in the United States Patent
and Trademark Office, the Canadian Trade Marks Office and in other
countries.

Visit Silhouette Books at www.eHarlequin.com

Printed in U.S.A.

LINDSAY McKENNA

Living in twenty-two places across seven states during the first eighteen years of her life provided Lindsay McKenna with a backdrop for her fictional writing. A U.S. Navy veteran, she was a meteorologist while serving her country.

Currently, as a homeopath, she writes books that introduce people to alternative medicine. When she was nine, her father introduced her to healing concepts that she utilizes to this day. Coming from an Eastern Cherokee heritage, she likes to write about Native Ameri-cans and introduce people to life as she lives it. Continuing to capture the beauty of our earth, Lindsay is an amateur photographer and can always be found hiking in nature, recording our natural world. She can be reached at www.lindsaymckenna.com or www.medicinegarden.com. As always, she loves to hear from her readers at docbones@gotsky.com.

Chapter 1

Layne Hamilton felt the man's presence even before she saw him. Up at the lecture podium, she leafed slowly through her text on Cantonese Chinese, casting a prudent glance in his direction. Her unruly black hair tumbled across her shoulders as she leaned over, pretending to hunt for something in her notes.

He was older than everyone else, although he didn't appear to be over thirty. Perhaps it was his piercing blue gaze or his resemblance to a lean, hungry wolf that made him stand out from the other students. His tanned, square face was unreadable as he lounged with deceptive ease at the rear of the room. His broad brow topped wide-set eyes, a straight nose and a firm chin. Only his mouth suggested leniency, the corners turning upward instead of down. Layne's fingers trembled perceptibly as she thumbed through her lecture. It fit. It all fit. He was one of *them*: a CIA agent.

Layne felt her heart tighten in her breast. Compressing her lips, she tried to put a lid on the cauldron of escaping memories. When she raised her head, she narrowed her eyes as she looked at him again. He was a Company man just as Brad had been. They never referred to themselves as agents, operatives or the CIA. No, within that elite group they called themselves the Company.

She stared at the intruder in her class. He didn't fool her. Coiled power emanated from the dark-haired stranger, and Layne found her throat closing with tears, her vision suddenly blurring. Oh, damn! She couldn't cry! Not here. This was her first class of the fall quarter. Anger suddenly swept through her, drying the impending tears. Damn him! Damn them all! She had told Chuck

Lowell she never wanted to see or speak to anyone from the Company again. And now one of his men was watching her from the back of the room, a curious flame burning in the recesses of his steel-blue eyes. What did he want from her? She was simply a widow of a Company employee who had died in the line of duty—nothing more.

"Well?" Chuck Lowell demanded, leaning in his rich, burgundy leather chair. "What do you think, Matt? Is she up to this assignment?" He steepled his fingers, watching Talbot closely.

Matt placed his hands on his hips, a giveaway of his Air Force training. "No," he replied, adding to himself, *but she's unforgettable.* His mind returned to his observation of Layne Hamilton earlier that day. He had tipped his head back against the wall, listening to her low, cultured voice. Nice, he'd thought as he studied her. But there was nothing to suggest she could possibly handle the assignment. She was attractive, yes. But was she a survivor?

Her voice had been soothing, pacifying his raw nerves. *Like warm, liquid honey.* The black hair framing her tanned complexion accented her luminous eyes and full mouth. Matt had found himself staring at her, surprised at his strong response. He had to admit that Layne Hamilton was indeed a woman of substance: a dangerous mixture of femininity, vulnerability and elegance nicely rolled into one very appealing package.

He'd had to mentally switch gears in order to recall his real purpose for being there. According to the data he'd been given, Layne had been widowed nine months ago. He could still see the ravages of that period. She was thin, as seen in the too-hollow curve beneath her lovely high cheekbones. And her clothes were loose on her five-foot-eight-inch frame. The khaki-colored Kathryn Hepburn-style trousers bagged slightly at her slender hips.

Looks were often deceiving; he knew that from many years of experience. But if this was one of the top Chinese language experts in the country, Layne Hamilton could have fooled everyone. She had been associated with George Washington University since her marriage to Brad Carson, and in spite of two prestigious scholarly books to her credit, she didn't look at all like a professor.

Matt could see her as a model for one of those women's fashion magazines…or maybe as the gracious wife of a career diplomat. Her throat was deliciously curved, and his eyes had followed the thoroughbred lines of her graceful body. She might have been a ballerina. But not a full professor at a university.

His mouth thinned. He couldn't see her as a combatant by any stretch of his imagination. And action was vital on this mission— including lightning reflexes that could mean life or death. He'd known when he received the shattering news at Nellis Air Force Base, where he was stationed, that it was going to be bad. And now it had turned from bad to worse. The vulnerable woman up at the lectern couldn't fight her way out of a paper bag, much less handle a mission involving—enough! Matt refused to think about the crisis or about his brother. He'd just do as he'd been ordered: check out Layne Hamilton to see if she could do what was needed.

"Are you sure?" Chuck now demanded, breaking into his reverie.

Matt looked his superior squarely in the eye. "Positive. She's a rabbit. And we're going into a wolf situation."

Lowell frowned, then returned his gaze. "Rabbit or not, she's got contacts we don't have. Look, go back and study her once more before you make your final decision. I'm afraid Layne Hamilton is the only person who can help us at this point."

"Well, how was the first day?" Millie Hamilton sang out as Layne stepped from the foyer into her mother's living room.

Layne tried to smile but it didn't work. She dropped her books on the coffee table and set her briefcase down beside the sofa.

"It was horrible," she admitted, sitting down dejectedly.

Millie stood poised at the kitchen door. At fifty-nine she looked ten years younger, her short crop of black hair barely sprinkled with gray. But now her brow creased with concern. "What happened?" she asked gently.

Layne nudged off her low-heeled sandals and propped her feet up on the table. She gave her mother a helpless look. "There was someone from the Company there, Mom."

"Oh, honey, are you sure?"

A tidal wave of suppressed emotion surfaced in Layne at last, and her voice broke. "I'm positive. He was wearing a jacket. You don't wear a jacket on a ninety-degree day unless you're wearing a gun at the back of your belt. And his look…" She shivered, shutting her eyes tightly. Hot tears scalded her lids, and she took a deep breath to try to steady herself. "He just looks like one of them, Mom—restless, piercing eyes, lean strength—giving the impression that if he moved, he'd explode like a bomb."

Millie came over to sit next to Layne and stroked her hair. "I believe you, honey. But why? After Brad died…"

Layne rose, unable to sit still an instant longer. She paced the length of a living room filled with Oriental memorabilia— memories of her family's past, of her growing-up years as an Air Force brat, of a famous father stationed in the Orient. Layne stared at the photo on the mantel of her father with his arm around her mother and herself. Bob Hamilton: Air Force test pilot extraordinaire, made of the Right Stuff. He had tamed the most sophisticated supersonic jets in the world until one had finally claimed his life five years earlier. Both of the men in her life had been snuffed out by metal. The exotic skin of an aircraft buckling under testing stresses had claimed her father's life; and Brad had been ripped away from her by an enemy bullet, unexpectedly freeing her from the prison of their marriage. She took a deep, ragged breath, fighting a threatening wave of tears and guilt.

Layne sensed more than saw her mother rise and move to her side to place a gentle hand on her shoulder. "Perhaps it was a mistake," she soothed. "Perhaps this man just looked like an agent. It's probably nothing, Layne. Why would they send someone from the Company to sit in on your class? You know Chuck Lowell would come over if they wanted something."

Layne raised her face, her amber eyes misty. "That's right. Their rule is 'Never use the telephone, it might be bugged.

Always try for face-to-face contact.'" Her head felt heavy. "God, Mom, I can still hear Brad saying that," she whispered.

"I know, sweetheart, I know…"

Taking a steadying breath, Layne muttered, "I just hope you're right, Mom. I'm still not over Brad or the CIA. Why doesn't it fade with time?"

Millie squeezed her shoulder. "It will, honey. First, you have to let go of all that bottled-up anger you had toward Brad. No one could have known how cruel and insensitive he would turn out to be. You need to let go of the guilt, Layne. It's eating you alive."

"I hate the CIA," she whispered rawly.

Millie gave her a small shake. "The way Brad turned out is not the CIA's fault, Layne."

Layne looked up in disbelief. "Since when are you siding with them? Brad was ruthless because of the CIA!"

"No."

After all this time her mother was defending the Company? Layne stared at her. "I suppose you're an authority on them?" She hated the surly tone of her voice but felt powerless to stop.

"Listen to me carefully, Layne," Millie replied in a low voice. "I've kept out of your handling of Brad's death. I felt that you would eventually understand that the CIA had nothing to do with Brad's behavior toward you. They don't mold men and women into coldhearted robots! They're anxious to see that their employees' families understand the rigors and pressures of their work. They don't condone or even encourage Brad's type of behavior."

Defiance rose in Layne. "Oh, really? And how do you know?"

Millie released her arm. "Common sense tells me that. Brad was like a bad apple, Layne, rotten at the core. And no one knew it until it was too late. Place the blame where it rightfully belongs, work through your anger and hurt," she counseled. "And then let it go, and get on with the business of living."

Layne's heart sank when she entered her classroom Wednesday morning. He was there again. And he was in the same seat, with the same imperturbable look on his face. She felt beads of sweat begin to form, and claustrophobia enveloped her. Her hands trembled visibly as she jerked open the attendance roster on the lectern. For the past two nights she had experienced reawakened memories of the nightmare of her marriage. Now anger broke through her haze of fear. She hated the man in the back—hated him for what he'd slit open in her just-healing heart. And she'd been surprised at her mother's defense of the CIA. Everyone from the Company was cold. It was natural and expected for them to show nothing outwardly, not even love toward family members.

As she completed roll call her fears were realized: the man in the back wasn't on the roster. Lifting her chin, she aimed a cool look at him.

"You're not on the roster here, Mr.—"

Glacial blue eyes assessed her own, but she maintained her ground, refusing to be intimidated by a Company man. Layne wanted to force his hand. Slowly, the man's mouth curved up in amusement. "I'm auditing the course, Professor Hamilton," he drawled.

She felt heat rise within her. Like hell you are—she bit back the words. No one was allowed to audit introductory Chinese without registering; it was a university rule. The tension strung palpably between them. Layne gripped the edges of the lectern, her knuckles whitening. "Your name." It was an order, not a question.

"Jim Ryder."

Liar. She knew he wouldn't tell his real name even under threat of death. She glared at him, on the verge of saying just that. But there was some indefinable warning in his features that told her to back off for now. It wasn't anything specific. Just the tension around his eyes. She wrote the name down, giving him a dark look.

"Your audit papers, then, Mr. Ryder?"

"I'll bring them next time I come to class."

Layne controlled her desire to explode at him. They were simply playing a game, and they were both aware of it. She shut the roster book with finality. "Don't bother coming back on Friday if you don't have them with you, Mr. Ryder."

Matt barely tipped his head in recognition of her order and let the amusement show in his eyes. So, she did have claws. Backed into a corner, she came out hissing and spitting. Maybe Layne Hamilton wasn't going to be a rabbit after all.

Layne controlled her rage as she watched Jim Ryder soundlessly rise to his feet and leave five minutes before the end of class. Had he known she was going to openly confront him afterward? He must have. She watched him disappear like a ghost who had come out of her past to haunt her once again.

Back in her Georgetown apartment at the end of the day, Layne tried to keep busy. She had lesson plans that needed to be filled out, but she found herself unable to concentrate. As she sat at the oak desk in one corner of her living room, her head resting wearily on the palm of her hand, the doorbell rang. She roused herself, frowning. Looking at her watch, she saw that it was nearly ten o'clock. Who could it be? Her mother had been over earlier to share dinner. Getting to her feet, she smoothed out the folds of her soft peach skirt. She crossed to the door and opened it.

"May I come in?"

Layne stood frozen, a succession of emotions racing through her. Chuck Lowell, dressed in his usual impeccably tailored dark pinstripe suit with matching silk tie, offered her an apologetic smile. He looks just the same, she observed numbly. Layne would never forget the day Lowell had come to tell her about Brad's death, Brad's giving his life for their country…. She should have felt remorse. Perhaps grief. Instead, she'd dealt with an avalanche of guilt.

"Layne?"

She winced. "Come in," she offered woodenly.

Lowell inclined his graying head toward someone standing slightly behind him. "I've brought someone with me, Layne."

She gasped as the man who called himself Jim Ryder materialized at Lowell's left shoulder. "You!"

"May we come in?" Chuck demanded tersely.

Layne's throat tightened, and she glared at Lowell's companion. "Do I have a choice?"

Chuck Lowell gave her an odd look but said nothing. They entered the apartment silently, Lowell walking easily, taking a chair in the tastefully arranged living room. Pale blue walls accented the delicate Oriental furniture. Lowell studied Layne gravely as she moved stiffly into the room after him.

"Sit down, Layne. We've got some very important items to discuss with you."

She swung her gaze angrily to meet his. "There's *nothing* you have to discuss with me, Chuck. I told you I never wanted to see anyone from the Company again." She shifted her look to Ryder. "And you—"

"The name is Matt Talbot."

She was momentarily taken aback by the warmth in his low, mellow voice. What breed of Company man was this? Suddenly exhaustion overcame her, and she swayed. He was there instantly, his hand on her arm. She jerked out of his grasp, her flesh tingling where his fingers had rested with a firm but gentle touch.

"I'm all right," she said sharply.

His blue eyes appraised her coolly. "You're pale. Sit down, and I'll fix you something to drink."

Layne stared up at him, at the hard, unyielding planes of his face. Yet his tone was caring, and she capitulated, no longer wanting to fight. Sitting down, she buried her face in her hands, fighting the tears welling up beneath her eyelids.

Lowell's voice broke in. "I'm sorry, Layne. I know this comes as a shock. But we haven't much time and we need your help."

Her head snapped up. "My help?"

Talbot walked over, handing her a glass. She eyed the contents warily, then looked up at him.

"It's your own Scotch, on the rocks. You looked like you could use a stiff one."

"I was just wondering if it was poisoned," she said coldly.

A slight grin pulled at Talbot's sensual mouth. "We're on your side."

She frowned. "I'm not so sure about that," she countered

tersely, but she took a fortifying gulp of the drink, gripping the glass with both hands.

Talbot moved with easy grace to sit facing her on the opposite couch. Almost reluctantly, Layne shifted her attention back to Lowell. "Why are you here?"

"We've just had an international incident, Layne."

She took another gulp. "So? I'm just an ordinary American citizen. Do you usually go around asking lowly civilians for help on the international intrigue front?" God, she sounded childish. But she couldn't help it. The beaded coolness of the glass felt good against her fingertips, and Layne concentrated on that instead of on Chuck's narrow face.

"Look, I know you're still grieving for Brad. And we have no business coming to you, Layne. But the incident I refer to needs someone of your qualifications."

She gave him a round-eyed look. "Specifically *what* in my background qualifies me for this cloak-and-dagger game?"

"You know Chinese. You were born in Japan and raised in the Far East while your father served at the Air Force bases over there."

"So? I know you have intelligence people expert in Chinese. Let's see, if I remember the 'spouse training' that the Company so generously supplied me with, you have both division offices and stations or bases for your clandestine affairs. Surely your penetration agents or specialists can get you out of whatever quandary you're in without my help?"

Chuck held up both hands. "You're also highly knowledgeable about the South China Sea area."

"So are your operatives."

Matt leaned back, assessing Layne's role in the tense exchange. Her honey-brown eyes had darkened in anger. He mentally reviewed what he remembered of her personnel file and life history. In brief, she was a woman whose sensitivity was balanced by keen intelligence. Chuck Lowell would have to be a magician to get her to agree to his plan, Matt realized. In fact, right now he'd put money on the Hamilton woman to win. His eyes narrowed slightly. Why was she so angry with the

Company? And with Lowell? He watched his boss struggle to maintain an air of neutrality beneath her scathing attack. No, she certainly wasn't the rabbit he'd thought her to be. A slight smile tipped one corner of his mouth.

"Believe me, Layne," Chuck was saying with fervor, "if we had any choice at all in this matter, we'd go with an operative. It's not our policy to recruit people off the street to help us get out of a jam."

Layne shot him a dubious look. "Then what was this man doing in my class? That was an ugly calling card, Chuck. The worst."

Lowell remained low-key despite the strain in her voice. "I sent Matt over because he wanted to see if you were up to the rigors of this forthcoming mission."

Layne took another hefty gulp of the drink, then directed her gaze at Talbot. Her lips parted as she saw the tenderness burning in his blue eyes as he met her glare. Why? she wondered, finding her resistance melting. Her eyes filled with hot, scalding tears, blurring Talbot's face.

Matt eased himself from the chair, sending Lowell a sharp look. "We've upset Mrs. Hamilton enough, Chuck. I don't feel she can do it. Why not leave her with what little peace she has left?"

Layne's heart wrenched, and she lifted her chin, staring directly into those azure eyes that seemed to understand her. Careful, she told herself. He's an agent, a robot taught to act and react, both on and off the job, showing no humanity or compassion. Swallowing tears, she choked out, "He's right, Chuck. Why don't you just leave? I've told you, I want nothing to do with you or your people ever again."

Lowell shot Talbot a glance, then rose. "All right," he said stiffly. "We didn't mean to upset you, Layne. I know it's been rough on you…"

She bowed her head. "Just leave, Chuck."

"I'll drop over and see if you're feeling differently tomorrow."

"Don't bother," she murmured, not looking up as the door quietly opened and closed. Layne stared numbly at her drink:

most of it was gone. Oh, well, she thought. Might as well kill the pain with the rest of it. She lifted the glass to her lips.

"Take it slow," came Talbot's husky voice. "That was a double."

Layne gasped, nearly dropping the glass. He stood by the door, watching her in the explosively charged silence. With a swift stride, he reached her, and his long, slender fingers closed around the drink in her hand. As their fingers met, Layne released the glass instantly, as if burned.

"I told you to leave!"

Talbot gave her a distant smile and set the glass down on the black lacquered coffee table. "You asked Chuck to leave, not me. Besides, I didn't feel you should be left alone just yet."

Layne stared up at him in disbelief, startled by the tenderness in his voice and eyes, as unmistakable as it was unexpected. Layne could have dealt with anger or even coldness, but not this kindness. Company men weren't supposed to show their emotions—ever. She felt warm tears begin to trickle down her cheeks.

Matt crouched down, his hands moving to caress Layne's raven hair. It felt like thick silk beneath his fingers. As he framed her pale face, he was struck by the pain in her luminous golden eyes. He had thought he was carrying enough of his own anguish around, but now… His brows drew into a slight frown.

She was pale beneath her tan; her skin pulled tautly across her cheekbones. And her lips…he groaned inwardly. Her full mouth could curve into a sunlit smile or tighten as it did now, with agony. Tears slid down to her soft lips, and she licked them away.

Matt opened his arms to her, drawing her forward until she rested against him. "Go ahead," he whispered thickly against her hair. "Cry. Get it out of your system."

The shock of seeing Chuck Lowell again had dredged up the shattered past Layne had tried desperately to forget. The instant Matt's hands had framed her face, she'd begun to cry. His touch was so male and yet so gentle, and his firm, strong body supporting her brought forth deep, wrenching sobs—sobs she'd suppressed for months. But the arms now cradling her against him had released her from her self-made prison of pain.

Matt closed his eyes, resting his head against her ebony hair. He inhaled deeply. She smelled good—like lilac—her body warm and yielding against his hard frame. He murmured endearments to ease her heart, feeling her tremble within his arms. Layne Hamilton was a woman of great sensitivity, he thought as he stroked her hair, burying his face in the fragrant mass and longing...longing...

Layne became aware of the deep, steady beat of Matt's heart in his taut chest. She gripped his shirtfront, her nails digging into it as her tears dampened the material to a darker shade of burgundy. His male scent was a heady aphrodisiac, awakening her dormant senses. He was, she realized, an intensely sensual man. She buried her head deeper in the hollow between his shoulder and chin as each stroke of his hand upon her hair released a little more of the old hurt from the five years of Brad's deception.

Another feeling was woven into the remnants of her grief: Matt Talbot cared. She could almost feel an imperceptible trembling of his long, expressive fingers as they grazed the crown of her head. He was still a stranger—one whose appearance had reminded her of five years she'd fought to forget. Yet he had remained behind, somehow realizing that she needed to be held.

"It's all right, kitten," he whispered huskily, "you're going to be all right now..."

A hunger for more than emotional support spread heatedly through her. The touch of his hands, his intoxicating scent and the hard planes of his body against hers unleashed a raw, aching need for closeness, for intimate contact. Unintentionally Layne nuzzled against his jaw, and she heard him draw in a deep, ragged breath. Then, trapping her face between his callused hands, he carefully lifted her mouth upward.

Matt groaned as he guided Layne's face to meet his descending mouth. God, he shouldn't be doing this! He knew better. But she was so warm and feminine, drawing him out as effortlessly as spring rain drew forth the first shoots from the cold, freezing earth. Her black lashes, thick with tears, were a sharp contrast to her golden skin. Her lips glistened, parting for his as he leaned down...down to claim them.

Layne uttered a small moan of protest as she felt his mouth settle firmly upon hers. But she knew it was hopeless. All common sense fled, and she folded against him as he molded his mouth hotly to her own, building a fire of longing that sent an aching need through her hungry body. Slowly she began to respond to his gentle exploration of her lips with his tongue. His breath was warm and moist against hers, his fingers imprisoning her face, tipping it to meld his mouth completely to her yielding lips.

"Let me taste you," he commanded hoarsely.

With a sigh, Layne acquiesced, her arms lifting, sliding about his broad, capable shoulders and drawing him to her. As her breasts brushed the wall of his chest a slight gasp broke from within her. Matt's tongue coaxed her further, cajoling her into heated participation as he stroked every moist crevice of her mouth.

Gradually Matt made himself draw back. He traced her swollen lips gently with his tongue to soothe any bruises he might have caused. Did she realize how much of an impact she'd had upon him? Her golden eyes were hazy with invitation, and Matt inhaled deeply, trying to get a grip on himself. He eased Layne back onto the chair, and in that heart-stealing moment, she seemed as innocent as a child. She reached her slender fingers up unbelievingly to touch her well-kissed lips.

"I didn't mean to hurt you," Matt said, his rough voice laden with desire. She looked so helpless. He could take her to bed; he knew she would come willingly. His body was screaming deep within for her warmth, her humanity, and he was hungry for her touch. But one look into those golden eyes, now filled with confusion, and he knew: He had to do the right thing for both of them.

"We have an old saying in the Air Force for women like you," he said huskily. A slight smile broke the planes of his lean face. "You're heady stuff, lady. The kind that dreams are woven from."

Chapter 2

Blood raced through Layne's veins, pounding in unison with her heart. Matt was so close, so incredibly virile that she was slightly dizzy. Raising her hand, she touched her brow. Even as she felt him rise away from her, she mourned the loss of contact with him.

"Stay here," he ordered gruffly, moving toward the bathroom.

Layne lay back against the chair, her eyes closed, experiencing a wild gamut of emotions. She didn't realize Matt had returned until she felt him press a cool washcloth against her hot, tearstained face.

"Here…let me do that," she whispered, forcing her eyes to open and taking the cloth from his hand.

Matt rested easily on the back of his heels, watching her in the comfortable silence. "Your mascara ran."

Layne grimaced, pressing the cold, damp cloth against her aching eyes. "I probably look a sight."

"No," he answered softly. "Just the opposite."

Her black hair tumbled across her shoulders and lay against her breasts as she leaned forward, burying her face in the washcloth. She tried to wipe away the mascara that had run from her unexpected tears, then she straightened, looking uncertainly at Matt.

"You didn't have to stay."

A wry smile pulled at one corner of his mouth. "I know."

"Why did you?"

He shrugged. "I'm a sucker for women with tears in their eyes who refuse to cry."

Layne knew he was referring to the meeting with Lowell. "I see...."

"I'm sorry we upset you."

She searched his lean face with penetrating thoroughness, seeking the truth behind his words. Brad had been a consummate liar.

"That would be a first—an operative sorry for his actions." She leaned back, pushing several rebellious strands of hair out of her face. And then Layne realized how harsh her sentence sounded after he'd been so kind to her. "I didn't mean to sound callous. I'm a casualty of the Company's attitude toward spouses. Wives are the last to know, if at all."

Matt rose slowly to his feet, unwinding from his coiled position. "There's some truth in that, I suppose."

Layne sat up, her eyes wide. "I'm sure I appear temperamental, but you don't understand why."

His eyes grew hooded as he looked down at her. "Just because I held you doesn't mean you owe me an explanation."

She felt chilled by his sudden withdrawal. "You might have had something to gain by your display of humanity," she pointed out.

Matt smiled calmly, watching the golden fire of anger igniting within her luminous eyes. "Is that your experience? Did your husband premeditate everything he did, including intimacy with you?"

Layne gasped, crumpling the washcloth in her right hand. "You have no right to information about my personal life!"

Matt suddenly looked weary, exhaustion shadowing his azure eyes. "That's the name of the game, isn't it? You think we all manipulate others in subtle ways, bending people's wills to overcome their resistance. Look, we're both tired. You've had a rough couple of days, and I think a hot bath and some sleep are in order." He ran his fingers through his short, neatly cut hair. What he really wanted to do was reach out, move into her arms and simply be held by her. He was so tired of the loneliness aching inside him.

Layne slowly got to her feet, standing mere inches from him, and tilted her chin upward to meet his shadowed eyes. "I lived with an agent for five years," she began tensely. "He was a master of the very thing you're talking about. I'd like to believe that what you did was out of human need and compassion, but I'm afraid all my conditioning tells me differently."

Matt's mouth pulled into a grimmer line. Carson must have wounded her deeply to make her this distrustful of his own intentions. He wondered how much of her sensitivity had been left intact over the years.

Matt reached out, taking a damp wisp of black hair curling along her cheek and placing it behind her delicate ear. Her skin was soft as a ripe peach. A rose hue stained her cheeks as she met his intense gaze. "I stayed because you needed someone, Layne. Good night."

Layne swallowed hard. There was a lump in her throat and her heart was pounding heavily. How could this man walk into her life and literally turn her world upside down in fifteen minutes' time?

"Wait!"

Matt rested his hand on the doorknob and turned his head slightly toward Layne. She looked almost ethereal, that glorious cloud of black hair surrounding her pale face, her lips parted breathlessly.

Layne slowed to a halt. "You haven't yet earned my trust, Mr. Talbot, but you don't deserve my anger."

"Prove it. Have lunch with me tomorrow."

Her heart gave a sudden thud. "Why bother?" she challenged him. "I already gave Chuck Lowell my answer."

"He didn't know how to handle you."

"And you do?"

"Why not wait until you hear what he wants before you turn him down?"

Her lips tightened. "You're very good at your job, Mr. Talbot. Keep victims off balance so they can't ferret out your real motive."

He offered her a hint of a smile, his azure eyes darkening with an unknown emotion. "It's Major Talbot, Mrs. Hamilton. And I'll pick you up at the university at noon."

Afterward, Layne stood in the foyer in stunned silence. Was he manipulating her, or was her paranoia from the past haunting her? Her mind spun with questions. But what difference did it make? She had sworn never again to get involved in any way with a man who worked for a government agency. So let Major Matt Talbot play his game of intrigue. It wouldn't get him anywhere.

Nervously, Layne gathered her sheaf of papers and put them into her desk drawer. Other teachers milled around, discussing the humidity and high temperatures. The desultory chatter set her on edge even more. She looked at her watch again—for the hundredth time, it seemed. Miserably she sat staring out the window overlooking the university campus. Maybe Matt wouldn't show up. Twice, Layne had almost picked up the phone to tell Chuck Lowell to have his man back off. She touched the collar of her plum-colored silk dress she'd accented with a hot pink sash. She had chosen the colors to strengthen her emotional state.

"Hey, Layne?" Dr. Fred Gerus called. "You have a visitor."

Layne forced herself to remain calm. She had purposely woven her raven mane into a chignon, softening it with wispy tendrils at the temples. Smoothing out the folds of the dress, Layne moved slowly toward the door of the teachers' lounge. Nothing, however, could have prepared her for what awaited her as she rounded the corner.

Matt Talbot was impossibly handsome in uniform, his lean, whipcord body attesting to his peak physical condition. He stood tall and relaxed, hands clasped before him. His azure eyes darkened with pleasure as Layne walked toward him. His blue Air Force uniform boasted a gold major's oak leaf on each broad shoulder. Layne's eyes widened as her gaze traveled downward. On the left side of his uniform were silver pilot's wings and rows of military ribbons attesting to his abilities. He was every inch a warrior, her mind told her. But her heart lurched anyway. He gave her a devastating smile of welcome, barely inclining his head forward.

"Mrs. Hamilton."

She gripped her purse. "Major Talbot." And then in a low, husky voice she whispered, "If, indeed, you are a major in the Air Force."

Matt grinned, confidently settling the officer's cap on his head, its black bill shading his eyes. "I am what I seem, Mrs. Hamilton. Shall we? I have reservations at La Fleur for twelve-fifteen."

Layne walked briskly beside him, wildly aware of his fingers on her elbow as he guided her out of the university. "La Fleur? That's terribly nouveau riche for someone on an officer's pay, Major Talbot."

"A classy place for a classy lady," he murmured, guiding her toward the parking lot.

"Butter wouldn't melt in your mouth, Major."

Matt smiled tentatively, guiding her to a shark-gray Lexus. "I prefer women with silky black hair and beautiful golden eyes," he corrected.

Layne observed him closely as they arrived at his car. Brad had gone through similar motions hundreds of times: carefully inspecting the vehicle before putting the key in the door. After all, a bomb could have been placed inside, ready to explode upon contact when the key entered the lock. Although it was ninety degrees and the hot sun was beating down upon them, Layne shivered.

Finally satisfied, Matt opened the door for her. Layne climbed in without a word, strapping the seat belt across her body. Then Matt slid in, deceptively relaxed.

"Why are you being so complimentary today?" Layne demanded as he guided the purring Lexus into the noontime traffic.

"Why not?"

Layne fumed inwardly. How many times had Brad answered a question with a question? She'd finally realized she wasn't supposed to ask questions at all, although she'd had many during the last four years of their marriage. Now, she gave Matt Talbot a murderous look.

"Because you want something from me, Major Talbot, that's why." And you're too handsome, she added silently, aware of his clean profile as he drove. A slight, inviting smile hovered around his mouth, easing the hard planes of his face.

"Why do you confuse my honesty with wanting something from you?"

Layne frowned and clutched her leather purse more tightly between her hands. "Since when did agents become honest?" she retorted scathingly.

"I'm an officer in the Air Force, Mrs. Hamilton."

"You also work for the Company."

"Sometimes."

"Like now. You're working for them now. This minute."

"Yes."

"And you've got the nerve to ask me why I don't trust your compliments?"

He slid a lazy look in her direction, then returned his attention to the driving. "Did you question your husband's compliments?"

Tears drove into her eyes. She felt as if someone had struck her in the chest with a fist. "That's unfair!"

"Any more unfair than questioning that I might compliment you because I think you're attractive?"

Her nostrils flared with anger as she glared at him. "You're very good at slipping a dagger between someone's ribs, Major Talbot. Did someone teach you to use personal assaults to net the desired response from the other party, or does it just come naturally?"

His eyes turned glacial. "Has anyone ever told you that you're paranoid?"

"It comes with the territory." Layne's knuckles whitened, and she stared straight ahead.

"There's an old axiom that the more paranoid the agent, the better he or she is destined to be—" Matt gave her a keen look "—but it's not recommended behavior for the family of the agent."

"It rubs off," she replied, tight-lipped.

As they walked into the elegant French restaurant located in a popular section of Georgetown, Matt leaned over. His voice was low, vibrating through her. "I owe you an apology. It's been one hell of a rough day, and I shouldn't have taken it out on you. Am I forgiven?"

One look into his eyes and Layne's retort melted. She avoided his searching look. "Let's just call it a draw, shall we?"

Matt laughed softly, guiding her into the darkened foyer of the establishment. "Now you see us as sparring partners in a boxing match."

"Aren't we?" she needled him.

He gave her an amused look, saying nothing.

Layne was not surprised when Matt shifted into fluid French with the maître d', and she reluctantly admitted his accent was excellent. As they approached a quiet, intimate table, Layne noticed that Matt was the only uniformed guest. The noontime trade at La Fleur mostly consisted of Hill people.

"You're getting quite a few daggered looks, you know," she said when he'd completed the wine order.

Matt's gaze settled hungrily on Layne. He liked her husky, warm voice. It reminded him of melting honey. "Does it bother you?"

She shook her head, folding her hands and resting her chin on them. "No. They probably think you belong back over at the Pentagon and not on this side of the Potomac."

He smiled, placing the menu aside and resting his forearms on the table. "There wasn't a restaurant like La Fleur over there. You deserve the best, Mrs. Hamilton. And if my uniform causes any of the patrons a bit of discomfort, I can live with that if you can."

"Men in uniform don't bother me, Major. It's agents in plain-clothes that I distrust," Layne reminded him sharply.

"Then I'm glad I'm in uniform."

Layne had the grace to blush. And then she recognized the sincerity in his softly spoken words. She felt as if he'd reached out and caressed her, the vibrant warmth of his voice again soothing her emotions. Last night she had lain awake a long time remembering his comforting words in her ear as she'd sobbed against his chest. And she remembered with vivid clarity the strength of his arms around her body, rocking her, caring for her simply because she was hurting and alone. Layne felt confusion rise within her as she met and held his gaze.

"Please," she begged softly, leaning forward, "why are you going to all this trouble? I know you want something from me."

Matt cocked his head, studying Layne with raw intensity. She was warm and outgoing by nature. And he had known her late husband, Brad Carson, off and on for years. Brad had been as cold as they came. Matt couldn't imagine Layne in Carson's arms. She was a woman of vulnerability, her sensuality as natural as moonlight. And Carson had never shown any response to others' feelings or emotions. How had they come together? Matt wondered.

Rousing himself, he forced a slight smile. "For you, I'm an open book."

Layne gave him a careful look that implied skepticism. "Oh, sure you are!"

He opened his hands in a gesture of peace. "Try me."

The waiter came, interrupting them, and Matt ordered their lunch. Once the waiter had left, he picked up his wineglass. "Shall we toast, Mrs. Hamilton?"

She picked up her glass filled with the chilled Chablis he'd ordered. "To what?"

"To the future."

Layne looked at him over the raised crystal. "What future?" she asked carefully.

Matt grinned, clinking his glass against hers. "On our assignment. *Salut.*"

She nearly dropped the wineglass, and her lips parted in stunned surprise as she set it down. "What are you talking about?"

"Do you know how beautiful you become when you're angry?"

"Stop it! Answer my question."

"I told you, I'm an open book to you."

"If you think you're going to con me into doing anything with you or—or—"

He reached over and gripped her hand gently between his fingers. "Rule number one—we don't mention any names."

She jerked her hand away, muttering an oath under her breath that raised his eyebrows. "I ought to leave. You're such an arrogant, self-assured—"

"Where did all this temper come from? I thought you had very little backbone when it came to fighting for yourself?" he teased, trying not to smile.

Matt watched her eyes darken to the color of ripened wheat. "That's none of your business, Major Talbot! Now, either you stop this little game or I'm getting up and leaving."

Settling his features into a more serious expression, he said solemnly, "Okay, start asking your questions."

"You're taught to lie."

"I won't lie to you."

"There isn't an operative alive who doesn't lie. That uniform could be nothing more than a cover!"

"I'm a major in the Air Force. And I am a pilot."

Her lovely eyes narrowed. "Be careful, Talbot. My father was in the Air Force. And he was one of the finest test pilots they ever had."

"I know that."

"Of course you would. You have my whole life history on microfilm somewhere in the vaults."

"I've read your file."

An Air Force pilot, indeed! Layne thought angrily. How many times had Brad assumed other careers, other covers to suit the purpose of his job? "What do you fly?"

He gave a lazy shrug of his broad shoulders. "Anything they'll let me get my hands on."

"Any idiot knows you're either a fighter or a bomber pilot, Major! Don't hedge on that with me. I'm afraid you don't know your cover very well. I'm not impressed."

"I'm a test pilot. Is that acceptable?"

Layne sat back, surprise followed by sadness welling up in her. Memories of her father came rushing back. She remembered his taciturn face as he'd climbed into the cockpit of the aircraft that would kill him on that hot October day. She forced herself to look at Matt Talbot again. Yes, he had that same look she had seen on other test pilots—the "look of the eagles." These men had an arrogant pride melded with the unshakable confidence that they could fly anything with wings attached to it.

"Where are you stationed?"

Matt sipped his wine. "Nellis Air Force Base."

Layne's mind ranged over the myriad bases her father had been assigned to during the twenty years he had been in the Air Force. "Nellis isn't a testing base. Edwards is where they test all the new aircraft." She watched him, waiting for an answer, but his face remained impassive. He said nothing.

"Well?" she prodded.

"I'm assigned to Tactical Air Command, Layne," he said, using her name for the first time since that evening. "Other than that, there are some things I can't tell you, so I'll remain silent rather than fabricate a story."

Her lips compressed as she glared at him. "Nellis is home of the Red Flag. It's where our fighter pilots sharpen their skills against specially trained U.S. pilots who fly like Soviets."

He gave her a nod of his head. "Yes. They're called Aggressor pilots and spend at least five hundred hours learning Soviet fighter techniques to use in training flights against American fighter pilots."

"But you're not an Aggressor pilot?"

"I was once, many years ago."

"But not now?"

"No."

"Nellis is right outside Las Vegas. It's all desert and sagebrush. What's a test pilot doing there?" she demanded. She felt frustration nestling in her throat. This conversation was reminding her of talks with Brad. Only Brad had always smoothly handed her a story, treating her like a child. Matt Talbot was at least telling her he wasn't lying to her, even if it meant withholding information. Which was better? she thought angrily. "Wait a minute, I saw an article in the *Washington Post* just last week about…" Her voice trailed off, then she straightened. "RAVEN. They say the RAVEN prototype is at Nellis for testing because the airspace there is off-limits to all civilians."

Talbot's face revealed nothing, but his azure eyes calmly met hers.

Layne grimaced. "All right. Don't say anything. By saying nothing you're practically admitting to me you're one of the men testing the RAVEN bomber!"

"I'd rather talk about why we need your help, Layne," Talbot returned quietly.

She slid her fingers around her wineglass. "I'm listening. Not that it's going to do you any good. I can say no to you just as easily as I did to Chuck Lowell."

The waiter arrived, bringing each of them a crisp salad topped with a special vinaigrette-and-baby-shrimp house dressing. Perhaps he wasn't lying. Why did part of her want so much to believe he was telling the truth? Because, her suspicious mind said, he held you last night when you were hurting so badly. He could even have taken you to bed and made love to you…. Layne gasped softly, stunned by her realization. Bed? Matt Talbot running his lean, powerful fingers over her hungry body?

"Chuck was right, we do need your services as an interpreter of Chinese," Matt said, breaking into her tumultuous thoughts. A self-deprecating smile tugged at his mouth. "I don't speak one word of Chinese, and we need someone who can."

Unwittingly, Layne found herself lulled into the conversation. "You're going to China?"

"I'm going, yes. But not to China. To Hong Kong."

She blotted her mouth with the napkin, intrigued. "I know Hong Kong like the back of my hand. My father made many friends over there while I was growing up."

Matt put the half-eaten salad aside, resting his elbows on the table, concentrating on her. "That's another reason why your name came up, Layne. One of your old friends contacted us while trying to reach you."

She frowned. "Who?"

"The last time you and your husband took a vacation, you went to Hong Kong and ended up writing a series of articles. Do you remember?"

The old hurt came up again. That had been the last vacation she had shared with Brad shortly before his death. "Y-yes, of course I remember it." And she also remembered Brad's cold, biting anger because she had insisted upon doing the articles. He had wanted to relax around the Princeton Hotel, taking it easy, while she'd been as excited as a child at Christmas at an offered chance to meet Kang Ying, *lao-pan*, or leader, of the notorious pirates of the South China Sea. During the interview she and the *lao-pan* had developed a warm friendship that had endured, although they had not seen each other again. Brad had been furious with her for abandoning him.

Matt saw her face contort, her topaz eyes darkening with momentary pain. Out of instinct he reached across the table, briefly capturing her hand and giving it a squeeze. "Are you all right?"

The husky tenor of his voice was like a balm to her aching heart. For once she didn't pull away from his touch. His fingers were warm, caressing the coolness of her own. The moment he moved his hand away she felt a stab of loss. Layne raised her head, trying to understand his actions. Either he was a consummate actor and knew when to touch her to gain her trust, or— she took a sharp breath—or he was a sensitive, caring man. Chewing on her lower lip, Layne fought to corral her emotions, not trusting her voice just yet to answer.

"I'm okay," she said finally.

Matt could see that Layne was upset and wondered why she'd suddenly withdrawn. "I didn't mean to stir up any muddy waters," he apologized. "Kang Ying sent a message through one of our agents on Kowloon that he desperately needed your help."

"The *lao-pan* himself?" Layne couldn't hide the concern and anxiety in her voice. "Why would Kang want my help? This doesn't make sense."

Matt watched the waiter approach with the main course. "Here's our meal, Layne. Let's talk later."

She couldn't resist a smile. Matt Talbot had shifted from an engaging luncheon companion to all business in those split seconds. He wouldn't want a shred of what they were discussing overheard by anyone—including a waiter. Oddly, though, his presence gave her a sense of security. As the waiter approached, setting Layne's plate before her with a flourish, she offered Matt Talbot her first genuine smile. And she saw a brief look of surprise flare in his eyes. Let him wonder why she'd smiled at him. Let him stew in his own juices for a while. She laughed to herself, suddenly feeling lighter and happier than she had in years.

Chapter 3

Matt watched Layne covertly as she picked at her meal. After awarding him that heart-stopping smile, Layne had visibly relaxed. Was she excited about the reference to Kang? Her love of the Chinese and the Far East was well documented throughout her personnel file. Or was she beginning to like him? He shut off those hopes ruthlessly, as quickly as they arose. There was no room in his life for any kind of emotional entanglement. His brother was either dead or had been captured, and his need to get to Hong Kong and find him was paramount. This elegant, attractive woman sitting across from him could lead him to Kang and, he hoped, to Jim and his copilot, also lost in the crash.

Layne waited until the waiter had cleared the table before resuming their serious topic of conversation. "I guess I shouldn't be surprised that Kang knows your people. The Company has its tentacles into everything and everyone."

"Kang's a criminal, we know that. But he also has access to the tongs and triads over there, as well as to agents looking for information." Matt rested his chin against his folded hands. "Time's at a premium, Layne."

Despite herself, she responded when he used her name. It felt like a caress. Trying to ignore her reaction to him, she frowned. "It's not a normal ploy to drag a civilian into your cloak-and-dagger stuff, Major."

He shrugged. "I agree with you. But we're not running this show, Kang is. The incident that occurred has made him a necessary middleman through whom we have to deal. And he said

he wouldn't consider working with us unless *you* act as interme-
diary." Matt's frown matched hers. "Apparently he puts great
trust in you, Layne."

She touched the tendrils at her left cheek. "I remember your
telling Lowell that you felt I couldn't do it. Do what?"

Matt gave her a quick look. "You heard that comment?"

"I miss very little. Even when I'm in the throes of sobbing my
heart out," she warned him. "Please answer my question. What
don't you think I'm capable of doing?"

Matt took a breath and dove in. "We're dealing with cut-
throats, Layne. I question Kang's reliance on you. A Chinese man
never places his reliance on a woman. Why you? It would be
beneath him. And you're an outsider, as well."

"Yet you're trying to coerce me into joining you on a jaunt to
Hong Kong to meet with Kang?"

"Lowell thinks you're up to it."

"And you don't?"

"No."

She gave him a close look. "Either you're the cleverest liar I've
ever met, or you're working against your own people, Major."

He remained silent, meeting her impertinent gaze.

"You're expecting trouble on this mission, aren't you?" she
demanded. "Of course, what mission doesn't have danger? You
don't think I can protect myself, do you? Kang is an honorable
man, even if he is a pirate. These men live by their own unwritten codes. He wouldn't hurt me, although it's true they dislike
Americans—they think we talk too much and can't keep secrets."

"I told you I wouldn't lie to you, Layne," Matt reminded her
huskily. "And frankly, I wish I had met you under any other circumstances. You're a woman of exceptional scope. Ordinarily, I
don't let anyone get under my skin…but you have. If I had my way
about this, you'd stay here. If we had a penetration agent among
the pirates, you wouldn't even have been considered." He gave her
a veiled look. "But then, I'd never have met you." Matt shrugged.
"We're both caught up in a web of events outside our control."

Layne's heart knew he was telling the truth. What agent would say I don't want you on this mission? And yet he was still hoping to convince her to come. "Has anyone ever told you that you're an enigma, Major Talbot?"

His boyish grin reappeared, relaxing his strong features. "I've been called many things, Layne. Enigma is just one of them."

"So tell me," she asked suddenly, "how would I explain to my colleagues that I'm taking a sudden vacation in the Orient?"

His eyes narrowed. "You'll come?"

"I'm not sure. I hadn't realized Kang was involved. But first, I want to know how you're going to handle this assignment, Major."

"We've arranged for a substitute teacher to take over your duties until you return," he said in a quiet monotone, as if reciting it by rote. "If you come, you'll pose as my wife. We'll be spending our honeymoon and combining it with a writing and photographic assignment for a leading national magazine. It's a perfect cover. You're already established as an expert on the South China Sea pirates since you published those three articles in *Life*. My cover as a photographer is well established, and anyone checking will find my credentials in order. We're scheduled to fly out of D.C. tomorrow at—" he checked the watch on his wrist "—8:00 a.m. From there we'll fly to Noreta Airport in Japan and disembark for about an hour. We'll catch another Northwest Orient flight to Hong Kong, where we'll stay at the Princeton Hotel for a day or two while we're waiting to be contacted by Kang. From there, it's his game, and he'll tell us how he wants us to play."

"What does the *lao-pan* have that you want, Matt?"

"I can't tell you."

Layne pursed her lips. "You're a test pilot they're sending over with me. It has to have something to do with planes."

He shrugged. "No lies, remember? It's safer for you not to try to piece it together."

"That's right. The less I know, the less I could spill to the enemy in case I'm caught and interrogated." Layne drew in a deep breath. "I know the Company has a compartmentation policy. Feed only necessary tidbits of information on a need-to-know basis to those involved. But I'm not one of your operatives. You're asking me to walk into a situation that's obviously got some danger attached to it and blindly trust you!" Her voice rose with feeling. "And I learned the hard way about trusting anyone from the Company."

Matt's mouth became grimmer. "Look, Layne, if I have my way about this, once the contact with Kang is made, you'll be staying in Hong Kong where it's safe."

A deluge of old emotions broke loose within her. "Why do we have to act like we're married? And why the Princeton?" Her voice held a note of anguish.

"It's necessary under the present circumstances to arouse no suspicions when we fly to Hong Kong. A husband-and-wife freelance team on a honeymoon won't stir up too much interest in enemy intelligence communities. I'll be contacting our CIA people and British Special Intelligence as soon as we land there."

"And the Princeton?"

The pain was evident in her trembling voice. Matt softened. She deserved a buffer zone of protection on the emotional front. "Kang's orders. That's where you stayed last time, and apparently he likes that location because the hotel sits right on the bay. An ideal strategic ploy if he or his people need to escape from the British officials who'd like to string them all up." His eyes grew tender. "I know it was the hotel where you and your husband stayed." He reached out, cradling her hand in his. "I hope it will be for only a few days."

Tiny tingles of pleasure arose from his touch, and Layne wondered if he realized how much his one gesture had halted her spinning emotional reaction.

"I— It's just that…it brings back some very unpleasant memories."

Matt frowned. "Unpleasant?" He'd assumed the opposite. "But you were on vacation…."

Layne withdrew her hand from his. "It's nice to know that not everything is in my file," she said sharply, suddenly refusing to meet his eyes.

"Files give facts, not emotional experiences. Didn't your husband want to vacation in the Far East with you?" Rapidly he searched the compartments of his memory for facts on Brad Carson's marital status with his wife. Outwardly, it had appeared to be storybook perfect. There'd been nothing to suggest that Layne was unhappy. But his gut had told him differently when he'd perused Layne's file. Carson had been ice all the way through, and after meeting Layne, Matt had recognized the chasm of emotional differences between her and her late husband.

"I suppose anything I say to you will end up in a report somewhere."

"No, it won't. It's none of anyone's business what your personal life with Brad was like."

Layne wanted to believe him. "It was my idea to try and find one of the pirate clan leaders for an interview. Brad wanted nothing more than to relax at the hotel for two weeks." Layne drew small circles on the white damask tablecloth with her index finger. Her voice became hushed. "I love the Far East. I was raised by my *amah*—my Chinese nanny—and could speak her language before I ever learned English." She gave a rueful laugh. "My mom and dad were chagrined, to say the least, when they found that out. Anyway, I practically begged Brad to take me to the Orient. I hadn't been there in seven years, and I was homesick." She glanced over at Matt. "Would it sound strange if I told you that I feel more at home living among the people of the Far East than I do here?"

He shook his head. "No. It's understandable. You spent the first fifteen years of your life over there."

"Funny," Layne mused, "Brad could never grasp that. He didn't want to go, and we got into a terrific fight over it. Brad hated tears. He called them a sign of weakness. And I cried a lot because I wanted to go home, just for two weeks. To make a long, complicated story very short, Brad capitulated and we went to Hong Kong." She shut her eyes against the memory. "If I had known that two months later he was to be killed," she said softly, "I'd never have forced the issue with him. I would have done exactly as he wanted. I should have let him have his way…."

"Maybe. Maybe not," Matt murmured, catching her morose gaze. "After five years of marriage you had never returned home. Why shouldn't he have allowed you that one request?"

Layne gave him a small smile. "Because we always went where he wanted to go on vacation, for each of those other four years." She sighed, raising her dark head to look at him. There was an odd catch in her voice when she spoke. "You have a gentle way of getting me to put it into perspective, Matt. Thank you."

The seconds spun effortlessly between them. Matt was aware of nothing in that moment except her. He felt a wrench in his chest, the blazing heat of desire uncoiling deep within his body. God, how he wanted her. "If you had been my wife," he said huskily, "I'd have made damn sure that you'd gone home to the Far East long before our fifth year of marriage. The Orient is as much a part of you as flying jets is to me, we all need our own kind of emotional sustenance in order to be happy."

"I agree with your analogy." A soft smile lingered on Layne's lips, and in her heart, as she tilted her head, drinking him in. There was an honesty to him that she'd never encountered in an agent before. "Are you working for the Company full-time?"

Matt shook his head. "No. Just on special projects. The rest of the time I do what I enjoy most—flying."

"A career officer, no doubt?"

"Does it show?" he asked, grinning.

"Yes, but it's becoming to you. You wear your authority well." And I feel heady, dizzy and wonderful, she added mentally. How could one man unhinge her so quickly?

"Since that's coming from an Air Force brat, I'll say thank you."

As Layne met his warm gaze, she felt a delicious wave of hunger course through her. She stared at Matt's mouth, a mouth neither so thin as to be considered cruel nor so full as to be overtly sensual. But it was the way he used his mouth that entranced her. One moment the corners would be drawn inward as if he were experiencing some silent pain; the next, they'd be curved generously upward into a genuine smile meant for her alone. She remembered his kiss, the branding fire of his commanding mouth as it took total charge of her parting lips. How many times in the past forty-eight hours had she recalled those moments of intimacy between them?

"Listen, Layne," Matt said quietly, breaking into her thoughts, "we've got to have your decision."

She remained silent a long minute, studying him. The bright September sun slanted through the floor-to-ceiling glass, back-lighting his head, broad shoulders and torso. He was an eagle ready to attack and a warrior from the past come to life again. He could be ruthless one moment, hot-blooded the next. She used her instincts, trying to probe beyond what he wanted her to read in his features. Fear raced through her, making her stomach clench in response.

"And if I don't go? Will you still leave for Hong Kong without me?"

"Yes."

"But you don't know Chinese."

"I'll have to rely on British SI to help me."

"And then?"

"And then I'll wait for Kang to contact me."

"That will be dangerous, Matt. No one approaches the pirates in ignorance. These men are straight out of the late eighteen-hundreds. They wield knives and axes instead of guns and attack ships grounded by typhoons on those little islands out in the China Sea. And when they swarm aboard those ships, they kill." She took a deep, unsteady breath. "And they never show mercy. You aren't any match for them."

Matt heard the tremor of fear in her voice. "Look, I'm not going to try to talk you into coming, Layne. Personally, I don't want you along. It could get very dangerous." His voice lowered to an intimate level. "I'd rather go alone and try to survive so I can come back and get to know you better."

Layne twisted the linen napkin in her lap. The aching honesty in his voice made her believe that he would want to renew their acquaintance without the pressures now surrounding them. He was drawn to her, as she was to him. Layne tried to separate her romantic feelings from the unfolding drama. She knew the Chinese mind. And she suspected Matt was unprepared for the way they dealt with outsiders such as himself. If she didn't go along… Pictures of him dying from knife wounds made her pale.

"Layne?"

"It's nothing."

Matt's eyes flared with disbelief as he watched her face whiten beneath her tan. "No lies, remember? What's wrong?"

"They'll kill you. You'll never get close to the *lao-pan* and his cutthroat clan. If you aren't one of them, they'll never accept you." Layne raised her chin, meeting his concerned gaze, then held out her hand, palm toward him. A thin white scar crossed the entire palm. "When I was looking for Kang, I was told by the junk people in Aberdeen Harbor that he hated all foreign devils. His youngest son had been killed by the British police on Kowloon. The only reason I'm considered part of Kang's family is because I helped his eldest son get admitted to a university in California. It was hoped that by educating Kang's son in the United States, the Dragon Clan might eventually stop their marauding as more of their people were enlightened."

"I see," Matt murmured. "And Kang's way of showing his thanks was to take a dagger to your palm?"

"It's a ritual among the Dragon Clan. Only the *lao-pan* may allow an outsider who isn't born of the clan to become a member of it. It was his way of honoring me—instead of lopping off my head." She grimaced. "I wasn't ecstatic about the idea, believe me." She gave him an embarrassed look. "When he cut my hand, I fainted. When I came to, his wife had placed healing herbs on my wound and bandaged it. I've shed my blood and mingled it with his. I can walk with safety among his people. If you don't have this mark, you'll be killed. They allow no outsiders to live to tell the rest of the world about their fortresses on the different islands."

Matt stared at the scar on her slender, artistic hand for a long moment, his lips tightening. "Didn't Brad go with you when you searched for Kang?"

Layne shook her head, slowly lowering her hand and tucking

it back into her lap. "No. He stayed at the Princeton for that week. I went to Macao in search of the pirates without him."

Matt swore softly, his entire body tensing. "He let you go by yourself?" What kind of idiot was Carson? Matt would never have allowed Layne to go into that nest of thieves by herself!

"Yes."

Matt put a leash on his anger, but it still came out in his lowered voice. "Well, I'll tell you something. If you were my wife, you wouldn't be traipsing off on some adventure without me. You could have been raped. Didn't you consider the risks? Kang could have killed you—or worse, made you a slave. We've got enough background data on the pirates for me to know that much." He let out a shaky breath, staring across the table at her. "What the hell kind of husband did you have?"

Layne's mouth pulled into a sad smile. "It's a long story, Matt. And too depressing." She leaned forward, urgently. "Just as you never would have let me go by myself to find the pirates, I can't let you go alone, either. The *lao-pan* wants to talk with me. He won't harm you as long as I'm there. He owes me a debt. If a *lao-pan* owes you, he must honor whatever you ask for— that's the unwritten Chinese code. And now I'll collect on it by asking him to help you in whatever way necessary."

Matt reached across the table, pulling her hands into his. "You're a special woman, kitten. Now listen to me carefully, I can't tell you much about this mission. It's all top secret. And it could become dangerous. I worry about you…I'm sorry, but you're not agent material, and that makes you vulnerable to attack from every quarter." His thoughts grew turbulent. It was like leading a lamb to slaughter. And yet single-handedly Layne had tracked down the pirates and met them on their own turf. There was a hidden streak of courage within her. His fingers tight- ened around her hands. His brother and the avionics were lost somewhere among the scattered islands ruled by the pirates of the South China Sea. And this woman with the childlike trust in her eyes was the only one who could help them enter that violent, bloody world to find Jim, his copilot and those black boxes. He knew that if they fell into the wrong hands, it could set the U.S. back ten years in electronic surveillance and defense systems.

"I trust you, Matt," Layne began quietly. "I swore I'd never get involved with another agency man. But you're different." She wet her lips, aware of the emergence of feelings she'd thought had died. "You'll protect me. I know you'll do your best. And I feel safe with you. I'll go. Just take me back to my apartment and I'll pack…."

She was coming! Matt stared at her, then gave her fingers one more squeeze before releasing them. "All right, let's go. I'll have all the papers and passports in order and pick you up tomorrow at 6:00 a.m." Numbly, Layne pushed back her chair. All she knew was that she had no choice. Matt needed her, and she was going.

Even though she was expecting it, the knock at her apartment door made Layne start. She hefted the last bag into the living room and ran to answer the door. The last few hours she'd alternated between bouts of fear, doubt and hesitation. The opportunity to see Kang Ying again was exhilarating. But the ominous note surrounding Kang's request left her with an icy feeling in her stomach. And then there was Matt Talbot, an operative. The sort of man she had sworn never to involve herself with again on any level. Yet she was drawn to him. Eagerly, Layne pulled open the door.

Matt stood there, leaning against the doorjamb. His smile said, Relax, everything will be all right. He was dressed in a pair of dark brown slacks, with a light blue shirt open at the collar. She liked the way his sport jacket accented his wide shoulders. Suddenly shy, she managed a smile, gesturing for him to enter.

"Come in, Major—"

"I think we'd better suspend the social formalities," he suggested easily, halting among her three suitcases. "Call me Matt."

Layne nodded nervously and shut the door. She wore a pair of designer jeans, low-heeled sandals and a sienna colored long-sleeved blouse that highlighted the color of her honey-brown eyes.

Matt gave her an appraising look that confirmed her choice of traveling clothes. "Scared?" he asked as he walked over to her.

"Yes. Does it show?"

"Just to me," he soothed. "Everyone gets butterflies beforehand." His mouth stretched into a softened smile. "I've got them, too."

She gave him a look that said she didn't believe him. "You look capable of handling virtually anything, Maj—I mean, Matt."

He was aware of her lilac perfume enhancing the warm scent of her body as he stood mere inches from her. "Looks are deceiving," he warned her. "Stand still." He saw a brief flicker of fear in her eyes as he reached behind her, gently loosening the confining pins that held her blue-black hair in the chignon.

"Did I ever tell you how beautiful you looked the first time I saw you?" he whispered huskily as he loosened the neatly twisted hair. The silken mass tumbled through his fingers to settle in a cloud around her shoulders and breasts, and he drew in his breath, aware of her femininity, her vulnerability where he was concerned. She did trust him, allowing him to caress her magnificent hair. "There," he said, his cobalt eyes dark with veiled desire. "That's how I like my wife—winsome, carefree and beautiful."

Layne trembled beneath his touch. Her knees were weak from the caress of his fingers coaxing her unruly hair across her shoulders. Closing her eyes momentarily, she felt a throbbing intimacy leap between them. When Layne reopened her eyes, she drowned in the flaring azure of his, losing her heart to this inscrutable man who touched her soul as surely as the sun kissed the uplifted face of each flower. At a loss for words, she took a step away from him.

"Remember," Matt went on gruffly, himself shaken at the sudden flare of intimacy, "you're my wife, and we're newlyweds. Anyone watching us would expect us to be in very close contact with each other." A glimmer came into his blue eyes. "This is the only part of the whole charade that I'm going to enjoy."

"What? Pretending that we're married?" she heard herself protest. But Matt's touch was anything but fakery. And Layne's instincts told her his feelings were genuine despite the circumstances. She realized she was becoming badly rattled. She didn't want to

be helplessly ensnared by his male magnetism and that special
flame of tenderness that surfaced whenever they were together.

Matt's brow wrinkled slightly, his eyes growing darker with
concern as he reached over, gently brushing her flushed cheek.
"Where does pretending end and reality begin?" he mused.
"Sometimes they overlap to become the truth." A disarming
smile tipped the corners of his mouth. "I told you before, kitten,
you're the stuff dreams are made of…the kind every man wishes
would come true." His brows moved downward and he caught
himself as he saw shock register in her eyes. What had Brad
Carson done to make Layne react like this? Perhaps aboard the
plane on the way to Hong Kong, he would have time to explore
some of the more personal facets of this complex woman.

Layne's heart was pounding, and she lifted her hand to her
breast. "This whole thing is a nightmare to me," she warned him.

"Even the idea of being married to me?"

"It's merely part of the plan. Nothing more!"

"And you aren't going to enjoy it?"

"Damn you, Talbot! You watch your step. Just because we
have to pose as man and wife doesn't mean I'll allow you to take
any liberties."

Matt's smile broadened as he watched her bluster, because he
knew how deeply he had affected her. He could tell by the gold
fire burning in the depths of her wide, heart-stealing brown eyes
and by the delicate flush of rose across her cheeks.

He pulled a small, dark green box from the inner pocket of
his suit coat. "Let's make this charade a little bit more genuine
and permanent then, shall we? According to the records, we
were married two weeks ago in a civil ceremony that was held
in Alexandria, Virginia." Matt claimed the hand that was resting
against her breast and slipped on the rings.

Layne looked down, a gasp escaping from her. The diamond
engagement ring and wedding band were fashioned out of old
gold; the diamond had to be at least three carats. "Oh, Matt!
They look—"

He placed the green box in a nearby desk drawer. "They

belonged to my grandmother," he explained, carefully noting the sentimental expression that replaced her shock. "She told me that if I ever found a woman who made me lose my train of thought and was in my mind every waking and sleeping moment, that I should give her these rings. And I just found such a woman." He pulled other essential papers from the left breast pocket of his suit.

Layne gave him a stricken look as she gazed down at the rings. A rush of joy suffused her heart for one heady second before it was replaced by fear. Brad had been just as smooth with his words before they'd gotten married. Was Matt the same? Was he, perhaps, lying to her for the sake of the mission? Yet Brad and Matt seemed as different as a glacier and a gentle, crystal-clear stream. Matt's warmth and care radiated outward to surround her. Brad had never made her feel like that. How could an agent—how could anyone—produce that sort of feeling if he didn't mean it? Her heart said he couldn't. Matt Talbot was more sincere and emotionally honest with her than any man she'd ever known. But even as she felt it, five years of the glacial past froze her fleeting joy. "I couldn't possibly wear these. I mean, what if—"

Matt lifted his head, meeting Layne's misty topaz eyes. Did she have any idea how vulnerable she looked? No, it was obvious she wasn't aware of her charms as a woman. He halted his spiraling thoughts. Business was their first priority—and then…

"I promise you, there will be no lies between us, Layne," he assured her. "The wedding rings are my personal property. And I can't think of a lovelier woman to wear them. It's a compliment, kitten, not a death sentence."

Layne touched her brow. "I'm sorry, Matt. It's just that so much is going on and—"

Matt placed his hand on her shoulder, giving it a quick squeeze. "You're doing fine. Let's get to some of the simpler details of this assignment." Handing her the new passport, he pocketed his own. "Your last name is now Talbot, Layne. Mrs. Matthew Talbot. Here's a copy of the letter from the magazine authorizing us to do a series of articles on the pirates. And here's a copy of our reservations at the Princeton." He smiled. "Women usually take care of these items, don't they?"

Layne was too stunned to answer, numbly taking each item as he offered it, slipping them all into her shoulder bag. "I—well, yes. Usually."

He nodded, placing his hands on his hips. The moment Layne saw that stance she knew that he was a fighter pilot; it was so typical of that breed of male to possess a languidly confident body language. And yet she could feel the tension radiating from him. But it wasn't nervousness; it was coiled power like an inner spring waiting to be released. Oddly, she felt her own nervousness dissipate in the presence of his alertness.

"Ready?" he asked, interrupting her thoughts.

She snapped her head up. "Yes, but I haven't gotten in touch with my mother."

"It's being taken care of," Matt soothed, realizing how affected she was by their departure. Layne was off balance, and he meant to restabilize her. He grinned, then moved toward her and took her hand. Layne relaxed visibly, then gave him a tremulous smile.

"I'm so nervous, Matt. I feel like I'm ready to explode inside. I worry about my mom. What will she think? She knows how I feel about anyone connected with the Company, and then I suddenly go off…" But Matt was on the move, checking over her apartment.

All windows locked, all lights off, Matt thought as he automatically completed his mental checklist. "Chuck will be driving over to see your mother at eight o'clock this morning to explain what's going on," he said, returning to Layne's side.

Layne gave him a doubtful look. "All of it?"

Matt picked up the suitcases. "Some of it," he amended. "Come on, kitten, let's saddle up. We've got a quick flight out of D.C. to Kennedy. We'll go through customs in New York, then board a Northwest Orient flight for Hong Kong."

Layne said little on the way to the airport. Once there, Matt had a porter check all their baggage except for one huge camera

case that he carried easily on his shoulder. Her heart leaped unexpectedly as he slid his hand into hers, leading her into the
airport facility. He glanced down at her, a casual smile on his
face. They were married, he had said. Remember—act like newlyweds. Layne squeezed his hand, remaining close to him, but
when she looked up at him he seemed a million miles away, as
if in deep thought. Then she realized he was scanning the endless
crowd around them, tabulating, categorizing, weighing each individual who passed near them. A sense of tightly controlled
power vibrated around Matt like charged electricity, and Layne
felt somewhat awed by him. Occasionally his grip would tighten
gently around her fingers, letting her know that everything was
all right, that she had nothing to worry about.

But within her, Layne admitted to herself, nothing was right.
Just the maleness of his hand capturing her damp, sweating
fingers made her heart pound with a new, aching awareness. And
in that moment she realized that Matt Talbot was far more dangerous to her newly awakening emotions than any outside danger.
Layne tried to turn off the sudden thought that they would be
sharing the same room. The same bed? She bit her lower lip nervously. It would certainly seem suspicious if they requested
separate beds. And if she remembered correctly, there was a
settee in each suite, but it wasn't long enough to sleep on. What
plans did Matt Talbot have for their first night abroad? she
wondered.

Chapter 4

Customs at John F. Kennedy airport in New York City jangled Layne's nerves. She tried to match Matt's cool demeanor as they inched forward toward the customs inspector, but she fumbled nervously with the passport between her damp hands. What if they guessed she wasn't Layne Talbot? What if they knew she was a fake? What if—

"Relax," Matt murmured huskily, and he leaned down, placing a light kiss on her hair. His arm went around Layne's shoulders, squeezing her reassuringly.

Layne glanced up and cast him a murderous look. "Do you realize what they'll do to us if they find out that we're not—"

Matt's eyes grew tender as he surveyed her flushed features. "My flighty little bird. It's all right. They won't suspect a thing unless you tell them."

"I'm just a case of nerves," Layne admitted softly. Was this what agents felt like whenever they went undercover? She felt Matt draw her tightly against him, and she released a held breath. Right now, at this very moment, all Layne wanted to do was sink into the protection of his embrace.

"I know. It'll all be over in a few minutes," Matt whispered, resting his jaw against the silken threads of her hair. His voice lowered to an intimate growl. "You smell wonderful, lady, like a meadow filled with springtime flowers."

Layne rested her head against his shoulder, responding to the caress of his voice. A faint smile edged her lips. "You're a poet, Matt Talbot."

She felt more than heard his soft laugh. "A poet and a soldier. Do the two fit?"

She raised her chin, melting beneath the warmth lingering in Matt's eyes. "They must," Layne murmured, confusion in her tone. "But I don't understand it. How can you be—"

"Next."

Matt picked up their luggage and gave Layne a quick smile. He ushered them to the waiting customs official. Before Layne could recover and grow tense again, they had been cleared.

"See," Matt confided, satisfaction in his voice, "it was over before you knew it."

"I'm glad," Layne said, suddenly shaky.

"Layne, talk to me. What's wrong? You're trembling like a leaf." One look into her wounded brown eyes made Matt want to sweep Layne into his arms and hold her close. He gave her a slight shake. "Layne?"

"I— It's nothing. Nothing, Matt. I'm just not used to all of this…charade." Layne forced herself not to lean against him. She managed a wan smile of reassurance. "Well, you yourself said I wasn't cut out for the spy business."

Troubled by her reaction, Matt pursed his lips. "Come on, I'll get us checked in on the flight and then get you a drink. That will help you relax."

The drink did more than settle her down. Layne had barely finished off the Scotch when the boarding for first class was called. By the time they had climbed the spiral staircase up into the "hump" of the jumbo jet, Layne was exhausted. Maybe Matt was right: this constant suspense and secrecy was far more stressful than she had expected. As she pushed her large, comfortable seat into a sleeping position, Layne knew it was more than the mission that was shaking her so.

Her violent reaction was partly the result of her realization that Matt touched her on levels that had never been brought to life within her before. Layne closed her eyes, allowing the anesthetizing power of the liquor to lull her toward sleep. Sleep would be a welcome escape from the unexpected turn her life had suddenly taken. Layne was only vaguely aware that Matt had retrieved a blanket and tucked her in as she snuggled deeper into the padded seat.

Layne awoke beneath the caress of Matt's fingers as he lightly stroked tendrils of hair from her brow. Drowsily she forced her heavy lids to open only to find herself drowning in Matt's azure eyes. Defenses down, Layne nuzzled against his palm now resting against the hollow of her cheek. This stranger invited familiarity.

"Wake up, sleeping beauty," Matt murmured huskily. "Come on…."

Was this how it would be if they slept together? Layne turned her cheek against his hand, resisting his request. In response, his mouth began to trail small, arousing kisses from her temple to her cheek. His breath was moist against her flesh, and Layne inhaled deeply of his masculine scent.

"Mmm," she whispered, "you smell so good…."

Against his better judgment, Matt leaned down once more, his mouth finding her full, sleep-softened lips. Touching his lips to hers, Matt gently cajoled her into awakening. He probed each corner of her mouth, tasting her, reveling in her trust. A moan slid from Layne's throat as he molded his mouth more firmly, parting her lips, stealing the breath from her body and replacing it with the fire of his longing. A small gasp of pleasure from those lips he now plundered fueled his desire, heating the icy core of doubt within him and making him believe in a future for them both. "Sweet," Matt groaned against her lips, "like honey and flower nectar…."

Layne's heart pounded wildly, fire racing through her as she drank from his strong, firm mouth. Her world tilted crazily, and she was aware of a fiercely tender man whose voice was thick with passion for her alone.

A marvelous blanket of languor filled her, and a tremulous smile touched her parted, glistening lips. "I've never been awakened with a kiss before…."

Matt shared an intimate look with her. "I think I'm going to make a habit of waking you like that," he told her, a glint in his sky-blue eyes.

Layne blinked again, the magical quality of the moment receding as she became more aware of her surroundings. There were only fifteen reclining beds in the hump of the jumbo jet, and they were the only two people in the area. As Layne sat up, her hair tumbled with carefree abandon across her shoulders. The look of sheer pleasure on Matt's face brought heat to her cheeks. He had crouched down beside her, his arms resting on the long, corded surface of his thighs.

"W-what time is it?" Layne asked, rubbing her eyes sleepily.

"It's 10:30 a.m. We're still over Canada, heading up toward the North Pole before we start the downward leg of our journey." He roused himself, giving Layne a tender look, and stood.

"Feel like something to eat? The stewardess keeps coming up here to feed us, and I think she's beginning to feel rejected."

Layne tipped her plush chair into an upright position, keeping the blanket around her lower body. Matt looked incredibly handsome standing above her, his hands resting on his narrow hips. She warmed beneath his smoldering gaze, still caught up in the evaporating magic of their shared kiss. And it had been a mutual kiss. "Let me wake up first," she murmured.

"Take your time. I'm going downstairs to get us some juice. It's always wise to eat lightly and drink plenty of liquids on a long flight like this."

"Make mine tomato juice."

Matt gave her a wistful smile. "Did you know how beautiful you are in sleep? Or in waking up?"

Layne's eyes widened. "I—no…"

Matt walked to the stairs. "Well, you are, kitten. I'll be back in a few minutes."

Layne shakily got to her feet. She found, to her surprise, that Matt must have taken off her shoes after she'd fallen asleep. She stood and folded the blanket, placing it behind the seat, then retrieved her purse. Still in her stocking feet, she padded to the lavatory. Once there, she splashed her face with cold water, first to wake up, then to try to douse her fiery reaction to Matt's last words.

Matt had arranged the juice on her chair tray when she emerged. Layne had deliberately taken her time in order to still her trembling fingers and racing heart. She had stared darkly at herself in the small mirror, giving herself a good lecture: He's an agent, Layne. Never forget that! He's used to using people. He has a talent for getting people like you to do what he wants.

"You look a little more awake," Matt greeted her, sitting down in his recliner, which paralleled hers.

Layne grimaced and sat down. "I look better, you mean?" Nervously she slid the cool glass into her fingers, taking a sip of the tomato juice.

"No, lady, you couldn't look better. You're pretty in or out of sleep," Matt assured her.

She gulped the juice, almost choking on it. Licking her lips of the salty liquid, Layne slid him a disgruntled glare. "Are you always so complimentary? Or does that go with the territory?"

Matt scowled. "I was being honest, Layne. Since when does honesty only come with certain territories?"

Gripping the tumbler, Layne stared down at it. "Brad once told me that sometimes when he lived a lie for very long, it became the truth for him," she whispered. "He said it was that way for any operative who was undercover." Lifting her head, Layne stared at Matt. "Yes, I question your compliments."

Matt gauged the hurt mirrored in her eyes. How could he say, *Look, you do something to me, Layne. I'm not sure what it is yet; all I know is that you make me feel like living and feeling again?* If he admitted the truth, she would find it too hard to accept and call him a liar. Instead, he said, "I told you when we started this that there would be no lies between us, Layne. I'm keeping my word."

There was a hint of apology in her husky voice. "And if I ask you about yourself? Would you still be honest?"

Matt nodded. "I'll tell you what I can." And then a brief smile eased his stern features. "Is this twenty questions?"

She shrugged. "I don't know. I don't even know why I want to know about you. You're an agent."

"I'm a human being first, Layne, a damn good test pilot second and a part-time agent third. But those last two are my vocations. They're not the whole of me. Just like being a professor of Chinese doesn't say who all of Layne Hamilton is."

Layne relaxed beneath the timbre of his voice. "I'll agree with you there up to a point. But Brad *was* the Company. His personality and vocation were identical. You couldn't separate one from the other."

"Tell me something, Layne. Did you ever mix with other Company wives or their families?"

She shook her head. "No. I have my academic circle of friends. Brad made it very clear that he didn't wish to mingle with anyone else—my friends or the Company people."

"He was a loner?"

Layne finished off the tomato juice, setting it on the tray. She pulled her legs up and placed her arms around her knees, then, resting her head against them, watched Matt through half-closed eyes. "Yes, he was a loner."

"No friends?"

"Brad never felt the need for any. He was totally self-sufficient." Layne grimaced. "Unlike me, who needed the help from family members and support from friends that he disdained as a sign of weakness."

Matt's eyes narrowed slightly. "So he never encouraged you to become part of the Company's family support system?"

"A support system?" she scoffed. "Come on!"

"The Company encourages spouses to take schooling with the employees and generally helps the wives and families cope whenever possible. In one way, the Company resembles military family living and has a similar plan to that of the services."

Layne looked at him in disbelief. So often the men in the military were away on duty and the wives had no one to turn to but one another. And if something needed to be repaired, the wife usually ended up fixing it. The lonely days, weeks and even months without a husband around to complete the family existence were eased by sharing with other military families in similar circumstances. "I doubt that."

"Well, it's a reality," Matt countered.

"Brad never mentioned it."

"He never brought home the newsletter that's circulated monthly to show events that families can participate in?"

Some of her initial disbelief dissolved. "No...."

"Each area has a newsletter, Layne. There's a human resource division within the Company concerned with the family of the employee. But if Brad didn't have that newsletter sent to you, how could you know?"

Layne gave him a guarded look. "What are you trying to do? Soften my opinion of them? Or of you?"

"No. I just want to make you aware of some facts so that you can make a decision based upon more evidence than what you already have. You seem to have gotten everything through Brad—whatever he fed you, you swallowed."

Anger stirred in Layne. "That's right, I did. For five miserable years. One can of lies after another."

Matt reached out, resting his hand lightly on her arm. "Brainwashing comes in many subtle forms, Layne. I met Brad Carson a couple of times. And I can tell you with great assuredness that he was unique among operatives."

"Meaning?"

Matt didn't wince at the tightness he heard in her voice. "Meaning he wasn't like most of us. Listen to me, Layne. Brad lived in his own world of fantasies. He acted them out. He had one foot in the cold, harsh reality of spying and the other in his dreamworld. And because of that, Brad didn't need any friends or—" he shrugged apologetically "—a family."

Layne felt Matt's fingers burning into her flesh. "After Brad was killed, I had an emotional breakdown." Her voice quavered with the difficulty of dredging up the determinedly buried memories. "I blamed myself for his death. I thought I had caused it by insisting upon going to Hong Kong, to my real home, the

Far East. He said he was stressed out and needed to get away. He wanted to go to Nassau and relax." She struggled, momentarily unable to go on. But one squeeze of Matt's fingers against her arm gave her the assurance to continue. "I don't know why I'm telling you this—you're a stranger...someone I met only days ago...."

"I care, Layne, and you know that. Regardless of what your past conditioning is screaming at you, your instincts are running true. You know I'm interested in your personal safety and welfare on this assignment. And the more I know, the better I can protect you."

Layne blinked back sudden tears, refusing to meet Matt's gaze. She pulled her arm from his grasp, burying her face in her hands. "The woman therapist I went to must have listened to twenty hours of my tears, guilt and reaction."

"And what was her opinion?" Matt asked gently, wanting to reach out and comfort Layne. But right now, he knew she would misinterpret his action.

"That Brad was schizophrenic, living different lives and not being responsible to me or—"

"Or?"

Layne dragged in a deep, anguished breath and then released it. "Or the family I wanted."

"Children?"

She nodded and wiped the tears from the corners of her eyes. "I love kids. Always wanted at least two of them." Layne met his warming gaze, melting beneath it.

A gentle smile pulled at his mouth, and Matt reached over, lightly caressing her unruly cloud of black hair. "You'd make a wonderful mother."

"Thank you," Layne whispered, blotting her eyes. Then a sudden, disturbing thought struck her. "What does your wife think about your double life as pilot and agent?"

"Jenny never knew I was working for the Company."

Layne's chin tilted. She heard carefully shielded pain in his voice. "You sound as if...I mean, are you divorced or something?" He had stated it as if she were a part of his past.

Matt tore his gaze from her concerned expression. His mouth tightened. "Jenny died three years ago from leukemia, Layne." Three years. Some days it felt like three months ago; others, three lifetimes.

Automatically, Layne reached out, her hand resting on his forearm. "I'm sorry…I had no right to pry."

Matt lifted his chin, giving her a slight smile meant to reassure her. "With you, I don't mind talking about it. Jenny and I shared six wonderful years together. We had a good marriage. She was a good woman."

And you're a good man, Layne added silently. Her heart wrenched in her breast as she saw the pensiveness in Matt's features. Her fingers closed comfortingly on his arm.

"At least you had six years of happiness, Matt," she whispered. "Most of the people in this world would give anything to have what you shared with Jenny." Layne removed her hand and gave him a rueful shake of her head. "I'd have given a lot to have one day of that kind of happiness in my five years of marriage."

Matt roused himself. "Hey, we're getting maudlin, kitten. Come on, let's get something to eat. There's something I want to discuss with you before we call it a night."

Chapter 5

Layne said little during their light lunch. She bypassed the heavier meat and starchy foods in favor of a salad and fruit.

"Want some dessert?" Matt asked, offering her the tempting chocolate cake.

"No, thank you."

His blue eyes crinkled as he placed the porcelain plate bearing the cake slice on her tray. "Go on, you look like a gal who loves chocolate. Besides, you need to put on some more weight."

The dessert did look delicious. Layne hesitated. "How could you know I like chocolate? Is that in my file, too?"

"No. Just a lucky guess."

Layne gave him a look that said she didn't believe him. "Somehow, Matt, I doubt if you leave anything to chance or luck."

He placed his tray on an empty recliner and leaned back, stretching like a satiated lion after a satisfying meal. "Meeting you was pure luck, lady. Good luck."

She picked up the fork, taking a tentative bite of the cake. It literally melted in her mouth. "Since when do test pilots rely on luck for anything?"

"I'm the first to admit that I don't have full control over the universe. There's an unseen element of luck or fate at work in everything." He laughed pleasantly, relaxing by placing his hands behind his head. His blue eyes sparkled with warmth. "Fate outdid herself this time, though. I couldn't have had a better partner on this assignment."

Layne's eyes flashed. "And just a few days ago you were

saying I was little more than excess baggage on this trip. Get your story straight."

Matt smiled good-naturedly. The petulant set of Layne's lips did nothing but remind him of their earlier kiss. Matt groaned inwardly, remembering her softness, her responsiveness. Tucking those passionate memories away, he focused on her rebellious attitude toward him. "I never referred to you as excess baggage. I felt and still feel that you aren't capable of defending yourself if it becomes necessary. What I meant was that I enjoy your company."

Layne stabbed at the cake. "Well, I don't like the idea of having you as a babysitter. But we each lack something that the other compensates for."

He saw the stain of crimson coming to her cheeks and felt the urge to reach out and reassure her. But in her present feisty mood, Matt knew she wouldn't stand for it, so he resigned himself to some more teasing. "This is one time I'm glad I don't know a language."

"You know, the Chinese are right—we are foreign devils."

Matt laughed. "Foreign devils?"

Layne finished the cake, satisfied that she now had him off balance, and she was in control of the situation, for once. Placing the tray on another recliner, she stood up. Smoothing out the wrinkles gathering on her jeans, Layne paced around the large, enclosed area. "What did they tell you about the Chinese, Matt? Anything?"

He lost some of his humor and sobered. "Let's put it this way: The *lao-pan* isn't a very nice guy. If the pirates don't like you, they get rid of you. They don't have many morals."

"Oh, they have morals; it's just that you wouldn't agree with them—or with how they see the rest of us."

"I get the feeling the Chinese don't like Americans."

Layne did a few minor stretching exercises to loosen her muscles. "It extends beyond Americans, Matt, so don't feel alone. The Chinese feel no one but their own kind can understand them. And anyone invading their country is considered a 'foreign devil.'"

"Is that stigma ever erased?"

Layne shook her head. "No. As much as the *lao-pan* respects me, I'm sure he still distrusts and dislikes me because I'm not Chinese."

"And yet, he made you part of their clan."

"It's an honor, to be sure."

"The alternative isn't particularly inviting."

"Yes, they'd lop off my head." She rubbed her arm, feeling goose pimples forming. "Kang is very clear about his rights as leader of his clan. They don't regard killing someone with the same horror or outrage that an American would."

"I suppose that's all tied up with their Far Eastern philosophy of reincarnation?"

"Partly."

Matt sat up and folded his hands between his thighs, a serious look on his face. "Are you sure they won't hurt you, Layne?"

Layne stopped her pacing, giving him a startled look. His voice held a depth of worry and protectiveness that sent her heart reeling. "As long as I play by their code and laws, the *lao-pan* wouldn't harm me. Why?"

He cocked his head, a cobalt darkness in his narrowing eyes. "Because there's no way in the world I'm going to lose you, Layne. This mission is dangerous at every turn." He briefly clenched his hands together, the knuckles whitening.

"I'll be okay," she assured him. "But it would help to know something about the mission, Matt. Can you tell me anything?"

His features became closed and unreadable. "Believe me, Layne, I'd tell you if I could."

"Don't give me that compartmentalized policy!" Her eyes grew amber with fury. "If I'm sticking my neck out on the same line as you, I should know what I'm walking into!"

Matt nodded. "Under any other circumstance, I'd agree with you, Layne." He motioned for her to come and sit down next to him. At first, she just stared at him, then finally acquiesced. "Look," he began in a quiet voice, "British Special Intelligence is in on this. And so is the Federal Bureau of Investigation. Not to mention the other side of the coin, which consists of KGB and People's Republic of China agents. Then we have the unknown entity in the guise of the pirates. As you said before, they live by their own codes and laws. They owe allegiance to no one."

"Except to themselves. You're sure that People's Republic of China has agents trying to find whatever we're after?" Layne asked.

"Positive." He leaned back, closing his eyes momentarily. "Right now we're walking into the biggest game in football."

Layne tilted her head. "The Super Bowl?"

Matt opened his eyes, staring directly at her. A wry smile surfaced. "I'll be the quarterback and you be my wide receiver. We'll win this game."

Her returning laugh was soft and lilting, stroking him like the delicate brush of a flower petal against his flesh. "Remember, I grew up in the Orient. I'm afraid I never liked football. Mind telling me what it's about so that I have a more complete picture of what we're getting into?"

Matt warmed to her team spirit. Layne could have said "what I'm getting into," instead, she'd automatically included him. That was good. It might save their lives at some point in the future. "As a kid I played football. I was a quarterback in high school."

"Sounds like you're good at being a quarterback."

"I am."

"And were you a state champion?" Layne guessed. With his natural athletic grace, she imagined him being highly competitive.

"I usually won my games." Matt grinned, then sobered. "And in this game, it's you and me on one team and the pirates on the other. Only they'll be throwing bullets or knives instead of a harmless ball."

Her flesh grew cool, and Layne lost her smile. "What are our chances, Matt?"

He heard the tremor of fear veiled in her husky voice. "Better with you along, that's for sure."

"Don't evade my question. That's a Company tactic."

Matt winced inwardly at the pleading in Layne's voice. "All right," he began grimly, "we stand a thirty-seven percent chance of completing this mission."

"That's what the computer has projected?"

"Yes."

"That still doesn't answer my question entirely."

His gaze rested on her. Again, Matt saw the flicker of a woman who could possess great leadership ability if she chose to bring it out and utilize that facet of herself. "We could get killed by KGB or PRC or the pirates."

"Not the pirates."

Grimly, Matt pursed his lips into a thinner line. "Look, we're not even sure if your *lao-pan* has what we want. There are other pirate clans out there in those hundreds of islands. And not all of them are friendly with one another. If it has fallen into other hands, we may need the *lao-pan*'s help in getting it from another of his factions. That would mean exposing ourselves to yet another enemy. It's not a pretty picture, Layne."

"Dammit, tell me what 'it' is, Matt! I'm tired of this pussy-footing around the object or thing we're supposed to get or find."

"You'll know soon enough after we contact the *lao-pan*, Layne. But not until then."

She glared at him. "Well, I've got some of it figured out. You're a pilot. Someone who's testing state-of-the-art aircraft. The Company wouldn't be sending you over here unless a plane of some sort was involved. I haven't seen anything in the paper to indicate that one of our aircraft has been shot down. So, it must be a reconnaissance aircraft. Or something our government was secretly testing that couldn't be tracked by radar. The RAVEN bomber is such a plane."

Matt gave her a grudging look of admiration. "Your father didn't raise you to be a dummy, did he?"

"My dad taught me to think on my feet," she returned sharply.

"Well, it isn't a RAVEN, so forget about that angle, Layne."

"All right," she continued, her eyes bright, "a reconnaissance aircraft. An SR-71 B-2. Maybe a U-2. Probably a B-2 because I know they fly that area off the coast of China, monitoring Russian as well as Chinese activity."

He said nothing, holding her challenging glare. He longed to share his fears and tell her that it was his younger brother whose life hung in the balance. Hell, he didn't even know if Jim was alive or dead. "No lies, Layne. I can't confirm or deny your conjectures."

Layne leaned forward, bare inches separating them. She could feel the heat of his body, smell the dizzying male scent of him, and it excited her. But she dove on, heedless of the dangerous tension that coiled invisibly around him. "A bird goes down. If it's a B-2 that means two pilots are involved. If it was a U-2, one pilot. Either way, there are lives at stake. Highly trained pilots who are the cream of the Air Force's crop carrying the most vital avionics technology in their heads. I'm sure the KGB would love to get their hands on our pilot and pull the secrets out of him."

She saw Matt's flesh tighten around his cheekbones and mouth, the color draining from his face. Layne instinctively retreated as he slowly turned his head, his thundercloud black eyes pinning her savagely.

"Leave it alone, Layne," he ground out. "Back off."

Shaken, Layne stared openmouthed for a second, assimilating the anguish behind his warning. Matt's hands were white-knuckled on the arms of the recliner. He appeared as if he were going to explode any second—at her. Taking in a gulp of air, Layne rapidly gathered her sharded thoughts. Matt was too emotional, which verified that she was very close to the truth. But no spy ever allowed the feelings that Matt displayed to surface. And that left her shaken. Was he really a test pilot working for the Company as only a part-time and rarely triggered second vocation? A part of her heaved a great sigh of relief if that were true; another part froze in abject fear. Matt was too human, then, for her own good. All that kindness and sensitivity in him was a natural extension of his true self—not some act to manipulate her like a pawn.

"Matt, I—"

"Drop it, Layne."

"But—"

He turned and faced her squarely, his features hard. "Not another word about it, Layne."

She reared back, fury etched in every feature of her face. "Don't try to treat me like some child! Brad tried that, too. I won't be parented. You either treat me like an adult or else."

"Quit overreacting and comparing me to Carson, dammit! I'm a hundred and eighty degrees opposite to him in every way. If you want this mission to go smoothly, you'd best start learning to trust and judge me as an individual, not as some counterpart of your late husband. I'm going to need your help, not your reactions." His eyes lost some of their initial hardness, his voice softening. "Don't fight me, Layne. Sometimes I have to stop myself from telling you everything. God knows I want to, but it's impossible right now." Matt reached out, his fingers wrapping strongly around her cold, damp hand. "Please trust me. It's the only thing that will keep us both alive during this mission. You've got to put your back up against mine as the enemy circles us. You've got to sense intuitively if I need your help or assistance. Don't keep needling me on what I can't divulge to you. You'll know soon enough."

A ribbon of shame flowed through Layne. This was the man Matt Talbot trying to reason with her, his voice trembling with conviction and concern. His hand was dry and warm and strong around her own. She chewed on her lower lip, feeling guilty. "I only wanted to say, before you kept interrupting me, that you were awfully emotional. And that isn't like a Company man."

Matt turned her hand over, studying her long, slender fingers. "And I don't spy for a living, Layne. I told you that before. This is a second job. One that I'm rarely called on to perform. If I had wanted to join the Company on a full-time basis, I'd have done it years ago. But flying is my life."

A small smile fled across her lips. "Your mistress?"

Matt managed a slight, strained laugh. "Yeah, I suppose you could call it that. I have the Air Force for a mother-in-law and my aircraft as a mistress."

Layne was acutely aware of his thumb tracing lazy circles in the palm of her hand, sending delightful tingles sizzling up her arm. Reluctantly she disengaged from his provocative touch, fighting a powerful desire to remain ensconced within his care. "My dad used to say he had the best of all worlds combined—a mother-in-law that understood his love of flying, a mistress who constantly challenged him and a wife who loved him, faults and all."

"Yeah, I can identify with that," Matt agreed huskily.

"What did your wife think of your test-piloting career?" Immediately Layne chastised herself; she was getting personal again. But the gnawing ache of wanting to know more about Matt simply dissolved those walls she had always hidden behind.

Matt began to uncoil and relaxed in the recliner, keeping his blue gaze steadily on her. "Jenny worried a lot. I even took her down to the operations building at Edwards Air Force Base and showed her the preparation behind a flight." He shrugged. "It didn't seem to allay her fears, but only increased them because she wondered if more errors couldn't be built into a test on any given flight."

Layne smiled. "That's interesting, because my dad did the same thing for my mom and me."

"And?"

"We both quit worrying a great deal about Dad's flights." Her brows drew into a pained position. "But a bird killed him anyway."

"What happened? Do you want to talk about it?"

Layne rallied beneath his roughened tone. "He was testing the fuel distribution pumps in both wing tanks on a prototype. I guess too much fuel was pumped into one wing when a valve stuck in the open position and there was no instrument to warn him of what had happened. The weight caused the plane to go into a dive, and Dad couldn't pull it out in time. He ejected at the last moment but the chute was shredded by the speed of the descent." Her voice lowered. "They told us later that he didn't feel a thing." Layne shuddered, reliving that October day.

"He wouldn't have—believe me, kitten."

She raised her head, lost in the blue of his eyes. "How long have you been testing?"

"Four years."

"I suppose you love it?"

Matt nodded. "Yes."

"I think you like living dangerously."

"But I don't see it as dangerous, Layne. Safety is the key phrase."

"And the rest is luck—or fate."

"There's that unaccounted-for ten percent that can go for or against you."

She rested her chin on her clasped hands, a faraway look in her eyes. "That's odd, Dad always said the same thing."

"Look at it this way, Layne. Fate brought us together. I feel like the luckiest man in the world getting introduced to you. Sometimes fate twists in the right direction."

"You'd better hope it doesn't turn its back on us, Matt Talbot."

"And you're blushing, Layne Hamilton."

She fretted, then rose. "I'm having a tough time dealing with your honesty, Major."

He grinned. "Better get used to it. I'm out to prove to you that even though I work for the Company, there can be such a thing as candor in an agent."

"What's the game plan once we land in Hong Kong, Matt?" she asked, changing the subject.

"I'll take you to the hotel and then I'll meet with British SI and the Company people."

"To be briefed?"

He nodded. "All contingents will be there."

"And then?" she asked, thinking that Matt would be coming back to the hotel to sleep. In their bed. The thought left her mouth dry, and her heart skipped erratically. What would it be like to be loved by him? A tremor of anticipation keened through Layne.

"And then I'll brief you as much as I can."

She ambled around the area, hands thrust into the pockets of her jeans, head bowed as she thought of the potential ramifications. "Upon landing do we have to be on guard?"

"One hundred percent of the time. But we also have to act like we're newlyweds and nothing's wrong."

"That's a tough act—be alert, yet melt into the crowd to look inconspicuous," she muttered.

Matt watched her pace. Layne's every movement seemed like that of a ballerina flowing through her lithe motions. "Just stay close to me and there'll be nothing to worry about."

Layne stopped and lifted her head, studying him darkly. "You know it's a serious crime to be smuggling a gun into Hong Kong. Only the police are allowed to have them."

He raised his hands. "I'm not carrying one."

She pursed her lips. "No?"

"No."

"What if your baggage is searched?"

"They won't find anything."

"You're telling me we're going into this without any weapons?"

"Relax. I'll get whatever weapons I need from our people once we land. Okay?"

She muttered something unintelligible beneath her breath. "I've never been around guns. I hate them. I hate the thought of violence…."

"So do I, kitten. You'll wear yourself out with all that pacing."

Matt picked up a magazine and began leafing through it. Layne stopped pacing and sat down next to Matt; she was finally beginning to relax again. She stared at him a long moment. Suddenly, she couldn't resist opening up and asking Matt about his past.

"I was born and raised on the Oregon seacoast," Matt told her, putting the magazine aside. "As a kid I fished off my father's trawler until I graduated from high school and went on to the Air Force Academy."

She stared at him for a moment, caught off guard. Matt had been a fisherman? The two images didn't agree in her mind. "You did?"

He laughed deeply, his blue eyes taking on a twinkle. "Yeah. I'm a grass-roots boy who grew up on the shores of the wild, untamable Oregon coast. Anything wrong with that?"

Heat surged into her face. "Well—it's just that you're such a professional in every way that—"

"People from simple beginnings can move in any direction they want," he countered, enjoying her amazement.

"I find it hard to equate fishing with flying."

"Both start with the letter *f*."

Layne burst out laughing. "Has anyone ever accused you of having a deadly, dry wit?"

His smile was devastating. "A few have. And if it brings a smile to that lovely face of yours and makes those eyes turn amber with happiness again, then I'm glad."

She wrestled with his praise as she always did, then chose to deal with it indirectly. "What I want to know," she said, smiling sweetly, "is who taught you to compliment? Your mother?"

"No. Actually both my parents did. They believed in positive strokes instead of negative ones."

"Oh, I see, raised on psychology. No spare-the-rod-and-spoil-the-child philosophy for them, huh?"

Matt grinned mischievously. "I wouldn't say that. I can remember getting the rod a few times."

"I'm sure you were a precocious child at best," Layne countered.

"No more or less than you, probably."

Layne hooted. "My *amah* made sure I stayed in line at all times. I didn't really get a chance to pull pranks like I'm sure you did."

He gave her an innocent look. "Me? Pranks? Jim was the one—"

"What's wrong, Matt?" Layne lost her smile, watching his eyes grow troubled as his voice trailed off on his brother's name.

"Nothing," he said a little too quickly.

"Who's Jim? Your brother?"

Dammit, why had he relaxed his guard? Matt chastised himself. "Yes, my younger brother."

Again, Layne sensed tightly controlled anguish around Matt, similar to the time she had interrogated him about the mission. A tenseness lay around the corners of his mouth, and instinctively she wanted to reach out and smooth them away with her fingertips. "How old is he?"

"A year younger than me."

She wanted to dispel the pain she saw in Matt's face. She smiled for his benefit. "Well, at least you have a brother. I always wanted a baby sister. My *amah*, Lao Shu, always complained to my parents that I was as much trouble as two children. So I guess my mom and dad believed her and decided not to have any more."

He smiled warmly, relieved at the turn in the conversation. "I take it an *amah* is like a nanny?"

"Yes. My mother was walking through an open-air market in Hong Kong when she was pregnant with me and Shu fell at her feet. She begged my mother to take her home with her. She promised to look after our family until she died."

"And what did your father think of all that?"

Layne smiled in memory of those days. "My dad had a soft heart, too. And Shu did stay with us until she died. I loved her dearly. Of course, she was a fierce old dragon when I would toddle off in search of adventure or play hide-and-seek on her."

Matt liked Layne's vernacular with the Chinese flavor. With her black hair and slightly tilted brown eyes, she could easily pass for a Eurasian beauty. "So, you said Shu taught you Chinese first?"

"Yes. She gave me my love of the culture. I was speaking fluent Cantonese by the time I was five. Later, I studied Mandarin and several other dialects such as Seiyap, spoken by the people of Hong Kong, and Haklo, spoken by the seaborne people who live on junks."

"I'm impressed. Chinese is one language I never had the yen to try."

Layne shared a smile with Matt over his terrible pun. There was an indefinable aura of enjoyment over sharing the small, but important nuances with him. "But you're fluent at least in French. Any other languages?"

Matt nodded. "Three, actually. But no Far Eastern ones."

"Now it's my turn to be impressed. How did you pick up your knack for languages?"

"Probably being a fisherman. Off the coast of Oregon, Washington, and California we met trawlers from every nation. During the summers my father let us go aboard a Chilean trawler and we picked up Spanish. The next year Jim and I spent time aboard a California tuna boat whose skipper was French. When he wasn't cursing at us in French, he was giving us orders in it." He smiled fondly, recalling those times.

Layne broke out in laughter. "I've heard that some of the French don't care for us. Oh, well, it can't be any more so than the Chinese. I think Americans abroad sometimes forget to try to integrate into the culture they're visiting, and people take an affront to that." Her eyes glimmered with mischief. "So tell me, were you a rough, tough boy growing up?"

Matt rubbed his jaw. "I suppose I was. At least until that sixteenth year when we worked on Cap Henri's tuna boat. My dad was a third-generation fisherman and had been bred to the sea."

"You defied family tradition by moving into the world of flying?"

A slight shadow veiled his azure eyes. "Yes. I left and then Jim followed me. It broke my father's heart."

"I'm sorry, Matt. I know how strong the Chinese are about family unity, pride and protectiveness. Your father sounds similar. It must have been rough on you, too."

Matt warmed with appreciation for her insight and sensitivity. "You know something, Layne Hamilton?" he said huskily.

She froze, momentarily stunned by the intimacy that fell around her like warming sunlight. "What?"

"I like you. I like your ability to see all sides of a situation. That's rare in today's world." He reached out, his fingers grazing her pale cheek. "The only good thing about this mission is that I'm going to find out everything there is to know about you. And I'm going to enjoy that."

Chapter 6

Hong Kong International Airport swarmed with activity, and Layne was intoxicated by the very fact that she was once again among her people. Fear that they might be followed by enemy agents meshed with her excitement at being in Hong Kong once again. Her heart surged with joy as Matt placed his arm around her shoulder, drawing her near as they walked down the spotless halls toward Customs. Singsong voices jammed the air as people ebbed and flowed around them. She glanced up at Matt, and her pulse raced at his tender glance.

"You're happy" was all he said.

"Very." Her amber eyes shone.

"You're home again."

Layne slid her arm around his waist, leaning her head against his shoulder. "Thank you for understanding." And she laughed, drinking in all the bustling people around them. "It's wonderful to be back here." She inhaled deeply. "I can smell Victoria Harbour, the tang of the salt, the odor of diesel from one of the many ships anchored there."

Matt smiled and gave her a fierce embrace. "For me, it's a lot of short people scurrying here and there, speaking in high-pitched voices and a half-dozen tongues."

"Hong Kong is the Far East's potpourri," she agreed. All she had to do was look around them to see lanky, ruddy-faced Australians, staid Englishmen, Africans in bright, colorful garb and Europeans nattily dressed in the latest Parisian fashions. There was no place like Hong Kong; it was magic. The air literally vibrated with frantic activity. And it was affecting her, too. And Matt? Layne lifted her chin, noting his alertness. He was reacting as he had at Dulles airport in Washington—a strange, coiled tenseness emanated from him.

Layne relaxed, realizing Matt's invisible radar was working to protect them. She wanted to let down after the exhaustion of the twenty-hour flight. Matt hadn't slept, telling her the best way for him to successfully hurdle jet lag was to wait and sleep that night at their destination. Luckily, it was 11:00 p.m. in Kowloon, where the busy airport sat out on the lip of Victoria Harbour separating them from the island of Hong Kong. They would be able to sleep and wake up refreshed tomorrow morning…. Her pulse began its usual erratic activity whenever she thought of Matt lying beside her. Would he try to make love to her? Layne wasn't sure.

Showing their passports, they were allowed to move on to the baggage-claim area, the last step of Customs. Layne knew from long experience that visitors coming into Hong Kong were rarely searched; it was only going out that the Customs people became stringent and thorough. She knew the airport well, showing Matt where the baggage would be unloaded. People milled around them, and the air was alive with at least fifteen foreign languages other than English. Matt pulled her against him, his back up against the wall near the baggage conveyer that would eventually yield their suitcases.

His arm draped casually around her shoulders felt comforting, and Layne relaxed against his hard, warm body. She tipped her head back against his shoulder, closing her eyes.

"How are you doing?" Matt asked, his voice husky near her ear.

Layne opened her eyes, drowning in the clear blue of his gaze. "Excited. Exhausted. Nervous. Do you want some more adjectives?"

His smile was distant as his gaze continued combing the large, spacious area containing hundreds of airplane passengers. "Those will do. I think they accurately describe your present state."

"How would you know?"

Matt's gaze focused back on her, and he studied her uplifted face and provocative mouth for a moment. "There's very little you can hide in those wonderful eyes or that revealing face of yours."

She wrinkled her nose, feeling deliciously taken care of by Matt. "That's not good, is it?"

He leaned down, kissing the tip of her nose. "For me, it is," he told her.

His deep, rough voice made her yearning explode into life. "You're incorrigible, Matt Talbot."

"I know. Aren't you glad?"

Layne's eyes widened momentarily, and she shared an intimate smile with him. "I'm not going to answer that."

His mouth stretched into a disarming, sensual smile. "Have it your way, kitten. I know the answer anyway."

She gave him a disgruntled look. "Know-it-all. I've never met a test pilot who wasn't."

Matt grinned, continuing to scan the crowd. "Yep, we're wonderful—once you get to know us."

She shook her head. Matt was so typically a test pilot that it sent an incredible surge of exhilaration through her opening heart. "You *are* incorrigible, Talbot."

"But likeable," he amended, returning his attention to her. God, Layne was completely relaxed in his arms for the first time. Was it that mysterious chemistry that always exploded between them whenever they got near each other? Was it the fact that she was finally beginning to trust him? Whatever the reason, Matt was grateful. He wanted to lean down and kiss her parted, smiling lips, drawing the honey and sweetness from her into his own starving body. And he knew that she would willingly give herself to him. But at what price to herself? To their budding relationship? Everything was moving too fast, too far out of control for his own comfort. Matt tore his attention from Layne, perusing the area again.

He spotted one Chinese man from their own flight who appeared to be other than a tourist. Had the PRC sent a tail on them from the States? Or was it British SI? Maybe a Company man. The scent of lilac mingled with his logical mind, and he glanced down at Layne who remained comfortably ensconced beneath his arm. She still had that devilish glint in her eyes.

"Something's up with you," he teased.

"Me?"

"Feigning innocence won't get you anywhere, *Mrs. Talbot.*"

Layne felt the heat of a blush spread rapidly across her face as he called her Mrs. Talbot. What would it be like to be married to Matt? If his behavior thus far was any indication, she ached to know more. But looks could be deceiving. No one knew that better than she. Brad had been a charmer on the outside, too. And Layne had fallen for that once. But never again. Time, a little voice whispered to her heart; give yourself time and Matt will show you his true colors. Was he a tiger in disguise? Someone who, after gaining her trust, would rip her apart, destroying her emotionally when her guard was down? But every time she looked into Matt's eyes, Layne felt buoyed and safe.

"What's the matter, cat finally got your tongue?" he coaxed intimately.

Layne lost some of her joy and shook her head. "Just thinking."

"Oh? About what?"

Layne shifted, lowering her lashes so Matt couldn't see the confusion she felt inwardly. "A lot of things. Dumb things, I suppose."

He chortled softly. "Lady, you may be a lot of things, but 'dumb' isn't a word I'd ever apply to you. Childlike, maybe. Or generous. Definitely warm. But not dumb."

"Now you're embarrassing me, Matt."

His fingers wove evocative patterns on her upper arm. "Just being honest, kitten."

Layne managed a partial smile, meeting the hooded cobalt eyes that suddenly seethed with desire…for her. Her mouth went dry and her heart began to pound heavily in her chest. She tried to recover, but she was too tired from the flight and her normal defense systems weren't in place because of it. Her words came out in a breathless hush. "Okay, you want the truth?"

"Never anything but that between you and me," Matt assured her, his voice deep and soothing.

"I—I worry what's going to happen when we get to the hotel."

Matt's eyes narrowed momentarily, and he immediately grasped Layne's dilemma. "It's not uncommon for one of the houseboys or maids to come into our room at any given time, Layne. I'd sleep on the floor, if I could. But we can't risk that. We can't afford to blow our cover to anyone." His voice dropped to a roughened whisper. "And to make you feel safer, I'd like to be able to roll up a blanket and put it right down the middle of the bed to prevent any straying…."

Color rose to a furious hue in her cheeks, and Matt pressed a kiss on her hair, inhaling her special fragrance. Layne forced herself to hold his serious expression, her heart hammering unrelentingly. "I'm afraid, Matt. Of you…of myself. I'm not ready. I'm so scared…."

Matt whispered an endearment, pulling her into his arms and holding her comfortably against his body. "I know that, honey. And I'll try and watch myself for your sake, although—" he took a long, unsteady breath "—God knows, since the day I saw you, I've wanted to make love with you."

Layne stood frozen in his arms. A part of her had wanted to hear those wonderful, tremulous words in that intimate growl that excited every nerve-ending in her body. But the other part of her shrank in abject fear, reacting blindly to Matt Talbot, the Company man.

Matt's brows drew downward as he felt Layne stiffen in his arms. "Don't worry, Layne. You'll be safe with me."

Layne relaxed visibly, momentarily sagging against him, her eyes shut. "Thank you, Matt. I'm sorry, I can't go to bed with just any man. I'm not built that way." She gave a nervous laugh. "Whether I like it or not, I'm conservative by nature." She looked up at him, an imploring expression in her eyes. "It's probably because I was raised in a conservative military environment. Or—" her voice dropped to a painful whisper "—maybe it's because I thought I could have a storybook marriage like my parents had. I'm an idealist, I guess—a romantic idealist who believes in love and loyalty for one person, forever."

Matt cupped her face, lifting it, watching those gloriously thick ebony lashes lift to reveal pain-ridden topaz eyes. "That's not idealism, kitten. Those morals and principles are to be applauded."

Layne's full mouth pulled into a grimace, and she rested her cheek against his steadying palm. "Brad had several affairs while we were married, Matt."

Matt drew in a sharp breath, realizing the implication of hurt to Layne. His fingers momentarily tensed against her flesh before he consciously relaxed them, not wanting to hurt her. "I'm sorry. He was the one who was screwed up, Layne. It wasn't you."

"He made me think it was me, Matt. He had me believing every marriage could endure an affair or two and survive."

His mouth drew into a grim line. "Why did you stay with him so long, Layne? Why didn't you leave him?"

Her face grew solemn and her eyes glistened with tears. "My idealistic attitude. I thought that if I changed enough, Brad might want me instead of those—those other women."

"No," he whispered violently, his voice seething with controlled anger. "Brad made you believe you were the one who was driving him outside the marriage and forcing him to have the affairs. Your attitude left you vulnerable to taking on the guilt he heaped on you, Layne. There's a difference."

He was right, Layne conceded. Again, she was stunned by Matt's insights into human nature and into herself. "You're right," she admitted. "I swallowed the whole thing—hook, line and sinker, to use one of your fisherman's adages. It's only been a short time since his death, and I'm able to see more and more clearly what was wrong with him every day. But I still haven't been able to trust men in general." And then she added painfully, "And Company men in particular. You've been on the receiving end of my distrust on that point."

Matt lightly grazed her hair in a caressing gesture. "Don't worry about me, I'll survive." And then a little more gently he added, "And so will you." He slid his hand across her drooping shoulder and gave her arm a reassuring squeeze. "I'm not going to take advantage of you in this situation. What you say goes.

Although—" Matt raised his head, a smile pulling at his mouth "—you're the most tempting woman I've ever had the pleasure of meeting. What a challenge—keeping my hands off you."

Just the way he said it made Layne snap out of her reverie involving her painful past. A tremendous load slipped from her when she realized Matt wouldn't try to pressure her. And yet…she longed to possess and be possessed by him.

"Did you hear me?"

"Y-yes."

A glimmer of mirth danced in his eyes. "Don't look so disappointed, then," he said, a catlike grin spreading across his mouth.

Layne shook her head. "You really are incorrigible, Matt Talbot."

He lifted his head as the baggage carousel began to operate and suitcases began to appear. "And aren't you glad?"

"Very," she agreed breathlessly, walking arm in arm with him to retrieve their luggage.

Customs was, as Matt put it later in the taxicab drive to the Princeton Hotel, like melting butter in a hot skillet: quick and smooth. Layne languished against him with his arm draped comfortably across her shoulders on the short ride from the airport to the Tsim Sha Tsui district of Kowloon. Her lids kept drooping downward despite her eagerness to drink in the black, reflective bay that separated them from the glittering island of Hong Kong. Layne had all but forgotten why she was here and the danger surrounding them, thanks to Matt's protectiveness shielding her.

At the hotel entrance, Matt gently shook Layne awake. He winced inwardly as she lifted those lashes to reveal sleep-ridden eyes. At that poignant moment, Matt wanted to take Layne into his arms forever and never let her go….

"Come on," he coaxed her gruffly. "It's time to check in and get you to bed."

The spacious lobby of the Princeton was inlaid with polished beige and brown marble, setting off the glittering array of crystal chandeliers that made the entire area look like a palace. Stumbling sleepily, Layne was grateful as Matt put an arm around her waist, drawing her near. The encroaching tiredness had reduced her to a sleepy-eyed child. The lights seemed too bright; even the softened sound of precise British English was too much to cope with. All she wanted to do was fall fast asleep in Matt's arms.

In no time, they had taken the elevator to the fourteenth floor. A houseboy brought fragrant jasmine tea and biscuits, placing them on the rosewood coffee table in front of the pale blue silk settee. Matt thanked David, their houseboy, who would be looking after them while they stayed at the plush hotel. Locking the door after David's departure, Matt walked back into the spacious suite decorated in blue silk-covered furniture. A king-size bed sat in one corner of the room. Layne was beginning to open one of the suitcases when he came over, placing his hand over hers.

"Let me do that. You get your bath started and then hit the sack."

She looked up, her eyes dark with confusion. "But—"

Matt led her into the marble bathroom and turned on the gold-leaf faucets. "You've got shadows under your eyes, kitten. What you need is a good eight hours and you'll be fine."

"What about you? I mean—"

"Let me get you settled first."

She was too tired to argue, allowing Matt to add orange crystals to the rapidly filling tub. "Sounds wonderful. Thank you," she murmured.

Matt dug through her suitcase and found her nightclothes. He was acutely aware of the white satin material of her nightgown as he picked it up. Layne would look incredibly beautiful in the floor-length gown. Muttering an oath under his breath, Matt knocked on the bathroom door and handed Layne the item when her hand appeared.

With the thoroughness of a detective, Matt checked every lamp in the place, turning each one over and examining it for any kind of sound device. He unscrewed the phone receiver, finding it clean. The potential for a bug or wire to be placed in the room was very real. As fatigued as he was, he shoved the weariness away, continuing his search while Layne took a well-deserved bath. He took the mattress off the bed, checked behind the rosewood headboard and made a sweep of each drawer in the dressers. Nothing escaped his attention in that half hour. Finally, standing with his hands placed on his hips, he was satisfied. He shifted his sharpened hearing to the bathroom: there were no sounds coming from it. Frowning, Matt moved to the door, knocking on it softly.

"Layne?"

No answer. He knocked more loudly, calling her name again. The doors were made of heavy, dark teak, the bathroom of tiled marble, while a thick, luxurious royal blue carpet felt like heaven beneath his feet. It was possible that the sound of the heavy knock wouldn't carry well. Again he rapped sharply on the door, calling her name. No response.

"Dammit," he growled, twisting the knob and pushing the door open a crack. "Layne?" His voice carried through the long, rectangular bathroom.

He stepped inside, aware of the steamy atmosphere created by the huge tub of water. His eyes lost their hardness and grew tender as he walked quietly to where Layne lay asleep, her hands clasping the washcloth to her breast. Matt forced himself to do the right thing: he retrieved one of the huge, fluffy white bath towels and knelt down next to where she lay. Layne's flesh was flushed pink beneath the water, attesting to the initial heat of the bath. The scent of orange blossoms filled the room, and Matt tried to ignore the vision that met his eyes and its physical effects on him.

As he reached out to gently shake Layne's shoulder, he hesitated only a second more. She had coaxed that glorious mane of black hair into a loose knot on top of her head; the multitude of tendrils curled languidly around her temples and neck in the steamy atmosphere. Dots of perspiration covered her relaxed features, dark shadows skirting beneath her black lashes. His heart wrenched as his gaze traveled down across her face and her full, parted lips.

A soft smile crossed his mouth as he touched her shoulder. Instead of shaking her, Matt slid his fingers across her shoulder in a slow, circular motion. He watched her lashes flutter and stilled his hand. Her flesh was slick and pliant beneath his hand as Matt waited for her to pull away from the fingers of sleep.

"Come on, kitten. Let's get you out of the water and into bed," he told her in a hushed tone.

Her lashes lifted as if weighted. Golden eyes stared up at him in drowsy bewilderment. Matt smiled tenderly and slipped his hands beneath her arms, pulling her upward. In one smooth, unbroken motion he lifted her from the tub and onto the rug where he stood. Then he wrapped the towel around Layne before she could gather her scattered senses. Keeping one arm around her shoulder, he coaxed the thick terry-cloth robe onto her.

"Matt—"

"It's all right, Layne. You fell asleep in the tub. I called you, but you didn't answer."

Her eyes were clouded as she reached up to touch the robe as he belted and tied it snugly around her waist. "But…oh, dear…"

Matt opened the door and then lifted her into his arms as if she were feather light. "Bed for you, my beautiful kitten," he said huskily. "Shh, it's all right. I've seen women undressed before."

Layne tried to drag herself out of the jet lag enough to feel properly embarrassed by having fallen asleep in the tub. Matt's rough voice wove warm magic, and Layne lay her head on his shoulder in surrender.

"That's my lady, just lie there and enjoy the ride." There was a hint of amusement in his tone as Matt carried her to the bed. He'd thrown back the covers previously, and now he gently settled Layne between the crisp white sheets.

The lamplight snapped off, and Layne was blinded by the consummate darkness. She felt Matt tucking her in, as if he were putting to bed a much-loved child. He leaned down, kissing her damp temple.

"I'll see you in the morning, Sleeping Beauty. Good night."

Layne mumbled something, but whatever it was came out in a garbled whisper. Her lashes swept downward and she willingly slid back into the welcoming arms of sleep, knowing she was safe because Matt was near.

* * *

The first gray hint of dawn was nudging back the cape of night as Matt wearily left the elevator and walked toward their room on the fourteenth floor. His eyes smarted and he rubbed at them to try to stop the ache. Carefully placing the key in the door, Matt slipped inside. The room was dark and quiet, just the opposite of the place where he'd spent the harrowing past five hours with British SI. Matt's shoulders slumped, and he stopped to observe the thin light of dawn coming up over Hong Kong. There was just enough illumination through the gossamer panels for him to see outlines in the grayness of the room. His gaze traveled to Layne, lying curled up like a small kitten in the wide bed, her hair free. One slender hand lay stretched out toward his pillow, fingers softly curled inward toward her palm. Matt didn't need any more of an invitation.

He ached for her nearness. He was almost past thinking as he placed the key quietly on the bedroom stand, shrugged out of his shoulder holster and placed the gun beneath the bed. He sat down, his head bowed. A hundred bits of information whirled through his mind, his emotions cresting as he thought about his brother Jim's desperate plight. Nudging off his shoes, Matt shifted his weight and turned, stretching out on top of the covers. He was too exhausted to take a shower. He was too exhausted to do anything but sleep. Tiredly, Matt turned on his side and gathered Layne to him.

A soft moan broke from Layne's lips as he brought her against him, her head resting comfortably upon his shoulder. *I probably smell like hell,* he thought wearily, inhaling the scent of oranges that perfumed her velvety skin and the sweet fragrance of her hair against his jaw. *Oh, God, Layne, I need you. Just lie here with me, and let me feel your softness, your sweetness.* A ragged sigh escaped him as Layne nestled more deeply into his arms. Did she somehow know he was hurting and lonely? His hand slid across the swell of her blanketed hip. She felt good to him, and the tension began to drain from his body. Matt nuzzled his face into her hair, the raw silk sheets clean and sweet against the sandpapery texture of his unshaven cheek. How long had it been since he held a woman like this? Not since Jenny.

The last coherent thought in the jumbled mass of problems ranging through Matt's mind was that he wanted the time to explore Layne. But she could never know that as long as her life was in his hands. He had to make sure she got out of this mission alive. He couldn't afford to impinge his own selfish desires upon her and risk throwing her off balance, making her lose focus on the mission. In the morning, he thought, in the morning….

Layne awoke slowly, a feeling of joy transcending her state of drowsiness. She stirred, the corners of her mouth curving with a soft smile. And then it dawned upon her: a masculine arm was draped across her waist. With eight hours of badly needed sleep having nourished her jet-lagged body, Layne forced open her eyes. The realization that she lay with Matt brought her completely awake. When had she come into his arms last night? Carefully, Layne extricated herself from Matt's embrace. Only when she sat up with the rumpled terry-cloth robe on, did she realize that he was still dressed and sleeping deeply. He hadn't pulled any covers on top of him. Her eyes softened with compassion as she looked at Matt's face, now shadowed with a growth of stubbly beard making his cheeks look gaunt. Reaching out, Layne's trembling fingers pushed a strand of hair off his forehead. In his exhausted state, he looked almost boyish. She got up and threw a light blanket across him.

Sunlight was lacing through the floor-to-ceiling windows. Layne walked over the plush carpeting and opened the panels to let the brightness cascade into the room like a golden waterfall. She stood for at least a minute, just drinking in the sight of busy Victoria Harbour where fishing trawlers, motorized junks and military ships from around the world floated by or lay at anchor. The island of Hong Kong sat in the hazy distance, with Victoria Peak proudly thrusting her velvet-green nose upward into the brilliant blue of the morning sky.

Turning back toward Matt, Layne mulled over the chain of

events from the night before. My God, she suddenly recalled, he had come into the bathroom! Her hand went to the plush robe at her breast. He had seen her naked! Had anything else happened? Layne didn't spare her foggy memory, ruthlessly retrieving as much as she could. No, Matt hadn't made love to her; she would have remembered. So why did she feel a little sense of disappointment, knowing that he hadn't?

Chapter 7

The polite knock on the door brought Layne to her feet. She glanced at Matt as she hurried into the hallway, making sure the noise hadn't disturbed him. Still dressed in the warm, comfortable hotel robe, Layne opened the door.

"Good morning Mrs. Talbot," said David the houseboy, whom they'd met on arriving. He bowed and his face broke into a welcoming smile.

Layne returned the smile, placing her index finger to her lips. "Good morning, David. My husband's still sleeping."

"Ahh, of course. I'll be very quiet, then," he promised as he wheeled in a breakfast cart.

"Thank you." Layne allowed the door to close, then followed David into the main area of the living room. He was dressed in a starchly pressed white housecoat and black slacks, and Layne felt nostalgia stalking her as she remembered her last stay at the Princeton. A soft smile hovered around her mouth as she watched the young, efficient Chinese boy bring the breakfast she'd ordered out of the heated box hidden beneath the pale pink linen of the tablecloth.

"That smells wonderful," she whispered, going over to her purse to find two American dollars.

"Good, good," he intoned, turning toward her. His eyes widened slightly as she handed him the money. "Thank you, Mrs. Talbot. You are most generous."

Her smile lingered. "My pleasure, David." Two American dollars were worth fifteen Hong Kong dollars. Layne knew David was probably part of a huge family living as one cramped unit in three-hundred square feet of space. His monthly pay probably amounted to less than three hundred Hong Kong dollars, so the two American dollars Layne gave him would keep his whole family fed for several days.

"And Mr. Talbot?" David asked, nodding in Matt's direction. "You ring and let me know when he's hungry."

Layne was careful not to reach out and touch David. Although it was a natural inclination on her part, the Chinese didn't touch one another under circumstances such as this; it would have been an insult. "I'm sure he'll be hungry as a horse when he wakes up, David. We'll give you a ring."

David bowed, then awarded her with a happy smile. "Good morning, Mrs. Talbot," he said, leaving as quietly as he came.

Layne stood staring down the empty hallway, happiness uncoiling within her heart. She loved the Chinese, with their industrious and hardworking philosophy. And to hear them speak British English better than most of the English themselves made her smile broadly: she loved watching American tourists raise their eyebrows when they learned that all of Hong Kong spoke the language fluently.

The savory odor of freshly cooked eggs, bacon and fried potatoes filled the air, and Layne inhaled appreciatively. She poured herself a cup of coffee, and the fragrant odor smelled like heaven to her. Later, after breakfast, she languished on the settee, her legs drawn up beneath her, a second cup of coffee in her hands. Glancing at the clock, she realized it was almost 10:00 a.m. Matt was sleeping deeply, and if it wasn't her imagination, the dark shadows under his eyes seemed to have miraculously disappeared.

Matt pulled himself out of the depths of sleep like a man drugged with fatigue. Was it the delicious smell of coffee and bacon that had tempted him out of the darkness? Or the faint scent of oranges surrounding him? He emitted a sigh, turning slowly over onto his back.

He sensed Layne's presence and forced his eyes open. She sat on the edge of the bed no more than six inches from him, and Matt's eyes widened with appreciation as he drank in her unparalleled beauty. She had brushed her hair until it shone with blue highlights, tumbling with careless abandon about her shoulders and breasts. Her eyes were clear, amusement flecked in their golden depths as she studied him in the sensual silence that swirled and wove around them. She wore a simple white lace blouse to perfection, Matt thought groggily. As he raised his gaze to her rosy lips his body automatically tightened with desire.

A slow smile began at her mouth and moved to her sparkling topaz eyes. "I've always heard the expression 'making love with your eyes,' but this is the first time I've ever seen it," she admitted throatily.

Matt managed a slight smile. "That obvious?"

"I'm afraid so."

"So much for being a Company man."

Layne lost some of her merriment, becoming sober. "I'm glad. It's kind of exciting for me to know what a man's thinking…or feeling."

Matt threw his arm across his eyes. "It's your fault, you know," he offered, his voice still thick with sleep.

She smiled, relaxing as she watched him wake up. The need to reach out and caress his face rose within her, but Layne forced her hands to remain in her lap. "My fault?"

"Yes, for looking so damn good this morning." He groaned and then moved his arm to study her again with his cobalt eyes. "As beautiful as you look and smell, I feel like ten thousand yaks not only trampled my body, but stampeded through my mouth, too."

"Are you trying to tell me you look and feel terrible?"

Matt grimaced. "That's about the size of it."

"Well, I can't speak for the ten thousand yaks tramping through your mouth, but I can assure you that you don't *look* that bad."

A boyish grin pulled at his mouth. "Yeah?"

Layne matched his grin. "Yeah."

"You just made my day, kitten."

Layne felt her self-control melting. Matt was a tousled little boy in rumpled clothes. "You must be terribly tired. I know you didn't get much sleep. Let me order you breakfast while you clean up."

He gave her a tender look. "Sounds good. Order me three eggs over easy and plenty of bacon. I'm starved." *Starved for you,* Matt thought, ambling off in the direction of the bathroom.

Layne puttered around the spacious suite while Matt showered. The day was beginning wonderfully. Even the sun had deigned to shed its warming rays on humid Hong Kong. The door opened and Layne turned, hands poised in midair from her duties of straightening up the bed. Matt padded out of the bathroom wrapped only in a towel.

Layne's eyes widened and she felt her mouth going dry. Matt's physique was magnificent. She knew he was in top condition; but now, his bronzed skin glistening from a recent shower and his brown hair gleaming, he took her breath away. The towel was draped unselfconsciously low on his hips, and her gaze followed the dark line of hair as it ran down his hard, flat stomach to disappear under the stark whiteness of the towel. Layne swallowed as Matt glanced in her direction.

"I forgot to get clothes," he explained, leaning over his one battered leather suitcase and opening it.

"Oh…yes, of course," she murmured, straightening, her fingers resting at the base of her throat. She couldn't tear her attention away from him, but Matt seemed supremely unaware of her blatant inspection of his almost-naked body. Matt wasn't heavily muscled, simply lean and tight, and each of his movements flowed smoothly into the next. He reminded her of a channel swimmer with his broad chest tapering down into a narrow waist and hips. She forced herself to resume her activity. Why was she behaving like a sixteen-year-old girl with a moviestar crush?

When Matt had padded back into the bathroom Layne took a deep, shaky breath. Standing before the bay window, she looked out over Victoria Harbour toward Hong Kong, trying to quiet her clamoring senses.

A light knock on the door short-circuited her nervous reaction.

David appeared with a second breakfast and quickly set up the table, wheeling the other one out as he left. Matt emerged moments later.

"That smells great!" he said, wandering into the room, handsome in a light blue short-sleeved shirt and well-worn jeans. He sat down at the small table.

"Come on, join me."

Layne laughed. "Me? I already made a pig of myself a little while ago."

He uncovered a basket of freshly baked croissants and cinnamon and Danish rolls, then poured her a cup of coffee. "Come on," he urged, smiling up at her. "I like your company."

Layne felt heat stealing into her cheeks as she took the chair opposite him. Why did it feel natural having breakfast with Matt? Her heart lurched with tenderness as she watched him eat like a little boy who had played hard all morning and was now coming in for a well-earned lunch. Matt's hair was neatly combed and dark from the recent shower. His skin was scraped free of the stubble of beard and his blue eyes danced with alertness. Layne nibbled on a croissant, languishing in his male aura.

"Cat got your tongue? What's going on in those shadowed topaz eyes of yours?"

Layne roused herself, stirring cream and sugar into her coffee. "I was just thinking that Brad and I never shared a breakfast like this," she answered softly. She looked around the room and then back at Matt. He had stopped eating and was studying her with naked intensity once again. "Well, I mean we ate together, but the feelings weren't like this…." She stumbled in explanation.

"Feelings?"

Layne was unable to look at Matt, and she reached for the marmalade, nervously putting some of it on the knife and then transferring it to her croissant. "I'm happy."

Matt's mouth curved gently as he watched Layne. Those two magic words flowed across him, and he reached across the table, claiming her left hand and giving it a squeeze. "So am I."

Just the contact with his strong, callused fingers sent a spiral of need through Layne. Shyly, she returned the squeeze, and Matt released her fingers to resume eating again. Swallowing hard, Layne bit into the croissant. "The last time we were here, Brad slept a lot. Of course he'd just come off an assignment and he was really tired."

"You never shared a breakfast like this?" Matt teased, removing the plate and pouring himself another cup of coffee.

"He made it clear that if I wanted to do anything, I was to do it alone. He was more interested in just sleeping or watching television." Layne shrugged. "That's how I stumbled onto the pirates in the first place. I was walking down by the Star Ferry wharf when I overheard some Chinese people talking about the pirates being active in the Macao area. So, I hopped a hydrofoil over to Macao and started to track down Kang's people."

Matt shook his head, his eyes glittering. "I'd never have let you traipse off like that by yourself."

She gave him a shy look. "No, I don't imagine you would. I feel as if you really do care what happens to me."

"I do." Matt grinned belatedly. "You're an easy traveling companion and you don't complain."

"If that's what you require in a traveling companion, then what do you like in a woman, Matt Talbot?" Layne asked, shocked by her own boldness. But Matt's whole demeanor seemed to invite that kind of intimacy from her.

He leaned back, crossed his legs and sipped the coffee contentedly. "I like a woman who's self-confident—someone aware of her strengths and weaknesses." His eyes crinkled. "I'm still enough of a chauvinist to want her to lean on me in her weak moments, but she'd also have to let me lean on her in my weak moments."

"That's the first time I've heard a man admit he might need to lean on a woman," Layne said—a little more harshly than she'd intended.

Matt tipped his head back, glancing up at the ceiling. "I think one of the gravest mistakes a man—or a woman—can make is trying to be strong all the time." He lowered his chin and looked directly at Layne, his blue eyes thoughtful. "I used to think I could handle anything or anyone, especially in the emotional department. I wanted Jenny to lean on me, but I fooled myself into believing I'd never have to lean on her. It was the old double standard. I was raised to believe a man was forever strong, although Cap Henri softened my views on that subject to a degree." His voice trailed off.

Matt allowed these memories to well up in him. He found himself wanting to share that part of himself with Layne; she was understanding and sympathetic in a way that appealed to him. "When Jenny contracted leukemia the doctors impressed upon me that she was going to die shortly, and it knocked me to my knees."

"And you cried?" Layne asked quietly, watching the pain in his eyes deepen.

Matt slowly turned the fragile china cup between his hands, staring down at it. "I didn't even know there was anything wrong with her. She never complained, either. All she did say from time to time was that she was tired. I had just gotten off a test flight at Edwards when a call came in from the base hospital that she had been admitted at Emergency. Our next-door neighbors, Paul and Alicia Johnson, had found her unconscious in the backyard. I dropped everything and went running out the front doors with my G suit still on and my helmet under my arm." Matt shook his head gravely. "Jenny was in a mild coma when I got there. I just stood in the doctor's office crying like a baby when he told me the diagnosis. A few days later, when they got her blood count back up and she regained consciousness, I felt broken emotionally. All I could do was hold her, cry and tell her how much I loved her."

Matt raised his head, his blue eyes dark. "As sick as Jenny was, she encouraged me to lean on her. Figure it out, she was the one dying a slow death, and she was comforting me, the one who would survive. It was then that I discovered the strength inherent in women. Men are brittle in comparison, Layne." He took a deep, unsteady breath. His smile seemed forced. "Through her illness I found weaknesses I had either ignored or hadn't been aware of. Jenny taught me to accept myself, weak or strong. I had a lot of guilt, but she helped me put it into perspective before she died."

The silence wove between them, and Layne felt hot tears drifting down her cheeks. She tried to wipe them inconspicuously away with her hand, but Matt caught her in the act. Layne knew she could be vulnerable with him. "Jenny must have been a very special woman."

"One hell of a woman," he agreed quietly. "With a marked degree of sensitivity, like you."

Layne squirmed. "I'm not in Jenny's class, Matt. I don't have her strength. If I knew I was going to die of leukemia, I'm afraid I'd be the worst coward in the world."

He shook his head solemnly. "No, I don't think so. If the chips were down, you'd be ready to fight, like a lioness protecting her cubs against an enemy. You wouldn't run and you wouldn't be a coward."

"Cowardice comes in many forms, Matt. If I'd had any sense, I'd have divorced Brad long before his death."

"Heroism on your part was in sticking it out with him and trying to make it work, Layne. You didn't run. You tried your best. If Brad hadn't died when he did, I imagine you would have divorced him eventually. You're too smart and too much in touch with your needs to allow anyone to destroy you. And he was doing that little by little, through humiliation and mental cruelty. I know his type—they're highly insecure and don't like themselves, much less anyone else."

Layne let his fervent tone wash over her like a healing balm. "I like the way you see the world and me," she said gratefully.

Matt managed a smile. "I'm tempered by life's experiences, believe me. When I was twenty-five I'd never have appreciated a woman like you. But at thirty-five, I can celebrate finding a gem among a bunch of uncut stones."

Layne warmed to his words. "There's the poet coming out again," she teased.

Matt sat down at the table, pouring both of them a fresh cup of coffee. "I don't show that side of myself to many, believe me. If Lowell knew, he'd probably be verging on cardiac arrest wondering if I could handle this job at all."

"You can," Layne assured him, taking the fresh coffee and thanking him. "And speaking of that—"

"We've got the day off," he interrupted. "We'll go to Macao tomorrow to start shooting some pictures of our topic."

Layne was momentarily confused by his abruptness. He was evading the topic. Was their room bugged? Quelling her natural curiosity, she nodded. "Okay."

"How'd you like to spend the rest of the day just playing tourist? With this kind of jet lag, we shouldn't be doing much at first, anyway."

Her eyes took on a glimmer of excitement. "You mean we can go shopping?" She broke into a dazzling smile. "Do you realize that Hong Kong is the world's largest shipping mart? It's Christmas every day of the year here! Gorgeous gemstones can be had for a tenth of their retail cost anywhere else in the world."

"The lady likes rocks, eh?"

"My passion is opals with red, green, blue or lavender fire in their depths. The kind you might find in Mexico or from the mines of Australia."

"How about diamonds?" Matt teased, looking at the wedding rings resting on her slender finger.

Layne gave him a wicked look laced with sensuality. "For marriage only."

Matt enjoyed her spontaneity. "Looks like I lucked out on that one."

"You couldn't have gone wrong, believe me." Layne held out her hand, admiring the rings. "They are lovely, Matt."

He caught her fingers and leaned over to press a kiss on her hand. "They were meant for you, kitten. Now come on, we've got a beautiful day ahead of us and nothing to do. What do you say we take advantage of it?"

Breathless at his unexpected gallantry, Layne could only nod. He was happy, too, she realized; truly happy. A new sense of expectation caught her up in a vortex of feelings that threatened to make her giddy. "Yes, let's go. I can hardly wait to walk the streets of Kowloon again. It will feel wonderful just to soak up the vibrations of the people and this wonderful land!"

It seemed natural to Matt to catch Layne's hand as they walked down toward the heart of the Tsim Sha Tsui shopping district. He reveled in her open excitement and ebullience. Her brown eyes sparkled and her lips held a smile of wonderment. The day was hot, with close to ninety percent humidity. Cumulus clouds took on ominous shapes far out over the South China Sea to the east of the island of Hong Kong, which sat in the distance. The crowds of tourists and residents of Kowloon rubbed elbow to elbow down Ching Yee Road as they walked away from the Princeton Hotel.

As much as Matt wanted to devote a hundred percent of his attention to Layne's utter enjoyment, he couldn't. He was grateful for the deep, uninterrupted sleep he'd gotten earlier, because he had to be alert as he and Layne wove their way through the jammed sidewalks. Each block offered stall after stall of merchandise and goods, the fresh smell of shoe leather mingling with the most expensive perfumes in the world. Open-air markets bulged with fresh produce, recently washed and ready to be sold in the feverish heat of bargaining. The odor of fish wafted on the wind, carrying down the winding streets and mingling with the fresh salt air.

Every crevice of space was utilized by the ingenious shop-keepers. Boutiques were laden with silk goods that hung from the ceiling of one merchandising stall like brilliantly colored raindrops falling from the sky. Turbaned Indians, quick-walking Chinese, arrogant Japanese businessmen and people from around the world ebbed and flowed around them. Matt glanced down at Layne, realizing she was in utter heaven with each new sensory experience.

"Enjoying yourself?" he asked.

Layne tossed him a delightful laugh. "It's wonderful, isn't it? I mean, look at the dress of the people! Women in saris from India, haughty Pakistanis, blacks in native African costumes and the starchy English in their ever-so-proper attire…"

"I think you look kind of fetching in your attire, lady."

Layne thanked him with her eyes. She wasn't prepared when Matt leaned over and placed a kiss on her parted lips. It wasn't a long kiss, but it was charged with meaning and left her pulse pounding. "What was that for?"

It was his turn to laugh. "Because, Mrs. Talbot. Just because."

Heat rose in her already flushed cheeks, and she brushed at some tendrils of her ebony hair that curled around her face from the humidity.

"Come on," Matt coaxed her, placing his arm around her shoulders. He led her toward the Grand Hotel on Cameron Road. "Let's take a breather from all this traffic."

Once inside the pleasant restaurant in the Grand, Matt made sure they got a comfortable booth away from most of the bustling activity. Layne noticed he always sat with his back to the wall so he could look out into the room. Layne settled onto the padded seat and propped her elbows on the table. "Is anything wrong, Matt?"

"No. I just needed to get you out of the Princeton and someplace where I was positive it wasn't bugged."

"I see."

The waiter came over, and Matt ordered them each a lemonade. After the waiter had brought their drinks and left, Matt got down to business. "You're a pretty savvy lady, you know that?"

The lemonade was ice cold and tasted wonderful to Layne. She set the glass down in front of her. "What do you mean?"

"You could have asked me what happened when I left you last night, but you didn't. And this morning at breakfast you took my hint not to discuss our mission."

Layne traced patterns on the sweaty glass surface. "I figured you'd tell me what I needed to know when the time was right. Why? Are we being monitored in that room?"

"It's possible. I searched it thoroughly last night, but that doesn't mean they didn't set up some sophisticated listening device in another room to tap into our conversation. And by the time we get back to the hotel this afternoon, they could have planted a bug." He frowned. "It means tearing the place apart all over again just to be on the safe side."

Her happiness dampened rapidly. "I feel a little guilty. I should have helped you search last night."

Matt grinned. "You were asleep in the tub. Remember?"

"Please, I'm trying to forget that!"

"I'll never forget it. I'd never want to." His voice dropped intimately. "Except for being skinny as a rail, you're beautiful."

Layne gripped the glass. "I wish you'd stop making me blush! Do you know how disconcerting that is, Matt Talbot?"

His blue eyes lightened with merriment. "I think it's becoming."

"You'll think I'm a naive idiot."

"Never an idiot. Sometimes heartbreakingly naive. But that's one of your endearing qualities, Layne." He reached over, capturing her hand and squeezing it. "Don't ever apologize for being yourself, kitten. It's refreshing to find someone like you."

"Let's talk about business, shall we?" Layne suggested, squirming under his praise.

Matt suppressed another smile. "Okay, you've got a deal. I was with our people until five o'clock this morning going over their latest information. Kang has sent word that he wants to meet with you in Macao. We're supposed to hang around the dock area after we disembark from the hydrofoil."

"Kang won't meet us, he's wanted by every policeman in the Far East."

"He'll send someone, we're not sure who."

Layne wet her lips. "And then?"

Matt shrugged. "We wait to be contacted."

"This reminds me so much of what it was like when I first tried to contact Kang. Everything's so secretive."

Matt picked up both her hands. "Yes, and dangerous."

She shuddered, her amber eyes darkening. "Matt, this is scary. I mean, Macao is right next door to China. What if PRC agents are following us? Could they kidnap us and take us into China?"

He rubbed small circles across her hands, feeling the velvet softness of her flesh. "We'll get help from British SI up until the time we're contacted, so we'll have a little protection against the other elements."

His fingers felt soothing. "For a moment I forgot why we were here." Layne gave a subdued laugh. "Hong Kong has that kind of magic, you know. The sights, the sounds, the excitement; I guess I just got swept away by the place."

"It's all right. My job is to keep us alive. Your job is to speak Chinese when we need an interpreter. You're doing fine, Layne. Matter-of-fact, I'd rather have you relaxed like this, it makes our cover look that much more legitimate to any enemy agents who might be interested in us."

A cold shiver wound its way up Layne's spine, and she reclaimed her hands. "You've made it easy to seem as if we're married," she confided quietly. "It's as if…"

"As if we really were married," Matt finished. "Yeah, I'm pretty comfortable in our relationship."

Confusion shadowed her eyes. "I'm frightened, Matt. For you."

He reached out, caressing her flaming cheek. "And I'm more frightened for you. I don't want anything to happen to you, kitten. You're special to me. One of a kind." Matt gave her an encouraging smile. "Buck up. We'll both survive this ordeal to pick up where we left off with each other back in Washington."

Layne managed a strangled laugh. "Oh, sure! I was so wary of you, I didn't trust the ground you walked on. It's not much of a past to build upon."

Matt's blue eyes darkened as he held her gaze. "Do you trust me now, Layne?"

She sobered, looking away to avoid his intense appraisal. "You invite trust, Matt," she began in a strained voice. Layne lifted her lashes, meeting his tender gaze. "I hope you are what you seem to be. God…I couldn't stand for this to all be some elaborately fabricated lie…."

"Layne," he whispered, "it's not a lie. Nothing you and I share is a lie. Believe me."

Layne swallowed hard, her eyes suddenly filling with tears. Tears! Matt had brought her to tears back at her apartment, and then when he'd told her about Jenny's fight against death. And now. "Oh, Matt," she began thickly, wiping her eyes, "you've made an absolute crybaby out of me. Do you know that?"

A smile lifted Matt's concerned expression. "I think it's a healthy sign."

"It is?"

"Absolutely. That means your heart trusts me even if that head of yours armed with Brad's past conditioning gets in the way. We've got nowhere to go but up."

Layne dug a tissue out of her purse and carefully blotted her eyes, hoping her mascara hadn't run. "You're the eternal optimist, I can tell."

He laughed. "Well, I don't like the other choice. Do you?"

"No, no, I don't. Is there anything else you can tell me about this assignment, Matt?"

"I wish I could, but I can't. When we leave for Macao and before we make contact with Kang, I'll fill you in on the rest of the details."

"All right."

Inwardly, Matt grimaced. Right now even he didn't know any more than he'd known in D.C. His brother Jim had been the air commander on the B-2 that went down. And no amount of searching by satellite had revealed the whereabouts of the downed bomber and its valuable contents or crew. His heart wrenched when he thought of his parents. They knew nothing about Jim's crash or the fact that their firstborn son was about to risk his life to bring Jim back. They could lose both sons.... And then he raised his troubled gaze and looked across at Layne. There was a serenity surrounding her; he felt it, craved it. He wanted to simply be held by her, to seek a moment's peace from the inner hell that plagued him before the outer hell exploded all around them.

Matt picked up her hand, cradling it within his own, feeling the softness and warmth of her flesh. What would it be like to have her slender fingers sliding up across his body, finding joy and release in making love with him? Matt sought out her gaze, drowning in the liquid amber depths of her eyes. He forced a smile he didn't feel for her benefit.

"Come on, there's a gift I've been wanting to get for you."

A startled look crossed her face. "Me? A gift?"

Matt rose, pulling her upward. "Sure. Why not you?" He put the necessary amount of Hong Kong dollars on the table and led her out of the restaurant. The pleasure in her eyes made him feel euphoric. And the smile she smiled was for him—a cherished gift in itself.

Chapter 8

Leaving the Grand Hotel, Layne and Matt swung into the jostling noontime traffic. The constant warning ring of bicycles flying by and the voices of people in the crossing areas mingled with the honk of horns and the general frantic atmosphere. Layne remained close to Matt, her hand firmly held captive by his as they wound through the nonstop hustling on the overly crowded sidewalks.

"I think it's going to rain early this afternoon," she pointed out, lifting her hand toward the towering thunderheads now building toward mainland China where Kowloon rested.

"I think you're right," Matt said. "Although, at ninety-percent humidity we're already wet for all practical purposes."

Layne agreed, noticing that Matt's blue shirt clung damply to his body. He was even hotter because he wore a lightweight jacket to conceal the gun carried at the back of his belt. "I hope wherever you're taking me is air-conditioned."

"It is," he replied enigmatically.

"Just how many times have you been in Hong Kong?" Layne demanded. Matt seemed to know the layout of Kowloon with the ease of someone who had been here more than once.

"Off and on throughout my Air Force career—about eight times."

Layne gave an unladylike snort. "And here I thought I'd be contributing to your lack of knowledge about the area. Now I really feel useless!"

He shared a smile with her and squeezed her hand. "Never useless, believe me. When I was flying B-2 bombers, I'd always try to get a few days of leave on a flight over to Australia and come to Hong Kong. It's one of my favorite cities here in the Far East."

"And in all that time, you never picked up any Chinese?"

Matt shook his head. "Oh, I'd try, but I'd slaughter it. I left the Chinese rolling in the aisles with laughter."

She gave him a flat look, one eyebrow crooked. "No self-respecting Chinese would ever laugh in your face for mangling his language."

He grinned happily. "That's true—they just stand there impassively staring at you. That's when you know you've screwed up. I never had the talent for climbing up and down that tonal range to get the right sound. I could never even manage to say 'Good morning' in Chinese without having the offended party give me that special stare."

Layne shook her head, smiling. The day was turning into a dream come true. It was as if Matt and she were simply tourists enjoying the sensual pleasures of Kowloon. She glanced up at him. Although he appeared more relaxed, his gaze nevertheless constantly roved the crowds, ferreting out any suspicious people or movement. He was still on guard.

As they left Nathan Road and turned onto Salisbury Road, Matt took her elbow and guided her toward one of the newest shopping centers, the New World. They moved easily between the crowds of people and into the cool embrace of the building.

"Whew! I've always appreciated air-conditioning over here," Layne muttered, running a slender hand beneath the mane of her hair.

Matt wiped a sheen of sweat off his brow as they halted out of the flow of the traffic. "That makes two of us. That's the only drawback to Hong Kong as far as I'm concerned—the humidity."

Layne dug through her shoulder bag and found a hair clip, then handed Matt the purse to hold while she gathered up her ebony tresses and formed them into a loose knot and anchored it with the clip. "There! I feel cooler now. I should have put my hair up before we left the Princeton."

Matt gave her a pained look. "You look beautiful with your hair down."

She slid her purse back onto her shoulder. "You are so typically male. Is there a man alive who doesn't like to see a woman with long hair? Did it ever occur to you how *hot* the back of your neck gets in weather like this? It's terrible!"

Matt held up his hands in surrender. "Okay, okay. I'm allowed to retain some of my chauvinistic male traits. And you're right: I like a woman with long hair. There's nothing like running your fingers through it, believe me," he added throatily. His azure gaze was like a caress. Abruptly he winked, surprising her. "Come on, let's get you that gift."

He led her to the escalator and they rode three floors up before finally stepping off. The shopping center was immaculate, with polished white floor tiles set off against the cinnamon-colored brick and the glass display windows of the storefronts. *Elegance* was a word that came to mind as Layne slowed several times to peek through the windows at the hand-knotted Oriental rugs or silk fabric. She gave Matt a weak smile.

"Last time I was over here, I must have spent five thousand dollars on gifts for everyone back home."

Matt placed his arm around her shoulders, drawing her near as they ambled down the polished hallways. "Well, all that good karma's coming back to you."

"Karma?"

"Sure. You know, what goes around, comes around. You get exactly what you deserve."

"You're a real dichotomy. Test pilots don't believe in fate. Or karma." Layne's eyes narrowed. "Maybe you really aren't one."

"Bet on it. I am. I just happen to have a different philosophy from most other test pilots."

"You're very different, period."

He smiled down at her. "Does it bother you to know I'm not

the straitlaced military type? That I'm not necessarily conservative by nature?"

Layne's eyes twinkled. "I'd say you're anything but conservative!"

"Yeah?"

"Yeah."

"And how do you feel about that, Layne Talbot?"

Layne felt pleasure arc through her when he used her "married" name. It was an odd, unsettling feeling. The give-and-take of good-natured exchanges seemed like something usually reserved for married people who really were in love with each other. Layne touched her brow, confused by the emotions that warred with the cold logic of her brain.

"Layne? Where did you go?"

"Huh? Oh, I'm sorry. I was just thinking…" She trailed off lamely.

"I see. I shocked you because you found out I wasn't conservative. Is that it?"

Melting beneath his warm blue gaze, she managed a wry smile. "A stuffed shirt you're not."

"Makes you wonder how I've managed to stay in the military so long, doesn't it?"

"No. You can be an individual in the military and survive nicely."

"The lady's pretty smart."

"No, the lady had a father in the military who was a very independent cuss, too."

"Your father was a pretty colorful character," Matt agreed.

Layne slowed to a halt, turning to face Matt. "Did you ever get to meet him?"

Matt rested his hands on her shoulders. "Yes, I met him several times. And I liked him, not only as a test pilot, but as a man. Your father had a thread of integrity in him that his daughter also possesses."

Layne's heart wrenched. "You did meet him," she whispered, her eyes suddenly bright with unshed tears. "I'm so glad…."

Matt cocked his head and studied her silently. "I was still in test-pilot school at Edwards when I met him the first time, Layne. I remember thinking that he was the perfect role model for all of us students. There was an open generosity to Bob Hamilton, and we always knew he'd share everything he knew with us. He'd drop over to the school from time to time and just talk with us— tell us about some of the problems we'd encounter as test pilots. Bob earned a place in all our lives, Layne. He was the sort of man who always left you feeling good about yourself." His hands tightened on her shoulders. "And you're no different, kitten. Just sharing time and space with you makes me feel good. You're a catalyst like your father: everything you touch, you transform. And I'm the better for it."

Tears blurred her vision and Layne again searched blindly for a tissue in her purse. "Thank you for telling me about that, Matt." She sniffed, then blew her nose. "For some reason, I'm glad you met and knew Dad. I'm sure he liked you a lot. You're so similar in many ways."

Matt drew the handkerchief from his back pocket and placed it in Layne's trembling hands. He hadn't meant to make her cry again. But moments of emotional intensity seemed a natural spark between them that both were helpless to fight. Not that either of them wanted to. He brushed several stray tendrils of hair away from her damp, flushed cheek. "I'm sorry. I didn't mean to upset you, honey."

Layne raised her eyes, meeting and locking with Matt's. "What's happening between us?" she asked hoarsely, her voice barely above a whisper. "I feel as if I've known you forever, Matt. I can feel again. Do you know how long it's been since I felt the full range of my emotions? I cry…" She looked down apologet- ically at his dampened handkerchief. "My heart wants me to ignore what my head's telling me and enjoy you."

Matt released a held breath, resting his arms on her shoulders and drawing her near until her body barely touched his. He pressed his brow against her hair. "I feel it too, Layne, if it makes you feel any better," he began huskily. "I've been living in a vacuum for the past three years since Jenny died. I buried myself in my work. Every time I met a woman, I saw Jenny instead. I'm afraid I ruined a lot of potential relationships doing that. But I suppose it's part of the grieving and healing process that I had to get through." He stroked her silky hair with trembling fingers. "Maybe I was ready to start living again when I met you. I don't know. All I do know is that when I did observe you those first couple of days, I saw you, not Jenny. And when we came over to your apartment, something snapped inside me. I had been feeling so cold and desolate inside, Layne. And just being in your presence, watching you wrestle with a backlog of pain and hurt, I started to feel again." He caressed her forehead with his lips. "At the apartment when Chuck left, I knew I couldn't go. I couldn't leave you to wrestle with all that anguish we'd dredged up for you again over your husband's death."

Layne gripped his arms, staring up at him. "And the kiss? Why did you kiss me, Matt? I wasn't expecting it, but something happened to me, too. You were so gentle with me...and kind. Brad had never been that way. You made me want to lean on you and just cry all that past horror out of my soul...."

A broken smile pulled at Matt's mouth as he caressed her cheek. "I kissed you out of instinct, need—I don't know. All I know is that you knocked me off my feet, lady. I felt warm inside with you in my arms. I felt like life might be worth living again. So much happened in those split seconds, Layne. I felt like I'd explode from happiness. All I wanted to do was pick you up and carry you to the bedroom to hold and love you.

"But I didn't pick you up. And I didn't make love with you." He ran his thumb across her parted lips, feeling the texture of them beneath his flesh. "I was content with the kiss, kitten."

A huge lump formed in her throat, and she could barely speak. "No one has ever been honest like this with me, Matt."

"Let's put it this way," he said wryly, "if we didn't have this job to do, I wouldn't let you out of the Princeton for the next couple of days, lady. You'd be in bed, next to me, where you belong."

Layne pressed the crumpled handkerchief back into his hand. "I don't know what to say...."

Matt neatly folded the handkerchief and slipped it into his back pocket as they resumed their slow walk past the storefronts. "Don't say anything. Looks, actions and expressions speak louder than any words can, Layne, believe me," he warned her. "Look, we'll talk more about this later," Matt promised her, searching her drawn features with tenderness. "I don't mean to put pressure on you, Layne."

"I know," she said softly.

"God," he groaned, "I feel like a snowball rolling downhill out of control."

A small smile crept to her mouth. "A sense of humor regardless of the circumstances. I like that about you."

And I like you, lady, Matt thought. *One hell of a lot.* He felt like a man who'd been in the desert, dying of thirst, and Layne was cool, pure water. She was life. "You know, test pilots have a deadly sense of humor, even at the worst of moments," he said, trying to put lightness into their conversation.

"Just don't laugh the next time you kiss me," she warned with a teasing grin.

"Touché, you scored a direct hit."

"Wounded but not out of commission."

Matt gave her a disturbingly sensual look loaded with unspoken promise. "I'm never out of commission as far as you're concerned," he growled.

Layne tried to quell her fluttering pulse and covered up her delight at his response with a small laugh. "Are we going to walk the length and breadth of this place just for exercise, or what?"

He pulled her to a halt in front of a lavishly painted gold and red storefront. "No, ma'am. We're here. Well, what do you think?"

Layne's eyes widened as her gaze moved up to the name. "House of Ming? Oh, Matt, this is the most expensive jewelry outlet for opals in the Far East." She quickly looked over at him, noticing the satisfied expression on his face.

"Really? Must be my good taste in choosing it, then, for your gift."

"But—"

He cupped her elbow. "But what? So what if it's expensive? It's the most reputable place in Hong Kong for fine-quality opals. Now close that beautiful mouth of yours and quit arguing with me. Come on, I know the owner's son, Michael Ming." Matt gave her a delighted smile. "We've known each other off and on throughout the past seven years."

Layne allowed herself to be led into the lavishly appointed jewelry store. Two armed guards stood at the doors. Inside, glass cases glittered with hundreds of the finest opals from around the world, as if clear sunlight shot through the fiery cut gems. The thick carpet was a welcoming apricot color, and the pale ivory walls were hung with expensive and very old tapestries. There were few customers, but then, the House of Ming invited only the rich and those who knew the quality of their gems.

Matt made a beeline between the showcases of the rectangular-shaped store to the rear, where several Chinese stood near the office door. Layne was busy staring at the bracelets, earrings, necklaces and rings mounted with opals of every size and description.

"Matt!" a voice rang out delightedly.

"Mike! How are you?"

A tall, lanky man broke away from the group, his hand extended enthusiastically. "It's good to see you again."

Matt gripped his friend's long, artistic fingers firmly. "Great to see you, Mike."

Mike grinned, exposing a set of even white teeth against his dusky complexion. He was neatly outfitted in what Layne was sure was a gray Savile Row suit from London complete with matching silk tie. "A pleasant surprise. A sign of good fortune." Mike demurred, his almond eyes settling pleasantly on Layne.

"I don't know about bringing you any more good luck than you've already got, Mike, but I want to introduce you to *my* good fortune. Layne, this is Michael Ming, heir to the House of Ming. Mike, Layne is my wife."

"Ahh, she is a lotus blossom. Truly beautiful." Mike made a slight bow of deference to her. "Welcome to our humble store, Mrs. Talbot."

Layne inclined her head, smiling warmly. "Thank you, Michael."

He waved his hand. "Call me Mike. Only my honorable mother and father insist upon calling me Michael."

Matt grinned. "Mike and I met years ago over at a very unique place called the Stoned Crow. I was just coming out of the restaurant late that night after a great meal of Australian food when Mike was jumped by a couple of hoods about half a block away. I ran over and scared them off."

"Don't listen to him, Mrs. Talbot. I was in the process of being robbed by six youths when your husband took them on single-handedly. They were holding a knife to my throat and stripping me of my clothes when he jumped them. Matt braved their knives and chains to save my life. If he hadn't rescued me I would have been found dead in some neighboring alley the next morning, I'm sure."

Layne gazed up at Matt. "You never told me…"

Matt shrugged self-consciously. "Never occurred to me."

"You really are a hero," Layne murmured and watched a slight redness come to Matt's face. He was blushing! Layne slipped her arm around his waist, giving him a quick hug.

"Indeed," Mike broke in, his English impeccably British, "he was like a tiger prowling among a cowardly group of jackals. After he scattered my attackers he carried me back to the Stoned Crow and had the restaurant owner call for help." Mike touched his forehead just above his brow where a thin white scar was visible. "I'm afraid I was in shock and bleeding heavily from a head wound. Your husband calmly gave orders, pressed a towel to my forehead and kept me from going into deeper shock." Mike placed his hand on Matt's shoulder. "From that night on, he has become a permanent friend of the Ming family, Mrs. Talbot. I tried to pay him, but he refused. I tried to give him a gift of some of our finest opals and he refused that, too. However, since then, we have always shared a dinner over at the Stoned

Crow whenever he comes to Hong Kong." Mike smiled broadly, patting Matt's shoulder with an obvious show of affection.

"That's quite a story, Mike," Layne agreed, awed by Matt's colorful background. "I'm aware that there are tongs and triads in Hong Kong. It's not unusual for people traveling the back streets late at night to be robbed. You're lucky Matt was there."

"My honorable parents say weekly prayers in thanks for Matt. Without him, I wouldn't be around to inherit our fine business."

"Well, without getting into any more of our war stories, Mike, I'd like to buy Layne the opal of her choice."

"Oh, Matt—"

"Hush. Give Mike an idea of what you'd like."

"Oh, I don't know, Matt. I mean—"

"Honorable friend, if you will allow me?" Mike interrupted, turning to Matt.

"Go ahead," Matt said dryly, "someone has to get her attention."

Mike gestured to Layne. "Please, Mrs. Talbot, follow me. I believe I know exactly what would suit your obvious taste. Come, come."

Layne could do nothing but dumbly follow Mike to the last glass showcase. With a flourish, he brought out an elegant Chippendale chair for her to sit upon. Matt drew up another one while Mike moved around behind the case. Before Mike could sit down across from them, one of the other employees had unlocked the teak case and laid out several individually wrapped gems on black velvet before them. Clearly enjoying his job, Mike leaned forward, the gold cuff link at his wrist glinting as he gestured toward the wrapped stones.

"Now, Mrs. Talbot, let me show you those of our finest opals that would be worthy of your beauty."

Layne groaned inwardly. My God, the price of *any* opal in the House of Ming would be high. Her mouth grew dry as she watched Mike lovingly unwrap each individual stone and place it on the background of black velvet to show off its natural colors.

"As you know, opals are not for everyone, Mrs. Talbot.

Wearers must be people of high quality, warm heart and un-selfish generosity. No evil may linger in their hearts or minds, or the opals will bring them only what they deserve—bad luck. But the gods have ordained that fire opals from some of the finest mines of Mexico are for those who possess extraordinary passion for life through the goodness of their courageous hearts." He picked up the first opal; it was milky white with traces of red and green fire in its oval depths. "From Australia, a fine specimen devoid of fissures or cracks. As you know, opals will become brittle in colder temperatures and even crack upon occasion. They're happiest when resting against your skin, where your own natural body heat will provide the proper temperature. This is why we fashion all our jewelry from gold, silver or platinum, which conduct the heat of the body and transfer it to the lovely opal, which lives for such human contact."

Matt watched silently. Layne was like a child at Christmas and completely under Mike's magicianlike salesmanship. He wove story after story for the stones he showed her with flair and flourish. Layne touched, stroked and held each gem as if it were a fragile, priceless living being. The soft parting of her lips, the velvet topaz warmth in her eyes made him want to take her into his arms and love her that moment. Would she welcome him into her arms with the wonderment and awe she displayed for the opals?

Mike watched Layne steadily as she passed her slender fin-gertips across the five exquisite stones. He glanced at Matt. "One more. Wait one moment." He turned and gave orders in rapid Cantonese to two hovering employees who waited nearby. In-stantly they disappeared behind a teak door adorned with a gold inlaid design. He rubbed his slender hands together as they brought out a small carved ivory box with gold filigree on its top.

Matt smiled to himself as he watched the ceremony Mike was creating for them: he was truly a master of the dramatic. He neatly unlocked the gold latch and eased it up with a flourish of his hand. Staring at the ivory box, Layne was completely mes-merized. Whatever was inside it, Matt promised himself, Layne could have it. He knew from spending time with Mike over the years, that the best jewelry never saw the glass case; all the truly valuable or exotic gems were lovingly stored out of sight in a safe.

"Now, Mrs. Talbot, I have purposely left the best for the last. I can see you admire the stones that are before you. But, as I sensed earlier, you are a woman of great quality whose pureness of heart could truly wear the most precious possession we have at the House of Ming." His manicured hand rested lightly on the top of the ivory lid, poised to open it as he turned it toward Layne. "This stone comes from Mexico. It was found at the end of an opal stratum where the fragility of the stone increases. This opal is rare many times over because the rest of the stone it was fashioned from crumbled. We tried to salvage the potential gems, but to no avail. Not even our most gifted and careful jewelers could cut and shape any opals from the rock. I was there, watching the heartbreaking failure as each possible opal fractured beneath the most caring and experienced of hands. There were tears in everyone's eyes. None of us were pure enough of heart to stop the wonderful gems from dying before our very eyes."

Layne was transfixed by the story. "That's terrible…oh, I'm so sorry. It must be a beautiful opal to have survived."

Mike smiled and nodded soberly. "We stood around, the five of us, looking at the ruin before us, Mrs. Talbot. There was one more piece of the stone left. None of us wanted to touch it, for we knew that the gods of the opal were telling us that only someone of absolute purity must touch it or it, too, would disintegrate before our very eyes.

"And then, Ming Shan happened to come in and take my arm." His eyes lit up with pleasure. "Shan is our beloved daughter, and I had had her training with our finest craftsmen to learn about the business. She is an impetuous child of nineteen, and she picked up that last bit of stone, extolling its beauty. Naturally, we all stared at her. And it was then that I knew. Shan was born out of love and had known only that, ever since leaving her mother's womb. I turned to her, my lovely child of my heart, and bid her to fashion what her feeling guided her to do with the stone."

Mike's voice dropped in tone, laced with feeling. "We all

know that opal contains a life spirit. The fire that glimmers from its depths is the soul of the gem. To be able to capture that fire and wear it is truly an honor and blessing from the gods, Mrs. Talbot. And now, I will show the stone fashioned by our beloved Shan. The opal tolerated her loving touch; she shaped and formed it according to what it told her. And I believe this is the only opal for you, with the goodness that shines forth from your eyes…."

He lifted the lid slowly. There, cradled and surrounded by black velvet, was a heart-shaped opal no larger than a penny, set in gold. Layne gasped, raised her hands to touch it, then hesitated in midair. The depths of the opal glinted fiercely with red, green, blue, lavender and a spectacular gold in a surrounding area of darkness.

"My God, it's a black opal, Matt. They're so rare, so expensive!"

Matt leaned forward, sliding his hand across her shoulders. "Then it's yours, honey, because you're like that opal: rare and beautiful. Take it. It's yours. It's you."

A gasp escaped Layne and her hands rested at her throat as she stared longingly down at the necklace. "I've never seen such beauty…. It's as if that opal weren't of this world…."

"Precisely," Mike agreed, pushing the ivory box toward Layne. "The opal was fashioned in heaven, and no ordinary person may have the privilege of wearing its fragile, fiery spirit. Please, pick it up. Touch it. Feel if it is right for you. You will know, Mrs. Talbot. You will feel it."

Layne felt Matt's fingers tighten on her shoulder momentarily.

"Go on," he urged huskily, "do as Mike asks."

"But—what if I drop it? Or it fractures…"

Mike shook his head with assuredness. "Pick it up, Mrs. Talbot. I can see even now how it glints fiercely with life as it comes in closer contact with your person. You must pick it up!"

Her fingers trembled as she lovingly grazed the heart-shaped opal with her fingertips. "It's so warm," Layne offered in a hushed voice.

"It's alive. Of course it's warm. But know this, Mrs. Talbot: the safe is kept at a controlled temperature of seventy-five degrees. It's not cool to your touch because it warms to your vibration. It needs your touch...."

Layne's breath lodged in her throat as she gently extracted the opal from its bed of velvet and cradled it in her palm. Her heart was pounding as she tipped her hand first one way, then another, watching the myriad of color leap from the depths of the rare and expensive black opal. "My hand, it feels warm. Almost hot!"

Mike traded a knowing look with Matt. "They say that when an opal heats your hand it is making a pact with your heart. Indeed, those who wear the opal are protected by all things good. It wards off evil." Mike closed the box with finality. "Do your wife the honor of putting the necklace where it rightfully belongs, my friend."

Matt uncoiled like a sleek cat and picked up the necklace. His fingers grazed Layne's neck as he slid it into position, and tiny tingles of pleasure shot through her as he gently worked the clasp closed.

"There," Matt murmured, satisfied. Coming around, he leaned over to look at the opal resting like a brilliant, living being in the hollow of her throat. "Beautiful," he whispered. "How does it feel?"

An employee quickly placed a mirror in front of Layne, and she gasped with pleasure, raising her fingers to touch the gem as she took in the sight. "It's lovely," she murmured, unable to believe that something so rare would be around her neck. Mike nodded his head sagely.

"Our black opal with the heart of fire has found a home at last. On you, Mrs. Talbot, the opal breathes. I can tell by the way the colors of its fire change that its spirit is happy at long last."

Layne reached out, gripping Matt's hand, all the while staring at the opal at the base of her slender throat. "I never dreamed something so beautiful could exist, Matt...never...."

Her barely spoken words wrenched Matt's heart with newfound joy, and he gripped her fingers tightly. "I could say the same thing about you when I first met you, honey. I'd never believed someone of your rare quality existed."

Tears came to her topaz eyes as her gaze met and locked with Matt's warm azure one. Was she truly his black opal? Something so rare that it defied existence until now? Her fingers lingered over the gem as if to reassure herself that both it and Matt's words were real. The words *I love you* were almost torn from her lips as she studied him through shimmering tears. She watched as Matt turned toward Mike.

"We'll take it, Mike. I knew you'd have something special for her. Thanks." He started to take his wallet from his back pocket but Mike gripped his arm and shook his head. Pleasure danced in his dark eyes. "I've waited a long time, my friend, to do this." He opened his hands before them. "I consider this black opal small thanks for saving my life. I knew that someday, somehow, I would find a way to reward you for your assistance."

Matt began to insist upon paying for the gem, but Mike stood. "We believe that all deeds and acts are rewarded, my friend. Let the gem created out of love and given with love be a fitting thanks to each other." He held out his hand.

"Okay, Mike," Matt murmured huskily, gripping his hand, "because of our friendship."

"Now and forever," Mike agreed warmly. "Tell me, will you be in Hong Kong long? We would be honored for you and your wife to have dinner with us."

Layne finally released her long-held breath of air, unable to tear her gaze from the mirror as she looked once more at the fiery opal. She heard Matt regretfully declining the invitation.

"Some other time then," Mike agreed. "Come back again. Soon. And next time plan some time to spend with our family. You must meet Shan, she is the lotus blossom of my life, as your wife is to you."

Layne was in a daze as they walked out of the jewelry store. Her fingers rarely left the opal as they walked arm and arm down the busy hallways toward the exit. Matt grinned. "Cat got your tongue?"

"Wouldn't you if someone had just given you the most beautiful gift you'd ever received?" Layne said breathlessly, meeting his gaze. He was so handsome! Her heart wrenched, and in an act of utter spontaneity, she turned and threw her arms around him, holding him as hard as she could. "Thank you," she whispered. "I never expected so much. I…"

"Come here," he ordered thickly, capturing her chin and turning her face toward him. In one telling instant his mouth moved across her parted lips in hungry adoration and abandonment. Her knees weakened as his mouth sought to bring her pleasure and joy, and she sagged against him, a willow against the hard oak of his body. Layne lost herself as his firm, warm mouth captured hers and coaxed it to a fiery life—just like that of the opal that lay at the pulse point of her slender throat.

Chapter 9

"If anyone had told me I'd be in Hong Kong in September enjoying myself, I would have thought they were crazy." Layne shook her head in wonder as they walked back into the spacious and elegantly attired lobby of the Princeton.

"After I found out about this mission, I didn't think I'd end up finding any happiness surrounding it," Matt agreed. He pulled her to a halt, glancing at his watch. "It's four o'clock. What do you say we take advantage of high tea here in the lobby and listen to the piano music?"

Layne's heart swelled, and she gave him a brilliant smile. "I'd love that! I think the British have the right idea, late afternoons make me feel so lazy. All they're good for is sitting back, relaxing, drinking tea and munching on cookies."

Matt grinned, leading her up into the plushly carpeted area filled with well-heeled patrons taking advantage of the English custom. They found a cozy settee in the corner, far enough away from the piano to be able to talk, yet near enough to be able to enjoy the soothing music. A Chinese woman dressed in a long black skirt and a long-sleeved white blouse floated toward them with the menu. Matt turned to Layne.

"Order for us while I check the desk for any messages?"

"Of course. Any special type of tea?"

"I like the cinnamon kind," he said, grinning as he rose from the table.

"Consider it done." Layne took the menu and asked for tea, biscuits, a small arrangement of finger sandwiches and freshly baked cookies to go with the order. She watched the graceful Chinese woman drift away, then leaned back and relaxed against the silk brocade of the ivory-colored settee. Her gaze returned to Matt, now standing at the desk down at the other end of the lobby. He looked capable and confident even in a pair of worn jeans. Brushing her wispy bangs off her eyebrows, Layne sat up when the tea was brought. A soft smile touched her mouth as she fingered the opal that rested in the hollow of her throat, unable to believe the magical quality of the day, which seemed to be lifting her higher and higher on a cloud of giddy euphoria.

"Smells great!" Matt said by way of greeting, sitting down next to her and reaching for his recently poured tea.

"You're so enthusiastic about life." Layne smiled, offering him one of the finger sandwiches composed of sliced cucumber and mayonnaise.

"Does it embarrass you?" he asked, making quick work of the sandwich and reaching for a second one. "Say, these are good."

Layne couldn't suppress her smile as she leaned back, enjoying him thoroughly. "Are you hungry?"

"Sure. We must have walked four or five miles this afternoon. Fresh salt air, exercise and a pretty lady at my side always make me hungry."

"Chauvinist."

His eyebrows rose and he hesitated a split second before consuming his third sandwich. "No way. I was being honest. Although I'll admit I like opening car doors for you, seating you at a restaurant and that sort of thing. But today has been nothing short of a small miracle, and I'm starved because of it."

Layne laughed softly, deciding that if she wanted at least one finger sandwich, she'd best get it now before Matt had disposed of all those remaining on the lazy Susan. "Miracle. You've said it all," she murmured, unable to decide which sandwich to choose.

Matt picked up her china plate and put two sandwiches and a variety of biscuits on it. "Here, you'd better take these."

She was touched by his ability to share.

"Do you really like doing this? I mean, taking part in high tea?"

He frowned momentarily. "Sure. Why shouldn't I? Is there an unwritten axiom somewhere that men don't enjoy the smaller pleasures of life?"

Layne nibbled on a coconut macaroon, looking at him through her black lashes. "No...I suppose not."

Matt seemed partly satiated after eating about half the biscuits, and he sat back, his teacup balanced on his crossed leg. "Before you met Brad, did you have many serious relationships with other men, Layne?"

She flinched inwardly. "By serious you're asking me whether I went to bed with them?" Her casual tone belied her tension.

"Not necessarily. It just seems that Brad's shadow has conditioned you to such a point that I suspect he was the first man to really get you involved in all aspects of a relationship," Matt said carefully. He watched as Layne colored and grew uncomfortable beneath his probing.

"I was twenty-three when I met Brad," she said softly. "I suppose you could say that before that I was terribly naive about men." She lifted her lashes. "I was practically raised in the Orient—and in a conservative military family. Both societies tend to discourage a lot of personal involvement with the opposite sex when you're a teenager. That, combined with my goal to achieve a doctorate in Chinese and the fact that I jumped several grades in school, left me very little time to explore any relationships."

"When Brad came along you finally had time and maturity on your side to get involved?"

Layne warmed to the way Matt had worded his questions. If she'd thought for an instant that he was asking about her sex life, she'd have told him it was none of his business. But she got the feeling that he was trying to understand how and why Brad had indoctrinated her, and his motivation made the exploration less painful.

"You might say I fell head over heels for him. He seemed in control of every situation. As if there wasn't anything he didn't know about or couldn't handle. I was in awe of him. I'd never met anyone like him." She took a sip of tea, and realized that the old pain was finally healing as she began to share it with Matt. "And to be fair, I was ignorant and wasn't able to realize at the time that his charm, manners and gallantry were all designed to coax me into bed."

"That's being a little harsh on yourself, Layne."

She shrugged. "Maybe. But looking back on it after five years of marriage, I think Brad stalked me, got me to bed…and that ended the challenge of the chase for him."

Matt set the teacup down on the variegated pink marble coffee table in front of them. "So why did you marry him?"

Layne gave him a sad smile. "I think in his own way, Brad fell in love with me. It wasn't the same kind of love I had for him, but it was all that he was capable of giving. And the first year was the best year." She stared down at her tea. "After that, it became a prison—for both of us, in our own ways. Whatever Brad had felt for me died, and he became like a stranger to me, Matt. To this day I carry some of the guilt about that change. I wonder if I triggered it. Wasn't I enough of a woman for him? Did my own career kill our marriage?" She tucked her lower lip between her teeth.

Matt reached over, sliding his fingers across the lacy fabric at her shoulder. "Listen to me, Layne," he said, his voice low with feeling, "you're enough woman for any man who has the intelligence to appreciate what you bring to him in a relationship. It sounds as if you were both infatuated with each other and jumped into marriage. Romantic love is fine as long as you realize it won't last very long. It's the worst kind of love to base a marriage on." His fingers grew more provocative as he caressed the nape of her neck with light, stroking motions.

She nodded, sliding a look over at him. "I realize that now. I'm older but wiser—isn't that how the saying goes?"

Matt nodded, a smile resting in his sky-blue eyes. "It's the only way we get wisdom, kitten."

"Matt, why do you have so much insight into people? You should have been a psychologist, not a pilot."

He caressed her cheek. "I guess I'm streetwise about people.

I learned everything I know the hard way, Layne. Coming out of the Air Force Academy, I was a cocky young bastard. But even before that, I was pretty popular with the girls. I broke a few hearts. Getting out of the academy, I enjoyed the groupies who hung around the fighter-pilot type." He picked up her hand, cradling it in his own. "I was pretty selfish for a long time. I used women, but then, they allowed me that privilege. And they used me in their own way. We each got the reward we were seeking— I got her into bed and she got to strut around with a fighter pilot on her arm."

Matt cast a look up at Layne and saw her distressed expression. "I was a typical jet jockey, Layne. Looking back on that time in my life, I can't say I'm exactly proud of it."

"But you're so different now. What happened? I mean—"

"I met Jenny." He stroked her opened palm lazily with his thumb, drawing invisible patterns across her soft flesh. A grin edged his mouth. "Remember me talking about karma—what goes around comes around?"

"Yes."

"Well, I fell like a ton of bricks for Jenny. But it was a one-way street, she disliked me for my arrogance and shallowness toward her. She was a classy lady and wouldn't take any of my famous lines or my B.S."

Layne smiled. "The shoe was on the other foot?"

"Was it ever. I chased her for a year before I even got one date out of her! All she'd let me do was walk her from her car to the base school and back, She was a teacher for the first and second graders. I had to talk fast. I soon found out she wasn't interested in my image as a fighter pilot. As a matter of fact, she flattened me on that point the first day, when we literally ran into each other over at the Exchange."

"You found out that shedding all that macho facade for the real Matt Talbot was better?"

"See? You understand." He grinned at her, his blue eyes dancing with merriment. "You know people, too. You just don't give yourself enough credit for it."

"Maybe," Layne hedged. "But go on. How did Jenny break and tame you?"

He laughed deeply. "That's a succinct way of putting it. At the end of the first year I had cooled my heels long enough that she agreed to go out on a date. Naturally, I reverted back to my inveterate aggressive and egotistical self…."

Layne couldn't suppress the smile blossoming on her lips. "And then?"

"Jenny shut me down, as she should have. She wouldn't see me for another six months. Well, by that time I was damned if I was going to let her get away. The first thing Jenny taught me was the art of communication. Not that I'm the greatest at it even today, but at least I know talking is the number one priority for keeping a relationship alive and moving in the right direction."

Grimly, Layne agreed.

Matt reached out, sliding his fingers over her hand. "There are some people who wouldn't open up even if they knew it was the right thing to do, Layne. I think Brad was one of those types."

She struggled to smile. "Tell me how you eventually 'caught' Jenny."

"She let me chase her until she caught me. After a year and a half of getting my cocky facade chipped away, all that was left was the real Matt Talbot. She settled for him instead."

"I can see why," Layne offered shyly. "You're so different from most men."

He finished his tea and rose, extending his hand to her. "A lot of men are getting there today. Don't give up on us as a group just yet. We may be thickheaded, but at least our hearts are in the right place. Come on, let's go upstairs. I don't know about you, but I need a quick shower to wash away all the sweat from that humidity."

Eagerly Layne agreed, gripping his hand. It seemed so natural to walk through the lobby, their fingers interlaced as if they really were married. On the way up in the elevator, Matt interrupted her fantasy.

"Remember, I'm going to have to search that room for any new bugs or listening devices. So, when we get up there, watch what you say until I give you a thumbs-up, which means we're fairly safe."

"But not completely?"

"Never," he answered quietly, giving her fingers a reassuring squeeze. "In this business you never trust anything—" his blue eyes took on a twinkle as he looked down at her "—except your partner."

The heavy brocade drapes had been drawn closed on the bay windows, shutting out the late-afternoon sunlight from their room. Matt ushered Layne into the hallway, flipped on the weak, gray overhead light and shut the door behind them.

"I'll get the drapes," Layne told him.

"Fine," he said, stepping into the tiled bathroom after turning on the light, already beginning his inspection of the premises.

Layne blindly groped her way forward, the settee barely outlined by the light shed from the hallway. Blinking, she wished her eyes would adjust more rapidly to the darkness as she fumbled for the drapery cord. Stretching upward, she slid her fingers along the sleek texture of the wall.

"Finally," she muttered, giving the cord a good, solid pull. Sunshine spilled into the room, momentarily blinding her, and Layne turned, wiping her hands on her slacks. Suddenly, her heart slammed into her throat, and she couldn't breathe. There, no more than a foot away from her, was a cobra. The brownish-black reptile hissed, slowly uncoiling from its position near the settee and rose upward, its hood opening.

She tried to scream. Nothing came. Frozen, Layne felt faintness sweeping through her as the cobra began to weave hypnotically back and forth in front of her, rising almost three feet above the floor. Its shiny black eyes were unblinking as it stared up at her. Then it opened its scaly mouth, revealing yellowed fangs as it hissed, shattering the silence once again.

"Don't move."

Layne felt the hot rush of tears as Matt's voice cut softly across her terror. The cobra continued to weave and hiss.

"Now listen to me," Matt said, slowly leaning down at the entrance to the hallway, "that's a common cobra. They can spit

venom up to three feet away into the eyes of their victim, Layne."
In one unbroken motion he lifted the right pant leg of his jeans
up to his calf. "Whatever you do, don't move. If you do, he'll
spit." His voice was low in intensity, breaking through the thickening terror.

Layne felt her throat constrict as she risked a flick of a glance
over at Matt. Her panic increased as Matt pulled an ugly-looking
weapon that resembled a small hunting knife from a sheath
strapped to his ankle. Her fingers were stiff against her taut
thighs. The cobra stopped weaving and eyed her evilly. She
didn't dare blink. Small dots of perspiration broke out on her
brow and upper lip. Was the cobra going to spit? Is that why he'd
stopped weaving? And Matt? My God, he was silently approaching the deadly snake from behind like a stalking shadow.

The cobra rose a few inches higher, his hood, with a white V-
like symbol on the back of it, fully extending. The reptile leaned
back, balanced by its huge, thick body, measuring the distance
to Layne. Its fangs gleamed in the sunlight as it opened its
viperous mouth wider.

Layne watched in numbing horror as Matt closed the distance
between himself and the cobra. If it suddenly turned on him, Matt
would be killed! When he was within six inches of it she saw him
draw the knife close to his body. A strangled scream gurgled in
her tightened throat. She saw the deadly knife come forward in
one fluid sweep, decapitating the cobra as if it were a blade of
grass before a lawn mower. The head of the cobra dropped and
bounced inches from her feet, splattering blood and venom
across her shoes and slacks.

Layne felt the viselike grip of Matt's hand on her upper arm.
The next second, she was jerked off her feet and into the safety
of his embrace. She sagged heavily against him.

"Don't move," he ordered harshly, breathing heavily. He kept
her in his grip, looking all around them as they remained in the
center of the room. The body of the felled cobra twitched and
jerked convulsively.

Layne's hair had fallen across her eyes, and she stared fixedly at the jaws of the cobra mechanically opening and closing. She muffled a sob as she watched venom leak from the yellowed fangs and disappear into the carpet.

"Listen to me," Matt grated, his voice taut, "there could be another one. Maybe more. I don't know."

"Oh, God—"

"Turn with me, Layne. Try to spot the other one as I move us slowly around in a circle."

Her heart had a rabbitlike beat. As she moved against Matt, probing every corner beneath every darkened, shadowed area of the dressers, Layne felt Matt's heart pounding heavily against her breasts. She smelled of sweat, of fear. One thought kept screaming through her head: Someone was trying to kill them. Who? And how had they gotten a cobra into the room? Layne gripped the front of Matt's shirt, feeling her knees knocking so badly they were actually hitting each other. Matt froze.

"There's another one. Under the nightstand." His grip loosened slightly, all his attention focused on the cobra, which was coiled and barely visible in the darkness beneath the low teak table. "Layne?"

"Y-yes?"

"Listen carefully. When I release you, I want you to go back over to the settee and climb up on it. I want you up off the floor. Do you understand? Get up there and don't move until I tell you to."

Matt's voice was low with tension. His fingers gripped her arm firmly. "Layne?"

"I— I'll do it…." Layne forced herself to stand on her own, her mouth drawn in terror as she looked up at Matt. "Be careful. For God's sake, Matt—"

"Go!"

Layne took two steps, then halted, staring down at the twitching body of the dead cobra. Blood was splattered all around the reptile. A shudder of revulsion crawled up her spine as she stepped across the carcass and climbed onto the settee. Her gaze darted about, as if she expected another snake to drop from the ceiling. Layne choked back a cry, her hands pressed against her mouth.

Matt had teased the second snake from beneath the furniture, and she could see that this cobra was even larger than the first one. It rose in a lightning attack, striking out. But Matt's movements were calculating: he gracefully evaded the first strike of the disgruntled cobra, who appeared to have been awakened by Matt.

Then Matt opened his arms and the cobra became confused, undecided as to which arm he should strike at first. Matt moved the fingers of his left hand, drawing the reptile's instant attention. But as the cobra turned to spit at his left hand Matt brought the knife in his right hand down in a violent, slicing motion.

Layne gave a weak cry. The second cobra head lay in the middle of the plush carpet. Matt moved like a lithe dancer back to the middle of the room, knife hand close to his body as he continued to survey the rest of the room. Sweat glistened on his hardened face, and his eyes narrowed to slits as he leaned down, searching for more cobras.

How long she stood on the settee watching Matt make a thorough search of the room Layne didn't remember. He carefully opened each drawer, each closet and receptacle that might hide another snake. A cold terror washed through Layne as Matt jerked back all the bedding, throwing the pillows on the floor, continuing his hunt. The idea of a deadly cobra waiting for them beneath the sheets of the bed made her weave unsteadily. The blade of Matt's knife glinted dully in the sunlight as he came back from the hall. His face was unreadable, his blue eyes almost black with intensity. But suddenly Matt closed off that side of himself as he lifted his head and focused all his attention on Layne.

"It's safe to come down," he told her, holding out his hand to her.

Shakily, her icy fingers met his. As she took the large step off the settee her wobbly knees buckled, and a small cry tore from her as she felt herself falling toward the body of the dead cobra directly beneath her. Matt broke her fall, pulling her into his arms and holding her tightly against him. He was so warm—so alive and strong. Those thoughts kept Layne coherent as she struggled to swallow the climbing hysteria threatening to consume her. She buried her head against Matt's shoulder, a little sob escaping her.

"It's okay, honey. Everything's all right," Matt said, stroking Layne's hair to soothe her. He frowned, feeling her begin to tremble in earnest. He kissed her temple. "You were brave, sweetheart. So brave…"

Layne managed a choked sound, wanting nothing more than the continued protection of Matt's arms around her. "Me? W-what about you? My God, where did you learn how to handle a knife like that? Or how to kill cobras?" The words tumbled out in a jumbled mass of stuttered fragments, and she felt as if she were blithering.

Matt pressed another kiss to her pale cheek and gently released her. There was a troubled look in his eyes as he drank in her wan features. "Will you sit here for a minute while I fix you a stiff drink?"

Layne nodded jerkily, staring down at the cobra only a foot away from them. Its thick brown body was finally still, a stark reminder of death on the royal blue carpet now stained dark with its blood. Layne shuddered and hugged her arms to her body as Matt led her back to the settee. The warmth and concern in his gaze told her volumes as he looked at her one more time before moving across the room to the refrigerator.

She took a hefty gulp of the Scotch on the rocks, gripping the crystal-cut glass in her white-knuckled fingers. Matt resumed his search for listening devices as Layne sat shaking uncontrollably in the aftermath. Gradually the adrenaline that had poured into her bloodstream over the nightmarish event began to disappear. By the time Matt was done, Layne had finished the drink. She was amazed by his coolness as he picked up the snakes, put them into a plastic laundry bag and deposited them inside the hall closet. He went into the bathroom, where he cleaned his knife and slid it back into the sheath beneath his pant leg, then joined Layne.

"How are you feeling?" he asked, crouching down in front of her, his hands resting on her tense thighs.

Layne pressed her lips together, shrugging. "I—all right. I'm just a little shaky right now…."

He reached out and coaxed the disarray of hair away from her face, taming it into place on her hunched shoulders. "That's normal, believe me," he said, studying her in the silence. "The place is safe now."

She drew in a breath and looked at him. "Who did this, Matt?"

"PRC. KGB. Who knows?" His mouth was grim as he surveyed the bloodstained carpet. "We can't go to the police with this, Layne. All it will do is arouse suspicions about us and blow our cover, if we have any left. As far as Customs and the Hong Kong Police are concerned, we're nothing but tourists over here for a good time. If they find out somebody's put cobras in our room to get rid of us, they'll know something pretty serious is up." His hands momentarily tightened on her thighs. "They'll make a big deal of it here at the hotel, and it will end up getting in the newspapers."

"W-what are we going to do, then?" She dreaded the thought of having to stay in the room. "Can't we get another room?" She squeezed her eyes shut as a tremor of revulsion clawed through her. "I mean, the blood…and…and—"

Matt sat down next to Layne, removing the tumbler from her hands and placing it on the coffee table. "Come here, love," he murmured, drawing her back into his arms. The fragrant scent of her hair drifted to his nostrils and he inhaled it like a man starved for fresh air. The cloying scents of blood, of his own fear-sweat and the odor of the cobras still lingered in the room. Matt buried his face in the silk of her hair, nuzzling against her, holding her tightly. Her heart was beating rapidly against his chest, and he began to stroke the length of her back in an effort to soothe her.

Most women would have screamed or become hysterical when faced with a deadly cobra, Matt thought. Layne had trusted him enough to listen, enough to stand still and let him stalk the reptiles. He tightened his hold on her momentarily. "God, you're a brave woman," he whispered against her hair. Just the thought that she might have been bitten formed a cold knot of terror in his stomach. She was too rare, too wonderful to lose. It was then that the nakedness of his feelings rose in him like an exploding volcano. *He was falling in love with her.* Matt shut his eyes, a shudder running through him. God, not now. Not in the midst of this unfolding nightmare of a mission, which could easily claim one or both of their lives.

Matt groaned as he felt Layne's lips against his neck. Her breath was warm and moist against his flesh as he slipped his hands up to frame her face. He lifted her chin, struck by the vulnerability in her wavering topaz eyes and the translucent color of her skin. Matt obeyed the impulse of his body, and his heart, and he leaned down to taste her lips. He groaned, realizing she had been silently crying in his arms.

"Cry, kitten," he whispered against her lips. "Let me taste your tears. Come on, let it all go. I'll be here. I'll hold you...."

A jagged sound tore from her as Layne buried her head against Matt's chest. Her sobs broke the silence in the room, the warmth of the sun cascading like a protective blanket over them as Matt held and rocked her in his arms.

Later, as the initial shock dissolved with her tears, Layne grew quiet in Matt's arms. Gradually she released her death grip on him and sat up, giving him an embarrassed glance. "I'm sorry—"

He reached out, gently stroking her hair. "I'm not. Don't ever apologize for being human, Layne. I want to share your feelings. Don't ever hide from me like that again. I don't care if you cry. Okay?"

She nodded, reaching for the tissues on the coffee table. "I was so frightened, Matt. Frightened for you..." Her voice dropped to an aching whisper. "I never realized...I mean..."

Matt slid his hand beneath her chin, cupping it gently. "Realized what, kitten?"

Layne swallowed against the lump in her throat. "H-how much you mean to me. When I saw you approach that second cobra, all I could think was that I didn't want you to die." She gave a painful shrug, unable to go on. Her lashes lowered to her cheeks. The words, once again, were on her lips: I'm falling in love with you, Matt. I have no right to—I'm so scarred and so scared. I'm not worthy of you. But the words remained frozen on her tongue, and she could only revel in his caress as he sought to reassure her.

Matt's heart squeezed as he stroked her flushed cheek, relieved to see some color coming back to her features. "I feel the same way, Layne," Matt told her huskily, watching her eyes open and widen. "Maybe it's the way you trusted me just now. I'm not sure." His fingers outlined her brow, his expression growing warm. "But whatever it is, I want to find out with you. And I know you feel something, too." He grimaced. "Hell of a poor timing on it."

Layne managed a choked laugh, relief cloaking her as the last of the adrenaline washed out of her charged bloodstream. "The very worst, Matt Talbot."

That same boyish grin broke the tense planes of his face as he ran his thumb across her parted lips. "But that won't stop either one of us."

Her heart took a sudden leap; his touch was electrifying and filled with unspoken promise. "No," she agreed tremulously, her own voice low with emotion, "it won't."

Matt embraced her gently. "You're going to have to be pretty brave in the next few days. But the way you've behaved today, I don't have any doubts about how you'll act from here on out."

Layne tried to protest, resting against Matt, grateful for his continued support. "I've never been a heroine, believe me. I've always believed it's wiser to retreat and live."

"Well, if this is your cowardice, I'm impressed. Listen, you get a bath and relax. I'm going to clean up this mess and get rid of the blood on the carpet. We can't have the houseboy coming in to see this or discover the snakes until tomorrow morning."

Layne sat up, staring at Matt. "Y-you mean we have to stay here tonight?"

He nodded. "We can't afford to arouse any suspicions, Layne."

She moistened her lips. "Whoever put those cobras in here may come in later to see if they killed us."

"Maybe," he agreed, rising but keeping a hand on her slumped shoulder. "The houseboy might be in on it, I don't know. It would be easy to transport two cobras up here in a wicker hamper, no one would suspect what was in the basket."

An icy chill gripped Layne and she wrapped her arms around her body. "Could whoever did it break into the room and finish us off?"

"It's possible. We're going to have to play a game with whoever's behind this, Layne. If they know we're alive right now, they may try again before tomorrow morning. If we let them think we're dead we might get some sleep before we have to try to make it to Macao."

If we make it, Layne thought numbly, realizing that all the wonderful magic shared between them had been shattered by reality. Her fingers touched the opal at her throat; it felt warm and reassuring against the coldness invading her. "Can't you contact our people?"

He nodded, going to the closet and pulling out his khaki vest. "I will. Why don't you get that bath?"

It sounded like a good idea under the circumstances. Layne got shakily to her feet, careful to avoid the blood on the carpet as she made her way to the bathroom. She paused at the entrance, turning and giving Matt a worried look. "You did search in here?"

"Yes, it's clean." He pulled what looked like a pack of American cigarettes from one of the many pockets in the vest.

"I didn't know you smoked."

Matt gave her a knowing glance. He carefully worked off the top of the pack. "Only when things get tense," he said. The false lid opened to reveal a small black gadget that appeared to be a communications device.

Layne took the hint and hesitantly made her way into the bathroom. Her heart began to pound as she realized how small a space she was in—just in case there was another cobra sitting in the shadows, waiting. Trying to talk herself out of the ridiculous reaction, Layne quietly closed the door and began to undress. Maybe a hot bath would help. As she folded her clothes and laid them on the counter, Layne reminded herself not to fall asleep in the tub, although after what had happened, she doubted she'd ever sleep again. Was it possible for a small, slender snake to slither up out of the drain in the tub and bite her? Rubbing the goose pimples on her arms, Layne chided her overactive imagination still trying to deal with the gamut of horror unleashed by the cobra attack.

Chapter 10

The dark slash of night increased Layne's tense state. The hot bath had relaxed her to a degree, but Matt's continued state of readiness made her feel as if a bomb were ready to detonate. When she got out of the bathroom, Matt cleaned the rug free of bloodstains. Layne couldn't bear to watch him; the specter of the cobra rising before her was too much for her to cope with. After he'd finished, only wet spots remained where the soap and water had washed the stains from the lush carpet. Her composure was further shattered when Matt placed a small revolver next to where she sat on the settee before he went to take his shower.

"The safety's off, Layne," he warned her, pointing to the mechanism on the gun. "If you have to pick this up, it will fire with just a light squeeze of your finger on the trigger. So don't touch it unless you mean to use it."

Layne stared fixedly down at the ugly black gun. "Okay."

Matt hesitated, watching her pale face. She was still in shock from the cobra attack, and he hated to reinforce her fear so quickly afterward. Releasing a breath, he placed his hands on his hips. "Sure? I'll only be a few minutes."

Layne uncrossed her legs, pulling the thin satin robe across her in silent affirmation that she would deal with the latest challenge. "Go ahead. If I can survive cobras, this can't be any worse."

Matt gave her a belated grin. "Yeah, guns spit bullets, not venom. I won't be long, Layne." He reached out, touching her damp hair, still curling slightly from her recent bath. Layne's taut features relaxed, and she gave Matt a tremulous smile.

Layne noticed her fingers were trembling as Matt disappeared into the bathroom. It seemed like torturous hours before he emerged again, freshly shaven and showered. Just the familiarity of him padding across the hall with the white towel draped around his hips gave Layne a sense of relief. He looked toward her as he dug out a fresh shirt and jeans.

"Okay so far?"

"I'll make it. But it's sure good to see you again."

Matt smiled. "I'll leave the bathroom door open while I dress."

Layne nodded, more relief flowing through her. After Matt had dressed in a pale green shirt and his comfortable jeans, he made them both a drink, joining her on the settee.

"What now, Matt?" she asked, taking the cool tumbler filled with ice and Scotch.

"We wait. There's nothing to do. I've made contact, and everyone's aware of what happened."

"And?" Matt saw that her eyes were shadowed and large with exhaustion.

"Nothing. No one will do anything unless whoever attempted to kill us moves in to try to finish us off—if they find out we're still alive. Our friends have the place staked out. There's been as much precaution as possible taken to protect us, honey."

Every time he called her honey, the endearment seemed to flow like warm liquid from his lips to soothe her raw, jangled nerves. "I'm glad," Layne whispered fervently, taking another drink of the liquor.

Matt rested his hand along her robed thigh. Under other circumstances, Layne might have misread his intent. But when she looked toward him, he was staring off into space, deep in thought. Layne realized the gesture had been an unconscious display on his part to reassure her. She shifted position, tucked her legs beneath her body and rested her hand against his broad shoulder.

"Here you've been asking me how I am. I should ask you the same."

Matt slowly turned his head, meeting her warm brown eyes. "I'm tense. Worried," he admitted softly, sliding his hand down her thigh, his fingers coming to rest on her knee that leaned against his leg.

"How did you know I was in trouble out in the living room?" she asked in a hushed voice. "I know I didn't scream. I couldn't. My throat just closed up on me, and all I could do was stare at the cobra."

He shrugged. "I guess I sensed you were in trouble. You were right, you didn't make a sound." He smiled wryly. "My sixth sense warned me."

She closed her eyes momentarily, pressing her cheek against his shoulder. "I'm so glad you have that sense."

"Me, too."

Layne felt the languor of the second drink beginning to steal through her, and she didn't want to move away from Matt. She felt his hand lightly skim her thigh, coming to rest midway up her leg. There was an incredible naturalness to their gestures toward each other, and she accepted his touch, needing it. "Do you always carry a knife with you?"

"When I have to. Sometimes it comes in handy."

"If you hadn't had it this afternoon, I'd hate to think what would have happened."

Matt nodded. "Knives don't make noise. I couldn't have taken out my gun and shot the head off that cobra, because the bullet would have hit you. And if I'd moved into the cobra's line of vision to try and line up a different shot, he might have struck out at you."

Layne barely opened her eyes, gnawing on her lower lip. "And if you couldn't have knifed him?"

Matt grimaced. "I would have had to try to grab him by the back of his head, but that's almost guaranteeing I'd get bitten. Common cobras have that hood, so you can't grip them behind their heads properly without a lot of experience behind you. They can easily twist and sink a fang into you."

"Where did you learn all this? I mean, about how to handle a poisonous snake—and the knife?"

"All Air Force pilots are required to go to survival school

every few years. We learned how to hunt snakes and roast them for food. First you've got to catch them."

Layne shuddered, burying her head next to his. "And the knife training?"

"Same place. Although I've been using knives from the time I was about eight. You do a lot of gutting of fish on board a trawler, believe me."

"I'm glad you were a fisherman, Matt Talbot. Very glad. You almost looked like a dancer poised out there. I couldn't believe how gracefully you moved on the balls of your feet."

He pressed his cheek against her hair, a soft smile on his mouth. "Feeling better?"

The warmth of his voice flowed across her and Layne nodded. "I think it's this second drink. I almost feel light-headed."

Matt roused himself. "Come on, I want you to lie down and rest."

"But—" Her protest was cut off as he turned and lifted her into his arms. Her hair swirled off her shoulders and across his arm, and she placed her hands around his neck, relaxing in his powerful grip. The scent of him entered her nostrils, and she inhaled deeply, content to languish in his arms as he carried her toward the bed.

Matt gently removed Layne's robe, then laid her down, pulling a sheet across her. He saw the lurking fear in Layne's eyes as she drew her legs up toward her body. "There's no snake in the bed," he reassured her in a whisper, leaning over and placing a kiss on her lips. Switching off the bedroom lamp, he stood over her for a moment longer.

"I don't know if I can sleep, Matt," she protested wearily. "Just the thought of a snake in the bed makes me shake."

An understanding smile softened Matt's hard features. "How about if I lie down with you for a while and just hold you until you go to sleep?"

Layne's face mirrored gratitude. "I feel like such a child about all this."

Matt turned off the other light and placed the holstered revolver on the nightstand. Taking off his shoes, he lay down on top of the covers and gathered her warm, yielding body into his arms. Propping a pillow behind him, he allowed her to snuggle next to him, his shoulder a cradle for her head.

"Better?" he asked, his voice husky as he stared off into the darkness.

"Much," she answered fervently. "Thank you, Matt. I—I'm so scared." Layne slid her hand across his shirted chest, reveling in the hard muscle tone beneath her palm.

"Listen, I heard that over in Nam if you didn't like somebody, you just threw a banded krait, a bushmaster or a cobra into his hooch and got rid of him," Matt drawled. "Lousy officers frequently were bitten by poisonous snakes."

Layne shivered. "Not very pleasant."

"War never is," he agreed.

She closed her eyes, feeling the deep growl of his voice reverberating through his chest. "We're in an undeclared war right now, aren't we, Matt?"

He caressed her shoulder. "The worst kind, honey. Now quit talking and go to sleep. I'll be here."

Snuggling more deeply into his arms and already half asleep from the effects of the liquor, Layne murmured, "Promise?"

Matt's eyes shimmered with tenderness as he took his attention from the hallway and gazed down at her. "I promise, Layne," he whispered thickly. He watched as her lips parted moments later when sleep claimed her completely. Isn't this what he had dreamed of so often since meeting Layne? Lying in bed holding her? Watching as her breathing softened and became shallow, her small breasts pressed against his chest? Matt took a slow breath of air and exhaled it. She was everything he had ever dreamed of: the fragrance of lilac subtly wooed his sharpened senses, the yielding warmth of her flesh hotly reminded him of how much he wanted to love her. Her lips simply invited him to lean over and worship them, forever.

The scintillating lights of Hong Kong across Victoria Harbour invaded the room through the gauzy panels. For over an hour Matt lay perfectly still with Layne lying against him. She was vulnerable, he thought wistfully, and trusting him even though her experience had taught her otherwise. His fingers caressed her arm and gently he disengaged himself from her. Almost immediately, she curled up into a kittenlike ball, hands tucked beneath her chin and long, beautifully curved thighs drawn upward toward her body. Leaning over, Matt placed two blankets across her shoulders and tucked her in. Then he stood for a long moment in the darkness.

Matt crossed to the closet and rummaged in a pocket of his vest, locating some white tablets. He padded into the bathroom and retrieved a glass of water, taking the drug that would keep him awake for a very long, tension-filled night. Placing the gun beside him, he made himself comfortable on the settee.

Dark shapes slithered toward Layne. She saw them appear out of the hall closet, their brownish-black bodies moving like silent, deadly wraiths toward the bed where she lay. My God, they were coming to get her! The larger cobra crawled up onto the bed. Suddenly it rose with deadly grace only a few feet away from her and began to weave hypnotically, its hood flattening out. The black of its eyes glittered fiercely as it swung its body closer. Layne opened her mouth to scream, but nothing came out. She watched the cobra's mouth slowly open, its fangs dripping with venom. She had to escape! The cobra stopped weaving, and its cold onyx eyes gleamed with a terrible light. Layne's scream lurched into her throat as she saw the cobra strike. Instantly, she felt the grip of its fangs sink deeply into her arm and she lunged away, another scream tearing from her lips.

"No! Oh, God...no!" she cried, her voice reverberating off the walls of the room. Layne jerked upright, fighting off the cobra that seemed to be winding itself all around her. Her hair swirled about her face and shoulders as she tried to wrench free.

"Layne! Layne, it's Matt. It's all right...it's just a bad dream...."

Her eyes flew open, a sob escaping from her contorted mouth. "Matt?" Her voice was wobbly and raw.

Matt crooned softly to her, taking her damp, trembling form

into the safety of his arms. "It's me, honey. Come here, it's okay. Just a dream, that's all. You're safe. Safe…"

Layne choked and fell into his arms, burying her head against his chest. "Oh, Matt, it was awful. The cobras… They came out of the closet and…and…they got on the bed."

He rocked her, holding her firmly in his arms. "They're dead. They haven't come back to life. I promise you, honey. I've been sitting right across from you all night, and I'd know if there were any more cobras around. Okay?"

Matt's voice penetrated the terror that still bound her, and Layne nodded her head jerkily, her fingers digging deeply into his shirt. Tears blurred her vision. "Hold me…just hold me, Matt. I need you. God, I need you so badly," she whispered rawly.

He groaned, his hand sliding down across her damp night-gown. "And I need you too, honey." His words were like a deep, resonant chant and Layne began to relax. Her grip on his shirt gradually loosened and her heart began to slow to a more normal rate. Matt kissed her temple, running his fingers through the unruly tresses, fingering the rich, curling silk of her hair.

Somewhere between her terror and awareness of Matt, Layne's heightened senses suddenly swung to him. She was aware of his hands trembling slightly as he ran his fingers through her hair, and the heaviness of his heartbeat accelerated power-fully as she lay against his chest. The scent of him, the feel of his taut muscles beneath her fingertips—all succeeded in arousing her, shoving the fear aside for the desire that exploded violently to life between them. Layne felt Matt's hands cradle her face, drawing her upward…upward to meet the hungry cobalt color of his eyes. Her breath caught as she realized he was going to kiss her. And then the air was being stolen from her body as his mouth molded forcefully against her yielding lips.

He seemed to be devouring her with his passion, and Layne drowned in the heady texture of his strong mouth as it moved against her lips. A wild, fluttering feeling uncoiled from deep within her body as he dragged his mouth from her bruised and swollen lips.

"Let me taste you," he whispered raggedly, his fingers spanning her jaw as he looked deeply into her wide, stunned eyes.

"Yes…" she said faintly, closing her eyes, leaning forward and entrusting herself to him in every way.

The second time Matt kissed her, he was infinitely more gentle. As if realizing he had hurt her the first time they had explosively come together, he pressed small, healing kisses at each corner of her mouth, licking her lips soothingly with his tongue, inviting Layne to take part in the feast of their mutual enjoyment of one another. The spark between them caught and became a blaze as his tongue moved between her parted lips to tease and stroke every delicate curve of her mouth. Her entire body trembled as the exquisite assault on all her senses escalated. She was wildly aware of his fingers as he peeled the damp satin nightgown from her shoulders. His firm touch sent a wave of heat radiating through her. She couldn't catch her breath; her heart hammered with the flow of fire through her veins as Matt's hands pulled the straps downward across her aching, swelling breasts, which seemed to scream for his knowing touch.

Matt drew away, his hands on Layne's glorious white shoulders, and stared down at her small, upturned breasts. The nipples were young and rosy with a life of their own, and he forced himself not to touch them. Not yet. His eyes moved upward to meet Layne's dazed golden ones. Her lips were parted and glistening, pink petals to be stroked by his tongue again, nibbled by his teeth. "Layne," he began, his voice thick with desire, "this has to be mutual. I want you. I want you so damn bad I ache inside. But you have to want me, too, or it won't be any good." His fingers tightened slightly on her shoulders as she wavered before him. He watched her face closely, watching her telltale eyes. She was exquisite in the gray dawn light—a warm, vulnerable woman he hungered to make his own. And yet…

"I—I want you, Matt," she whispered huskily, her fingertips grazing his cheek. "But I—I'm not as experienced as you." Layne lowered her gaze, feeling wretched, unable to stand the look in his dark blue eyes.

"Wait." Matt whispered hoarsely, giving her a small shake. "Don't turn away from me, kitten."

She tried to take a breath of air, tried to steady her throbbing, on-fire body—a body that seemed determined to vibrate out of her dissolving control. "You're disappointed…."

Matt uttered a low growl, cupping her chin and forcing her to meet his gaze. "The look you saw in my eyes wasn't disappointment. It was me telling you that I want to grab hold of you and never let you go." He reached out, his fingers caressing her cheek, loving her more than he'd thought he could ever love again.

"I feel inept," she admitted.

A tender smile pulled at his mouth. "I want what's in your heart, honey, not your experience or lack of it. Just give yourself to me; that's all I'll ask. And I'll give myself to you. The gift of ourselves to each other. Feelings are what count, Layne—nothing else."

She gave a little cry, throwing her arms with abandon around his shoulders. "Love me, Matt. Please, darling, I need you so desperately," she whispered against his ear.

The instant his callused hand brushed the curve of Layne's swollen breasts, she gasped softly, her fingers digging deeply into his back. And as he pulled her away from him and bent his head to suckle upon the waiting nipple, she felt faint with desire. The heat and moistness of his mouth captured the tensile point, and she arched into his steadying hands, her dark hair spilling in tumultuous waves across her shoulders, her slender throat exposed. Electrifying pleasure radiated outward from each breast as he lavished his attention on the proud nipples, reducing her to a mindless state. She was barely aware that he'd gently laid her back onto the bed and had stood up to disrobe. Layne stared up at him as he stood in the light from the ever-lightening sky. He was built sleekly; there was not an ounce of fat anywhere on his body—from his magnificent chest laden with dark, curling hair to his slab-hard stomach or his perfectly formed legs. Her heart started another pounding frenzy as Matt slid like a graceful cat down beside her. He was like an animal barely leashed by civilization, her hazy mind warned her: sleek, powerful and dangerous.

Matt eased his hands down across the curved flatness of Layne's belly, inviting the rest of the satin nightgown away from her body. He rose on his knees before her, drinking in her naked beauty. Leaning down, he lightly caressed her breast. "So beautiful," he murmured. "You're mine, kitten, all mine." He sampled each nipple, feeling her writhe beneath his hands. She was guileless, he thought, as he sucked on the sweetness her breasts offered. Her naiveté was touching, and her trust in him made his heart swell with such a fierce feeling of protectiveness that it took his breath away. Her reactions were too fresh and awe-inspiring to be feigned.

He trailed a series of wet, provoking kisses down between her breasts, his tongue weaving fluid patterns across her taut, damp flesh as he neared the silken triangle of ebony hair. He felt her momentarily tense, realizing she had never discovered this most intimate form of loving another.

In one smooth, unbroken movement, he rose beside her, placing a kiss upon her waiting lips. Gently, he slid his hand down to her silken carpet, parting her thighs. He eased his hand against her heated moistness, watching her eyes dilate with golden pleasure. For an instant, there had been shock in her eyes. He nibbled on her delicate earlobe, his breath hot against her skin. "Relax," he soothed, "just feel, kitten. This time is for you. Relax and let me please you as you should be pleased."

A moan of utter surrender rose in Layne's exposed throat as she gave herself to Matt's guidance. The throbbing hotness of his hand meeting, melding with her body sent jolts and spasms of white-hot pleasure arcing through her. She felt the growing pressure building, building, and a startled cry tore from her as an explosion of desire melted her totally. Matt saw the look of utter satisfaction on Layne's stunned features as she fell back from her arched position. He caressed her damp cheek, kissing her languidly, tasting the offered sweetness of her drugged lips. "That's the way it should be, kitten. You're hot, you're all woman," he whispered raggedly. "All mine. You've given me the most precious gift a woman can give her man…."

His words inflamed her, set her on fire in a way she'd never experienced. As Matt drew her beneath him, she welcomed him into her arms. She gasped in delight as he sheathed inside her. He froze suddenly above her.

"Did I hurt you?" Matt rasped.

Layne could barely move her head. "No…never hurt me. You just feel so wonderful inside me…. How can I explain?" she murmured, her voice throaty as she met and held his burning cobalt gaze. She followed the magnificent line of his chest, her fingers trailing upward to capture his face. "Love me, Matt. Love me…."

He twisted his hips, moving slowly to give her a full measure of pleasure, and she sighed rapturously, gripping his arms. "You're a dream…a wonderful dream," she said softly.

Matt gripped her hips, pulling her closer, moving her against him, watching her eyes cloud with dazed euphoria. "No, kitten, you're the dream come true. For me. Forever…." He watched as her eyelids closed, her lashes fluttering with each stroking plunge into her hot, fiery depths. She was honey; she was life. He felt the building explosion of his own body, wrestling to control it for her sake. He wanted her to experience the kind of love that only two people who gave selflessly to each other could achieve.

With sure movements he brought her into a fiery rhythm that matched his own, and leaned down to claim one of her hardened nipples between his lips. He felt her arch against him, her fingers digging convulsively into his shoulders. Without breaking the magnificent throbbing beat that joined their two bodies as one, he brought her to a climax that shook her like a leaf in a raging storm. Her breasts went suddenly taut and her body strained, then froze, a cry tearing from her milk-white throat as she yielded to her femininity. He prolonged the orgasm for her, watching as she suddenly became limp and almost faint, her arms dropping weakly to the tangle of sheets surrounding them.

Layne's breath came in shallow gasps, and she felt the perspiration run between her glistening breasts as Matt tenderly cradled her in his arms. Weakness flowed through her limbs, and she was barely able to move her head and place a kiss on Matt's sweaty jaw. He tasted of salt, the scent of him a heady perfume to her flaring nostrils. "I never knew," she whispered faintly, closing her eyes. "I never knew it could be like this."

Matt kissed her closed eyes, her nose and finally her softly smiling mouth. "It can be like this all the time, honey."

A tremulous smile pulled at her full lips and she reached up, fingertips trailing along his strong jawline. "You're a miracle, Matt. Simply a miracle."

He gave a low chuckle, moving inside her, reveling in her tight, wet heat. "Life is a miracle," he countered throatily, kissing her lips. "Love is a miracle. And lady, I've got to tell you, you're one hell of a lover."

Tears suddenly sprang to her eyes. "Hey, what are these for?" he asked, raising a finger to her damp cheek.

Layne felt the tears running down the sides of her face and soaking into the hair at her temples. "I thought I was frigid," she sobbed.

A crooked smile pulled at Matt's mouth. "Lady, you're like a fiery thoroughbred. You were born to love. You give and take. There's no selfishness in you. Believe me when I tell you, you're not frigid in any way, shape or form."

Layne blinked, her heart swelling with such a tidal wave of love for Matt that she could barely comprehend the deluge of feelings. "I believe you," she whispered. Buoyed by her incredible experience, she became bolder, moving against Matt now, watching the ragged desire mirrored in his face. The fact that she could give him pleasure and see it register there thrilled her.

"God, Layne…" he gritted between clenched teeth.

She moved sensuously beneath him, delighting in each new discovery. The wonderful power she had over his body with her own made her feel humble. She could use her body as a loving vessel in which to drink Matt into her, giving back to him all the pleasure he had just shared with her. Instinct moved her hands as she placed them against his powerful hips and drew her legs around his, arching deeply, watching him shudder with need. He groaned again, covering her with his body, his fists gripping the tangled sheets beside her head as she moved strongly against him.

Matt's heart pounded heavily in his chest and he thrust deeply, feeling the tightness bear down upon his swollen, aching body. It was as if she instinctively knew what it took for him to lose control until his senses shattered into a million pieces. Seconds exploded into a world of animal pleasure as he gripped her hips, lost in a brilliant world of spinning, satiated desire. Matt cried out and fell against her, gasping. She smelled so good, so clean as his face nestled in the silken strands of her hair. Seconds later, he lifted himself, not wanting to crush her beneath his superior weight.

Matt rolled carefully onto his back, taking Layne with him, not yet ready to free himself from her sweet confines. A pool of ebony hair fell around him and he smiled contentedly, slipping his arms around her long, graceful back.

"You're heaven," he whispered, leaning over to press a kiss on her cheek.

Layne nuzzled beneath his jaw, her fingertips making light patterns across his damp, curly chest hair. "We both are," she confided. She felt his arms tighten around her momentarily.

Matt's eyes opened. "Did I hurt you?"

She shook her head. "You'd never hurt me."

"Not intentionally," he admitted, giving her rounded rear a pat. "Lady, you made me lose total control, and that's when I was afraid I'd hurt you."

Layne's lashes lifted, and a smile of wonder lingered on her lips. "I have a question to ask you. You won't laugh, will you?"

Matt framed her face, his eyes solemn as he searched her joyous golden ones. "I'd never laugh at any question you ask, Layne."

Wetting her lips, she closed her eyes. "This losing of control. Is that good?"

He traced the line of her winged brows. "The best. It takes a special partner to make a man or woman lose all control and inhibitions, honey. Like we just did with each other."

Layne stretched slightly, her lips caressing his mouth with great tenderness. "You've given me so much tonight...."

"You gave me back life, Layne. After Jenny died, I lost interest in living. But now…" He caressed her cheek and shared a gentle smile with her. "Come here, just let me hold you a while longer."

Layne acquiesced gladly, lying back down on his wonderful male body. "I'm so sleepy now," she admitted, closing her eyes.

"Go to sleep then," he coaxed. "We've got another hour before we have to get up."

"What about you? Did you get any sleep?"

Matt ran his fingers through her thick ebony hair, delighting in its texture. "I'll be okay. You sleep, honey. You're safe now."

Almost immediately, Matt felt her relax against him. She felt good on top of him. Managing to snag the corner of a sheet, he pulled it across them, making sure Layne would stay warm. This was how it should be, he thought, feeling the first fingers of tiredness brought on by good loving. His woman. Layne was his woman. There was a primitive desire in him to protect her, to keep her out of harm's way, to always be there when she needed him.

As the sun rose, lending a pink radiance to Victoria Harbour, Matt pondered many questions. Did Layne love him? He found it hard to think she didn't. Layne wasn't the kind of woman to have affairs. And the look of undisguised joy in her gold-flecked brown eyes told him the depth of her feelings.

Time, Matt thought. They needed time. And they didn't have a shred of it left to them. He raised his arm, glaring at his wristwatch: in another fifteen minutes he'd have to wake her. And then they'd have to shower, dress and leave to catch that hydrofoil to Macao. If they even made it as far as the ferry dock. His brows drew down in a scowl as his entire being, training and instincts began once again to focus on their survival.

The first golden rays of sunshine were peeking into their room as Matt gently roused Layne. Her lashes fluttered and she nuzzled more deeply into his shoulder. A soft smile pulled at Matt's mouth as he leaned over, kissing those parted, provocative lips.

"Layne? It's time to wake up. Come on, honey."

Matt's voice poured over her like rich, golden syrup, and Layne smiled in her sleep. She felt his mouth upon her lips and

fire leaped to life within her, moving jaggedly from her respon-
sive breasts to the warm glow that seemed to inhabit her lower
body. She responded to his searching, tender kiss, her lips
moving hungrily against him. Layne heard Matt groan and was
vaguely aware of his hand gripping her hips to him. She was
filled with a wonderful sensation of being loved totally and un-
conditionally. Slowly raising her lashes, she focused on Matt,
poised above her. "Are you hungry, Matt?" When had he changed
position? She didn't remember being moved. And her body was
taut with desire for him all over again. Layne's eyes widened with
surprise at the thought.

"What is it?" Matt asked, taking a tendril and nudging it back
behind her ear.

She gave him a smile and rubbed her eyes like an awakening
child. "I was just thinking that I want to love you all over again!"

Matt grinned and kissed her lightly on the lips. "I think I've
created a monster."

Layne struggled to rise, her hair cascading in a delicious
ebony waterfall across her shoulders. "You didn't answer my
question, Matt Talbot."

He reluctantly climbed out of bed, standing before her, devilry
dancing in his darkening eyes. "I'm not just hungry, woman, I'm
starved—for you. But that's got to wait. Now come on, let's get
a quick shower. We've got one hell of a day ahead of us."

Chapter 11

There wasn't time to categorize or savor the new warmth that reveled through Layne. From the instant she'd gotten up, an unsettling tension began to thrum through both of them. She had purposely worn a dark green tank top, a set of jeans that were probably older than the pair Matt was currently wearing and comfortable white sneakers. She'd tucked her hair into a chignon at the nape of her neck, leaving wispy bangs and tendrils at her temples to soften the severe effect.

Matt raised his head and stopped packing the camera lenses while he drank in the total effect. This morning there was a heart-wrenching shyness in Layne that endeared her even more to him. Her modest glance drew him from his duties, and he straightened, walking over to her. Wordlessly he opened his arms to her and she came to him. He uttered a soft groan of pleasure as she fitted beautifully next to him. Matt leaned down, inhaling the scent of her skin, burying himself in the warmth of her as Layne's arms slid around his neck, drawing him closer.

"You smell good enough to eat," he growled, finding her slender neck and kissing her slowly. "Mmm, you taste good, too," he added, running his tongue beneath her right earlobe. He felt her laugh and dodge away, holding him at arm's length, and he smiled, drowning in the life he saw in her gold-flecked eyes. "That's better," he coaxed, running his hands lightly across her shoulders. "You look absolutely ravishing when you smile."

Layne basked in the light of his love, giddy and incredibly happy. "You are an irrepressible little boy lurking in a man's body, Matt Talbot. Do you know that?" Her voice was husky with desire as his touch sparked another ache of longing through her.

Matt's eyes twinkled dangerously and he gently framed her face with his long, spare fingers. "Aren't sorry, are you?" he asked, suddenly sober.

Layne barely shook her head. "No, I'm not sorry about this morning, Matt," she said gravely.

"Me, either."

Her eyes clouded with confusion and her lips parted as if to ask him a question. Matt leaned down, claiming her completely, drawing her back against his hardened body and pinning her hips against his to let her feel his arousal. "See what kind of an effect you have on me?" he goaded thickly, running his tongue gently across her lower lip.

Shakily, Layne opened her eyes, drowning in Matt's azure gaze. Her knees were wobbly with desire, her heart pounding wildly in her chest, and her nipples hardened beneath his hands as he skimmed her breasts in an intimate caress. She never wore a bra except at the university, but now she wished she had one. Every time she rested against Matt's hard flesh, the sensitive peaks tingled hotly from his touch. Matt's gaze trailed heatedly from her parted, glistening lips to the curve of her throat where the fiery opal rested, and then lower to her breasts. A smile of satisfaction lingered on his masculine mouth.

"You're beautiful," he said simply, caressing her back and hips. "And that opal is you—a fiery woman who knows how to love."

His throaty words sent a shiver of longing through Layne, and she momentarily closed her eyes. "Matt, before we go, I have to talk to you," she whispered. She forced her lashes open again and met his concerned gaze.

"What's bothering you?"

She wet her lips. "Us. I mean, me."

He gave her a small shake. "Going to fall back on that trap of taking all the responsibility for this relationship like you did for your marriage?"

Layne blinked, trying to understand Matt's question.

He caressed her flaming cheek. "Going to bed with you this morning and loving you was mutual, Layne. This involves both of us." His face grew tender, the lines of hardness melting from around his mouth. "From the first day I met you at the university I wanted you, but more than just physically. I was taken by you as a person. I wanted to find out what made this flighty woman run on a steel cable of taut nerves, what made her so distrustful of men in general and why she remained vulnerable through it all." He brushed her lips with his thumb. "I liked what I saw then, Layne. And I like you even more now. And I want the chance to explore our relationship." Matt lifted his head and grimaced. "All we have for now is stolen moments—a brief reprieve in which to reach out and love each other."

Layne swallowed against a huge lump in her throat, close to tears. "I didn't know you felt that, Matt. I—I thought maybe all you wanted was a short-term affair." She gave a helpless shrug. "I feel so damned helpless by my lack of experience with men!" She reached up to let her fingertips stroke his cheek and jaw.

Matt gave her a reassuring smile. "I know. And I realize you aren't the kind of woman who finds a one-night stand or a sexual fling a part of her lifestyle." He drew in a deep breath, gripping her shoulders firmly. "Just continue to trust me through this, Layne. Let's survive this mission. When we get back to Washington and things settle down, we can have the time we need. Sound good?"

"Does it ever," she quavered.

"It sounds good to me, too," he said thickly. "Come on, we've got to get going, kitten."

Matt released her, crossed to the bed and picked up the three cameras and the case. He gave the case to Layne. "That hydrofoil leaves the dock in twenty minutes. We'll take a taxi to the wharf."

Layne mutely agreed, the warmth spun between them dissipating rapidly as reality settled in around her shoulders. She watched as Matt donned the sleeveless khaki vest, which hid the revolver clipped to the back of his belt.

"We aren't walking over?"

"No, it's too dangerous." Matt halted beside her, giving the room one last glance. "Wherever we go, I always want you on the inside of me, Layne. Stay at my shoulder and don't walk ahead or behind me. I'll walk on the street side." His voice lowered. "If I tell you to hit the deck, drop like a rock and flatten out. And then, if possible, crawl to anything that might give you cover from whoever might be shooting at us." His face took on its usual lines of hardness as he studied her frightened features. "The second gun is in that camera case. All you have to do is unsnap the safety and it's ready to fire."

Layne's mouth went dry and she found it hard to talk. "D-do you think they might try to gun us down on the way to the hydrofoil?"

"I don't know. Nothing's stable from this point on, Layne. We don't know who put the cobras in our room. Could be the Soviets or the PRC. Just stay close to me, honey, and do as I tell you."

She nodded mechanically.

Matt opened the door, looking both ways before motioning her out into the long, carpeted hall. Layne stayed very close; he had rolled the sleeves of his shirt up on his forearms, and the comforting touch of the dark hair brushing against her bare arm gave her a measure of solace.

At 8:00 a.m. the lobby of the Princeton was just beginning to get busy. They wove through groups of hotel tourists waiting for their buses and walked out into the coolness of the Hong Kong morning. It was less humid right now, but Layne knew that by 10:00 a.m., the day would turn hot and muggy. Matt hailed a cab and gripped her elbow, helping her into the backseat. Layne pressed her hand against her heart, wishing that it would quit pounding so hard. But it wouldn't. She stole a glance at Matt, cold washing across her. He looked like a deadly hawk scouting the area—a predator ready to attack anything that moved.

The cab ride took only seven minutes through the bustling morning traffic of honking cars and the flurry of bicyclists. Matt paid the cabbie and opened the door. Layne waited, realizing that as he stood, he was sizing up the situation. The long concrete wharf housed two different ferry services that plied passengers to and from the island of Hong Kong across the harbor. Over a thousand Chinese moved in an unchoreographed dance of dodging one another in order to make the next ferry or scurry toward their destination on Kowloon. Matt held out his hand and Layne gripped it with icy fingers. She remained close as the cab drew away, her gaze darting across the sea of humanity. How could Matt possibly know if there was an enemy agent among all these people? She was grateful when he slid his arm around her shoulder and led her toward the Sham Shui Po Ferry Pier, which housed the jet foils, hydrofoils and Hovercraft that plied their trade to and from Macao on a daily basis.

A sleek yacht type of hydrofoil bobbed at the pier. Matt produced the tickets, and they were among the first to board the ship. He guided Layne to a corner where their backs would be against a bulkhead and chose seats next to a window. The seats were a crushed blue velvet that invited them to lean back and relax. Layne tried to appear as if she were a tourist, but her hands trembled as she paged through a tour map of Macao. Matt said little, watching the wandering stream of tourists coming on board. The ship was filled to capacity within fifteen minutes, and the Chinese crew scampered dockside, releasing the lines so the hydrofoil could leave the wharf for the open waters of Victoria Harbour. Unconsciously, Layne gave a sigh of relief, slumping more into her seat.

Matt reached out, tucking her hand into his, giving her a silent smile with his eyes. "Relax" was all he said.

She nodded, feeling the ship begin to lift onto the foils beneath its hull and rapidly gain speed. Soon the craft was skimming the dark green surface of the bay as it headed out toward open sea. White, frothy spray leaped beside their window, and a low, growling hum throbbed throughout the acoustically protected cabin. Within an hour, they would be in Macao, the Portuguese stronghold on the Chinese border. The gambling capital of the Orient, it sat on the South China Sea, a tiny city etched out and claimed by the Portuguese. Layne looked around, realizing that most of the people were probably gamblers, for which Macao was famous. She and Matt would be doing some gambling of their own, she thought grimly.

"Layne."

She snapped her head up, shaken by Matt's low command.

"It's all right," he soothed. "I just wanted to talk with you now that we've got the privacy we need to tell you more about the mission."

Closing her eyes, Layne nodded, her heart trip-hammering in her chest. "You scared me, that's all," she murmured, leaning her head momentarily on his shoulder.

"Sorry, honey. We're both edgy. You're doing fine, though."

She gave him a warm smile and his fingers tightened on her hand. "What can you tell me?"

Matt leaned toward her, allowing his restless gaze to move across the cabin. The vibration and noise formed a natural barrier so that nothing of their conversation could be overheard or recorded. Matt began to speak in a low voice, his head tilted slightly toward her as he remained alert.

"A B-2 was cruising at a top-secret altitude when it suddenly developed what we think was engine trouble. We're not quite sure what happened, because they maintain no communication when they're flying off the coast of Russia and China. One of our reconnaissance jets was loitering in the general area and got the B-2 on radar scope. They were the ones who reported it was rapidly losing altitude. Unfortunately their radar was at optimum range when the problem occurred, and they saw it disappear off scope at ten thousand feet. The B-2 never returned home to Beale Air Force Base in California with its two-man crew."

Layne grew sober. Because her father had helped test the phenomenal B-2, she realized the seriousness of the situation. The two pilots were in special pressurized suits with a full life-support system. At its top speed of over Mach 3, the temperature on the bluish-black titanium skin of the B-2 reached twelve hundred degrees Fahrenheit. On reentry from seventy thousand feet, the temperature could drop to minus sixty-five degrees. The blood of the pilots would boil at that altitude if they weren't encased in protective suits and the space-type helmet they had to wear during the mission.

"Have you ever lost a B-2 before, Matt?"

"Only one, and that was as a trainer some time ago." His mouth flattened. "This is the first one we've lost on an actual mission."

Layne felt an unexplained emotional frustration around Matt, and she twisted around in her seat, watching him closely. "Was it shot down by the Russians?"

"Not to our knowledge. The Pentagon's thinking is that the bird experienced some sort of malfunction. We know from the radar info on board the aircraft that the B-2 was in semicontrolled flight on its way down. It's as if the pilots were trying to keep it stable."

She chewed on her lower lip. "Did they eject when they reached a safe altitude?"

"Not that we can detect." Matt shook his head, worry apparent in his azure eyes.

"And your only lead is through Kang?"

"Yes. He contacted us and the Russians, saying that he had captured two American pilots and had certain black boxes from the aircraft in his possession. They'll go to the highest bidder. That's if Kang is telling us the truth. We have no evidence that the pilots are alive or if he has those black boxes. All we have is his proposal."

Layne drew in a deep breath, realizing the implication. "I don't think Kang would lie about that. He's a hustler and a gambler, but he wouldn't lie about something this international in scope. Matt, those Air Force pilots are the cream of the crop."

Matt stared down at his tightly knuckled fists. He raised his head. Layne's brown eyes were wide with compassion. "There's one thing I haven't told you: The air commander on that flight was my brother, Jim."

"Oh, my God…no!"

Matt felt his throat tighten with tears. Layne reached out, caressing his forearm, and it stopped the spiraling grief that threatened to knot his stomach once again.

"No wonder you were so upset." Layne's grip on his arm

tightened. "I don't see how you've been able to stand the pressure, the not knowing. And the delays." Layne's face grew pale. "And I'm the one who delayed us coming over here."

"No!" he growled ominously. "Don't even think about buying into that one, Layne. I won't let you. You couldn't help your feelings about the Company. I certainly don't blame you. If Jim's alive, we'll find out pretty soon. There was also a Major Frank Walters who was his copilot. It's possible Kang's holding both of them. They could be injured, we just don't know. Kang's refused to answer any of our questions through his envoy who's in contact with the Company in Hong Kong. He'll only deal through you."

Tears gathered in Layne's eyes and she blinked them back. Right now Matt needed her courage, not her emotions. She watched as he tried to control his feelings. My God, the torture he had carried around inside of him since the B-2 had disappeared.

"Listen, I know something about those B-2 pilots. My dad told me plenty about their caliber and quality, Matt. They're a very special breed of pilot. They're keenly intelligent. I know that if Jim's still alive, he's assessed the situation and is dealing with it. I just feel that."

Matt mutely squeezed her hand.

"When pilots eject, there's supposed to be a radio receiver that sends out a signal from their parachute pack to locate them," Layne said, mulling over the problem.

Matt nodded. "Ordinarily we'd have sent a search aircraft in to get within range of that radio signal and zero in on it to rescue them. But Kang's territory is off-limits to everyone. He's made it clear if he sees one search aircraft from any nation, he'll kill the pilots, pitch the avionics he's stolen from the B-2 and wash his hands of the whole deal." His eyes narrowed. "That's why we're hamstrung. If Kang is telling the truth, then potentially we'll have killed two pilots, and the avionics may fall into enemy hands. Kang's made it clear to both parties involved that he won't tolerate anyone breaking his rules on this venture."

"You'd better believe him. Kang's merciless when it comes

to meting out punishment, Matt." Layne shivered suddenly. "My God, if Jim so much as tries to talk back to Kang, he could have him beheaded."

She fought to ignore her vivid imagination and what Kang might do to the captured pilots. "Then, whoever pays Kang's ransom demand gets the pilots and avionics?"

"That and information about where the B-2 is located. For all we know, this could be one big bluff, Layne. With cloud cover all over that area, our satellites are useless. We can't verify if the plane's on an island, in the shallows or completely swallowed up by the ocean."

"Didn't Kang send any proof that he was holding the pilots?"

"No, he didn't need to. Russian, Chinese, British and American radar all saw the B-2 going down. We all know the general area where it went down. It's highly probable the bird is very close to Chinese territorial waters. The pirates are playing a dangerous game with the Chinese if the plane is in PRC waters."

Layne's eyes grew distant as she continued to ferret out possibilities. "I would think it's outside PRC waters, Matt. If the B-2 was in their jurisdiction, the PRC would take over, no doubt about it. But they have just as hard a time with pirates as everyone else does when the game shifts to the pirates' backyard—the hundreds of islands right off Chinese territorial waters."

"I hope you're right," Matt added fervently. "If KGB agents get hold of Jim and Frank…" He closed his eyes. There was no sense in telling Layne of the horror that lay ahead for any enemy of the KGB. He flexed his fists in an effort to drain the tension from his body. Just the gentle touch of her hand sliding down his arm helped to soothe his inner chaos.

"I know Kang well enough to believe he does have them, Matt. The Chinese are gamblers at heart, and they're also good bluffers. But I don't feel Kang would contact the interested parties without holding the pilots or equipment."

"I hope like hell you're right. Jim's wife, Irene, is expecting their first child a week from now. I want him home where he belongs, with Irene and their new baby."

The catch in Matt's voice didn't go undetected by Layne. She laid her head on his shoulder, closing her eyes. "I'm sorry, Matt. So sorry."

Matt's face became closed, his mouth set. "I wished it had been me instead. I had nothing to lose—no wife or baby to come home to. Just a lousy, sterile apartment outside of Nellis."

Her grip on his arm became firmer as she raised her head, her eyes awash with tears. "No," she protested softly. "Then we wouldn't have found each other. Out of every tragedy comes something good, something clean, Matt. There are hidden reasons why this happened to Jim and not you. But I want both of you to survive to come home."

He briefly bowed his head, then managed a strained smile. "I can't change what's happened to Jim," he admitted, "but I thank God I met you. You're the one thing about this whole convoluted mess that's good and decent."

Layne pressed a kiss to his clenched jaw. "Jim's alive. I know it. I feel it here, in my gut. And my gut instinct has never been wrong, Matt. Never."

They sat there for long minutes, both wrestling with their own special emotional nightmares. Finally, Matt roused himself. "When we dock at Macao, we're to meet someone on the wharf. Whoever it is will use the following code word. I'll spell it out for you since it's in Cantonese: S-H-A-O."

Layne's eyes widened. "That's the name Kang gave me! It's Shao, and it means beautiful springtime."

Matt grinned. "The wily old bastard has an eye for beauty, at least."

Their laughter mingled, and both took a needed moment of reprieve from the net of circumstances tightening around them.

"After Kang sliced my palm open with his evil-looking knife, he knelt over me and told me from now on I'd be called Shao. He said the white color of my skin and my gold eyes reminded him of the sea in springtime; frothed with whitecaps crashing toward the yellow honeysuckle shrubs that bloom all over Tantai in May of each year. I thought it was rather sensitive of him to put two and two together and come up with that name for me."

"Frankly, I'm jealous of him. Sure Kang doesn't have his eye on you as another wife for his harem?"

"No. He knew I was married. At least he respected that."

"And you're going to tell him that you've remarried, Layne. It's important that he believes you're my wife."

She nodded. "I wonder how he'll react when he realizes you're my husband and not just an agent for the U.S. government?"

"I hope it will be a bonus. He didn't hurt you, and he respects you. It might be the one thing that persuaded him to deal with us."

"How much money is Kang asking for?"

Matt smiled grimly. "No paper money. He's asking for gold. How much depends upon what Russia antes into the auction."

"Kang is typical of all the older generations of Chinese, Matt. They want their money in precious metals. They distrust paper money and banks." Her brows knitted. "Does that mean that agents representing the Soviets will be there with us?"

"I don't know. I have no idea how Kang has got this thing jury-rigged," Matt muttered. "And we won't know until we get to Tantai, his island fortress."

The hydrofoil cut power, slowly sinking back into the grayish-green sea, making its way toward Macao's busy docks filled with milling people. Matt waited until everyone else had disembarked before he pulled Layne to her feet and led her to the upper deck of the hydrofoil and onto the wharf. Layne glanced overhead at the churning clouds covering Macao; it felt as if a typhoon were stalking them. Gripping the camera case and Matt's hand, she slowly threaded her way through the merrymakers going to gambling casinos.

She barely got a chance to look around at the old-world charm that Macao offered. The citadel of Sao Paulo de Monte stood pristine and archaic on a hillside far above the bay area. The rococo church, the fortresses bristling with century-old cannons and the winding cobblestone streets lined with green, blue, pink and lavender stucco houses made a picture-postcard backdrop. Layne rapidly drank in the familiar Portuguese environment. A small brown hand reached out, tugging insistently on the hem of her tank top.

She turned and found a young Chinese boy with a crop of straight black hair staring up at her. Expecting him to hold out his other hand for money, she dug into her pocket for a few coins.

"Here," she said, pressing them into his palm.

"Shao?"

Layne straightened. Matt turned toward the boy who appeared to be no more than twelve years old and frowned, then exchanged a glance with Layne.

"Ask him to repeat it."

She switched to Haklo, the language of the seaborne people and the boy nodded emphatically. "Heya! You are Shao?" he jabbered excitedly, his brown eyes lighting up with pleasure as he eagerly pocketed the proffered coins.

"Yes, I'm Shao."

"Show me your right palm."

Layne opened her hand toward the alert boy, who reminded her of a high-strung colt. The boy leaned close, observing the thin white scar that ran the length of Layne's palm. He rubbed his slender fingers across the scar to make sure it wasn't fake. Layne had to suppress a smile, maintaining the correct attitude of respect toward the young messenger.

"Heya! It is good. I'm Mai Geng, honored Shao," he greeted her, bowing. "Come! Come quickly. We must go!"

The moment Matt started to go with them, Mai Geng turned, a puzzled look on his face.

"Who is this, honored Shao?"

"Matt Talbot, who represents the Golden Mountain. Why?"

Geng frowned, scratching his head. "They said only you were to come, Shao. They spoke of no one else…."

Layne glanced worriedly at Matt and translated.

"Tell the boy you go nowhere without me," Matt said.

Shrugging, Geng flashed her a smile. "Captain Qin Jun will decide. Come!"

Mai Geng's scrawny body was clad in typical seaborne people's costume; he was barefoot with loosely fitting black cotton pajamas. He was thin—too thin, Layne thought as they followed at a fast walk, weaving in and out of the tourists.

Layne gripped Matt's hand as he took the lead behind Mai Geng's retreating form. They walked for more than a quarter of a mile before breaking free of the heavily populated dock area. Mai Geng tossed a look over his shoulder occasionally, and his little legs pumped into a trot. Down the concrete pier, several bobbing sampans awaited them at the end of the wharf. Once there, Mai Geng halted, his small chest barely rising and falling from his exertion.

Layne looked over the four sampans as Mai Geng waited with barely veiled impatience. Hooped green canvas covered the middle half of the boats, which rode the incoming waves like bobbing corks. Matt eyed them speculatively, his hand tightening around Layne's, as if to silently reassure her. She tossed him a tight smile and focused all her attention on the boy.

"What now, Mai Geng?"

His round face blossomed into a smile. "You may call me Geng, honored Shao. Step into this sampan and we will take you beyond the breakwater."

Layne looked up, studying the ugly green sea in the distance. The waves foreboded danger for a boat of that size. She chewed on her lip for a second. "Geng, the waters look unsafe out there. What if the sampan turns over?"

"No, no, the gods are with us today, honored Shao. Please, please, step aboard. Quickly. There is no time to waste. We will have *joss*. Do not worry so!"

"*Joss*," Layne muttered, watching Geng leap nimbly aboard the craft. Another man, seated near the tiller, eyed them but did not move from his position. He was dressed similarly to Geng, a bamboo hat protecting his head.

"What?" Matt asked, helping her down into the rocking boat.

"I said *joss*. It's a Chinese word for luck. Good or bad." She explained the rest of Geng's conversation as Matt carefully got into the sampan. Both of them ducked down beneath the hooped canvas. Geng scrambled back to the bow, quickly casting off the line and giving a signal to the man at the tiller to start the engine. The sampan skittered away toward the moody sea coming up rapidly beyond the breakwater, leaving the busy dockside far behind.

Matt got Layne settled in the center of the sampan cabin. The area was surprisingly clean, and small rugs and pillows surrounded them. The sampan lurched up and down, its small engine puttering away, pushing it through the heavier waves it encountered. Layne had turned pale and Matt divided his attention between her and the sour-faced tillerman. He saw no weapons around, and he watched Mai Geng scamper back to join them in the cabin, where they were safe from the spray created by the bow of the swift little boat.

Geng plopped down in front of them, smiling broadly, his eyes gleaming with pride. He crossed his spindly legs, resting his hands simply before him.

"Honored Shao, this is a man from your government?"

"Yes, he's my husband. His name is Matt Talbott."

Momentary confusion clouded Geng's intelligent eyes. "Husband? But the *lao-pan*'s eldest son wrote and told him that your husband was dead. Has he come back to life?"

Layne smiled slightly. "No, Geng. This is husband number two. We married recently."

"Ahh…*joss*."

"Yes, very good *joss*."

Geng tilted his inquisitive face, studying Matt. "The *lao-pan* said only you were to come, Shao."

"That's not the message that was given to us. Perhaps I can discuss this more with the captain?"

"Heya, Captain Jun will talk of this, Shao."

"Geng, can you tell me about the pilots? Are they safe?"

"I'm sorry, honored Shao, I cannot answer your requests. The *lao-pan* has instructed me and One-Ear only to attend to your comforts for the journey. If we answered you, the *lao-pan* would chop off our heads." Geng made a quick, cutting motion at the back of his neck to emphasize the point.

Layne bowed her head in deference to Geng. "I understand and will honor your request, Geng."

Geng brightened. "You are perhaps thirsty? Hungry? We are to make you feel as one of us, honored Shao."

She smiled gently. "Thank you, Geng. First, call me Shao. And this is Matt," she said, touching Matt's arm in way of introduction.

Geng became serious and bowed his head to Matt.

"What's going on?" Matt asked.

"I'm making introductions. Call him Geng."

"Does he speak English?"

Layne turned to Geng and asked. The boy shook his head. "Only the weak land-dwellers take up the foreign devil's tongue, Shao. I mean you no disrespect, but we seabornes won't taint ourselves with the British."

"And One-Ear?"

"He would slice off his other misbegotten ear if he spoke anything but Haklo!" Geng laughed gaily. "Your husband has *joss*, Shao. He has you to be his mouthpiece. *Heya!*"

Layne relayed the information, steadying herself with one hand on the edge of the craft and the other on Matt's arm. The jostling of the boat became more violent as they plunged into the South China Sea. She turned to Geng.

"Isn't this dangerous, Geng?"

"Our junk waits just beyond the wall, Shao. We must stay out of British-controlled waters, as you know, or risk imprisonment. Soon we will be aboard and you can relax." He offered her a dazzling smile meant to make her feel safe. "Old One-Ear has many years of fighting the gods of wind and water. He has *joss* with them. The *lao-pan* knows the devil winds are coming, so he chose the best man to sit at the tiller. One-Ear will get us there."

The sampan was maneuvered skillfully to crest the top of each wave only to slide back down into the next greenish trough. Layne felt her stomach turn in warning and she clenched Matt's hand.

"How are you doing?" he asked.

"Not good. Oh, God, I hate getting sick on the ocean. There's nothing like it."

Matt pulled open one of the zippers on his vest, producing two pale yellow tablets. He pressed them into Layne's hand. "Here, take these. They're anti-motion drugs, the kind the astronauts use. They ought to stop your stomach from rolling."

Geng dug out an old, battered thermos from beneath a series of brightly colored pillows, expertly pouring her some lukewarm tea without spilling a drop. Layne murmured her thanks, grateful that Matt put his arm around her to steady her. A while later, Geng crawled out into the bow for a few minutes and then came back in. He gave them a brilliant smile.

"Soon, Shao. Soon we will be aboard the junk." His smile disappeared as he turned to Matt, holding out his hand. "Shao, ask your honorable husband if he has any weapons on him. I must have them before we board."

Layne heard the note of hardness in Geng's youthful singsong voice; his dark eyes were suddenly very serious as he stared at Matt.

Matt's arm tightened around her. "What does he want?"

"Your weapons. All of them, Matt. When I went aboard the *lao-pan*'s junk the first time, he had his wives strip me naked and look in some unmentionable places for any kind of a weapon I might have been carrying to kill him with. It was an embarrassing search, to say the least. You'd better hand over your gun and knife. You can't afford to have the *lao-pan* distrust your intentions. I'll give him the gun from the camera case. They'll look in all of our equipment, anyway."

Matt eased her away from him, sliding the knife from its sheath on his calf. He carefully handed it to Geng, butt first. The boy's eyes widened considerably as he reverently touched the double-bladed weapon.

"*Aiyeee*, he uses a knife such as us!" There was respect in Geng's eyes as he placed the knife nearby.

Layne shivered, recalling all too vividly that it had severed two cobra heads as easily as if it were a hot knife slicing through butter. She couldn't share Geng's obvious pleasure in Matt's weaponry.

Matt handed over the holster clip and revolver to Geng, and Layne gave him the other revolver from the camera case. The boy bowed respectfully, put the weapons in a soiled sack and wrapped it tightly with a piece of twine. He then threw it to One-Ear, who nudged the sack beneath the tillerman's seat, his face expressionless. Geng turned excitedly to Layne.

"Shao, is your husband a warrior?"

She blanched. "No, he's a test pilot, Geng. He tests flying machines for a living."

Geng's face fell in disappointment. "I was hoping that the agent from the Golden Mountain would teach me his craft while he was with us."

"That would depend upon many things, Geng. I don't know how long the mission to help our pilots will take. Or what the *lao-pan* requests in exchange for them."

"Do not worry, we will have time, Shao. Once we reach the *lao-pan*'s cave fortress on Tantai, there will be time. I would value your husband's knowledge of such a knife as he carries. Will you ask him for me?"

Layne's stomach turned sickeningly, and it wasn't from the roiling sea around them. Geng was just a child! She tried to reconcile herself to the fact that he lived in an entirely different world than she did, but he was asking if Matt would show him how to kill with that murderous blade. Matt looked inquiringly at her as she turned to him and related Geng's excited request.

"You decide," Matt said. "This kid seems to have a lot of prestige and power for his age. Can I say no and live to tell about it?"

Layne gave a miserable shrug. "I don't know. I don't remember Geng from last time. If Kang entrusted him and this guy called One-Ear to pick us up, they must be trustworthy as well as good at their jobs."

Matt gave her a humorless smile. "Twelve-year-old kids carried sapper's explosives and grenades in Vietnam. Geng may be small, but he's not dumb. The kid has savvy. Let's use his enthusiasm to gain his trust. We might need it sometime soon. If I have something he wants, maybe we can use it to barter with."

"You're not dumb, either," Layne commented wryly, swallowing her smile. She turned to Geng. "My husband tells me that if the pilots are alive and unharmed, then he will show you how to use the knife."

Geng's eyes lit up and he clapped his hands. "*Heya!* Then I will have him show me everything he knows! *Joss!*"

Layne drew a sigh of relief as she turned to Matt. His face was shadowed in the semidarkness of the covering. "Apparently the pilots are alive and well."

The hardness melted from his eyes for a split second. "Alive? Uninjured?" He shot the questions at her.

"Y-yes. Geng implied that they were all right when I told him you'd teach him to use the knife if they were alive and safe."

Matt slipped his hand over hers, squeezing it tightly. "You aren't so dumb yourself, lady. And I love the hell out of you."

Layne's eyes widened, tears forming instantly as she gazed at him through the grayness of the cabin. Matt stared at her hard, his hand almost painfully gripping her fingers. But Layne didn't care; his fervent admission rushed through her like a molten river of euphoria. He loved her! He loved her....

"*Aiyeee!*" Geng sang out, scrambling toward the bow. "The junk! Be calm, Shao, we'll soon be aboard!"

Layne barely heard Geng's joyous cry. She saw the teak structure of a small junk loom darkly before them as they rapidly approached it, but none of it mattered at that moment. Just as the sampan bumped solidly into the side of the junk and lines were being thrown to secure the bobbing boat, she saw Matt's lips once again form the words: *I love you.*

Chapter 12

A tattered rope ladder was thrown over the side of the wallowing junk as it struggled with the mounting anger of the ocean around them. Geng motioned Layne forward, and she crawled on her hands and knees, losing her balance once and crashing into the side of the sampan. Geng grinned, offering his small hand to help Layne right herself. Spray slapped into the bow of the boat, soaking her. Although the temperature was probably in the eighties, the spray was a cold shock to Layne as it soaked through her cotton tank top. Looking up, Layne immediately recognized one of the *lao-pan*'s most trusted captains, Qin Jun. With his pinched features and speculative gaze, he considered her as a fox would its quarry as he rapidly perused her wet, upturned face.

"*Heya!* It is Shao!" he roared, giving the signal for Geng to help her up the ladder.

Never had so many thin, darkly browned arms reached toward her as the pirates steadied her precarious ascent. Strong fingers gripped her arms, and Layne allowed them to help her onto the steadier deck of the junk. She was instantly surrounded by six of them, all dressed in their loose khaki clothing. Some had leather straps sheathing knives across their thin chests. Others had malevolent knives or curved swords hanging from their hips. Qin, whose left arm was missing up to his elbow, stood at least six inches shorter than Layne. He bowed. "Welcome, honored Shao."

Layne gripped the railing, trying to produce a decent bow in return. In China and Japan, a formal bow was as important as the correct curtsy would be to the Queen of England. The deck was awash with sea spray and it made it tougher to keep her balance, but Layne managed a bow that brought a smile to Qin's mouth. His gold-capped teeth flashed beneath his thin lips, a startling contrast to his pinched and weathered face.

"Thank you, Captain Qin. I'm honored to be among you once again."

His triangular face remained jovial, his head swathed in a gray turban that was little more than a filthy rag. Many of the pirates wore headbands to keep their long, black hair out of their eyes. Then Qin leaned over the rail, sizing up Matt, who sat there with an expressionless face.

"Who is that with you?" Qin asked, turning to her.

"My husband, Matt Talbot. He's a pilot from the Golden Mountain." Layne licked her lips, tasting the salt of the sea upon them. Her pulse beat anxiously as she saw confusion and then wariness mount in Qin's dark eyes. "We were married three weeks ago," she added. "The government felt it best to send a pilot because a plane's involved, Captain Qin."

The pirate remained contemplative, as if mulling over the unexpected problem. He spread his bare feet apart to stabilize himself on the fretful, rolling junk. Layne felt her stomach begin to knot as Qin stood there in thoughtful silence.

"He carries the authority of the devils from the Golden Mountain?"

"Yes. Full authority."

Qin's closed face became a scowl as he turned to Layne. "The *lao-pan* wanted you, no one else. You were to have the authority. The *lao-pan* trusts no one but you."

The sentence came out in a cold growl and Layne's face turned ashen. My God, Qin meant to either leave Matt behind or kill him!

"Captain! You must allow Matt to come with me to see the *lao-pan!* I cannot negotiate for the Golden Mountain. I'm only a mouthpiece—someone that the *lao-pan* trusts. My husband carries access to the gold that Lord Kang wants. Only he can negotiate." She compressed her lips, trying to glean the slightest reaction from the sea captain.

"The *lao-pan* asked for you!"

"My husband and I were told the *lao-pan* asked for both of us," she lied boldly, squarely meeting Qin's glittering gaze. "And if you do not bring him aboard, I will return to the sampan with him. He's my life, Captain Qin. I won't go without him." It was a reckless statement, Layne thought, feeling weakness stealing into her knees. She forced herself to stand, her back rigid, putting on her best stubborn look. It was a life-and-death gamble. But surely the captain wouldn't dare kill her or set her adrift on the ocean with Matt. She was one of Kang's clan, and therefore, protected.

Qin rubbed his pointed jaw, sliding a look in her direction. "*Aiyeee*, honored Shao, you are like all women, weak without a man."

Layne managed a shadow of a smile, her eyes narrowed with anxiety. "Yes, I am." She pointed down at Matt. "He's an honorable man, Captain. Like myself. I wouldn't bring a dragon into the rabbit's den."

The pirate relaxed slightly, grinning. "The *lao-pan* is hardly a rabbit, honored Shao. But I understand." He leaned over, giving Geng orders to allow Matt to come aboard.

Layne stood back, supporting herself against the teak cabin built out of the lower deck of the junk. She saw every crewman go on guard as Matt leaped aboard with the grace of a cat. Geng was next, scurrying up the ladder as if he had been born to the task. The pirates, like the boat people of Aberdeen Harbour in Hong Kong, lived and died aboard their junks, rarely setting foot on land for any appreciable time. She saw One-Ear give the captain the sack containing their weapons.

"Come—" Qin waved "—let us get out of this evil weather. The gods are angry, and the devil winds are fast approaching."

Layne was allowed to go to Matt, and she reached out, feeling his arm slip around her shoulder. She would have sagged against him in relief, but she had to maintain a show of strength before the pirates.

Qin led them into the safety of an interior cabin. The walls were swathed with expensive, handwoven tapestries depicting birds, fish and the ocean. It gave the large room a feeling of coziness that Layne found welcome under the circumstances. Huge mountains of pillows ranging in color from dark green to silver to deep gold were scattered over a worn brown carpet that was well cared for. Layne imagined Qin's female members picked up the dirt with their patient fingers. He gestured for them to find a place to sit.

"My number one wife, Peng Li, will serve you tea. I'll be back shortly, honored Shao, and we will talk further."

Layne nodded. "As you wish, Captain Qin."

Matt watched the wiry pirate. Qin had a machete blade in a worn and knicked leather scabbard hanging at his left side. Matt turned and focused his attention on Layne. As soon as the captain shut the door, she sagged momentarily against his strong body.

"That was close," she whispered, casting a glance up at him. The wind had tousled Matt's hair, and she saw the hard planes of his face soften as he looked down at her.

"What happened? It looked as if he wasn't going to let me come aboard." Matt guided her toward several pillows and leaned down, arranging them so they could sit in relative comfort.

"It was worse than that," Layne admitted, her voice trembling. She sat down, keeping a grip on Matt's hand as he settled next to her. "Apparently the *lao-pan* wanted only me to come and represent our government."

Matt's eyes narrowed. "Somebody screwed up on the message to our government from Kang, then."

She felt herself becoming shaky. "Kang is known to twist things, Matt. He may have said two people at first and then changed his mind later. Or the British Consulate in Hong Kong could have misunderstood. I don't know. I don't care."

"I see," he muttered. Matt reached out and wiped a bit of water from her cheek. "Why did he let me come aboard, then?"

"Because you're my husband." Layne lifted her chin, meeting, melting beneath, the steadiness of Matt's gaze. He seemed so cool and unperturbed! "Qin knows that the *lao-pan* doesn't want me unhappy. For all intents, you're here under my protection because I'm a clan member. It's the only thing standing between you and murder at their hands…." Her voice trailed off into an aching whisper.

Matt slid his arm across her tense shoulders. "It'll be all right," he soothed. "You're doing great. Up there on the deck you looked different: like a real take-charge, assertive lady." He pulled Layne close, feeling the tension draining from her.

"There's a price to pay for it, Matt. My insides feel like they're torn apart."

He kissed her damp hair, the smell of the sea and the lilac scent mingling around his nostrils. "You hide it well."

Layne became more serious. "And I'm going to have to continue to hide my fears."

"It's called bluffing." Matt embraced her, wanting to give Layne solace. "You any good at poker?"

She gave an unladylike snort. "Are you kidding me? I was the one who got five cards in stud poker and couldn't make anything out of them."

"Not even a straight?"

"Nothing. I always lost."

"I see."

"I was good at Monopoly, though."

"Well, just consider getting us to Kang is like buying up Boardwalk."

Layne grimly stared around at the luxurious cabin. "It all depends on the right roll of the dice, Matt."

"All my money's riding on you to win, Layne."

Her eyes darkened and there was a huskiness in her voice. "The Chinese would say it depends on the gods." She gave Matt a sobering look. "And it does. You'd better hope that ten percent of fate is riding with and not against you from here on out, or we're both in a lot of trouble."

Their conversation was interrupted when a stooped woman of indeterminate age slipped through the teak door at the other end of the cabin. Her gray and black hair was frazzled and uncombed around her thin face. Matt watched her progress as the junk rode the waves. He admired the woman's balance as she deftly brought them a tray bearing a white teapot and small cups.

Layne bowed, welcoming Peng Li in the soft singsong language of Haklo. The Chinese woman wore an expensive silk brocade jacket and loose, black silk pants. Her tiny wrists were adorned with silver and gold bracelets, probably stolen from a yacht or freighter that had blundered unwittingly into the pirate's territory. Like all fisher people, she was barefoot. The wife of Qin never raised her head to meet their eyes. She served the fragrant tea without spilling a drop. Layne thanked her and Peng Li bowed, leaving them as silently as she had come.

The tea was strong and good. Layne hadn't realized how thirsty she was until now, and she drank two cups before Qin returned. He entered the cabin, a dark scowl on his weathered features.

"Ah, I see you are comfortable at last, honored Shao." The captain sat opposite them, picking up the unused third cup and pouring himself tea. His slitted eyes moved to Matt. The two men stared silently at each other.

Layne's grip tightened on the cup. The hair on the nape of her neck stood up. Qin's unreadable face suddenly relaxed into a wary grin as he gestured toward Matt.

"Honored Shao, have your husband remove the vest he wears. I've never seen one with so many pockets. They must contain many things, eh?"

"I—I suppose," Layne stammered, turning and giving Qin's request to Matt.

Matt unzipped the sleeveless khaki jacket and handed it to Qin. The pirate set aside the quickly emptied teacup and spread the vest over his crossed legs. His hands nimbly began to unzip all twelve pockets.

"Ah, this is like a maze," he muttered. "What is this?"

Matt listened and nodded. "Tell him it's a survival jacket. Whenever someone goes into a hostile environment and doesn't know what to expect, this is worn."

Layne leaned forward, giving Qin the information. The pirate nodded as he pulled out a packet of white tablets. He studied them critically, holding them up to the gray light slanting through the window.

"White powder?"

She suppressed a smile. White powder was opium. "No. It's aspirin for headaches." She touched her head.

Clearly, Qin was disappointed. He methodically went through each pocket, pulling out the contents for identification by Matt. Qin's face lit up with pleasure as he pulled several fishing hooks and the filament line from the last pocket. "*Aiyeee*, he's a fisherman!"

Layne laughed, some of the tension easing in the room. "He says he is."

Qin was delighted with the silver and gold hooks of various sizes, watching them dangle and glimmer before him like baubles.

"Tell Captain Qin he can have the hooks if he wants," Matt instructed her. "But I want that vest back. There's medication and antibiotics in there in case those pilots need treatment before we get them to proper medical facilities."

"If he wants it, he'll take the vest, Matt. We can't stop him."

"So tell him I'll give it to him as a gift just before I leave with our pilots."

Qin's face became impassive as Layne relayed Matt's gesture. The pirate ran his hands over the sleeveless jacket, contemplating the offer. He picked it up, as if to decide whether there might be some other secret compartment on the inner side of the sewn fabric hiding a weapon that he hadn't found. Satisfied that the vest was harmless, he gave it back to Matt.

"What is the Chinese name for him, honored Shao?" Qin asked.

"They call him Steel Tiger, Hu Gang, Captain."

"Ahh," the pirate murmured, rubbing his jaw and nodding as his sharp eyes inspected Matt. Layne knew that being named after the powerful symbol of the tiger was important and said much to Qin about Matt, who sat like an imperturbable Buddha before him. "So, he is a brave man? It is a good name. A worthy name."

"Yes, he's a brave man, Captain. A man of honor and integrity. And like the tiger, he eats only when he's hungry. He's not a jackal who nips at his friends' heels."

Qin nodded, a twinkle dancing in his eyes. "Do not wake a sleeping tiger, however, honored Shao."

Layne nodded. "That is so. Among his people, he is revered for his skills at flying. That is why he is here—a flying machine and his fellow pilots are involved."

"I see." Qin gestured above him. "A tiger who stalks through the skies."

"Protecting those who are loyal to him and killing his enemy when necessary."

Qin's face lost a bit of its impassiveness as he cocked his head toward Matt. "Hu Gang is powerful?"

"He's *lao-pan* of the sky, just as Lord Kang Ying is *lao-pan* of the seaborne people."

"*Aiyeee*, then the devils from the Golden Mountain aren't as stupid as I first thought them to be." Qin broke into a grin, his gold-capped teeth visible. "I think the *lao-pan* will allow him to remain with you."

Layne maintained a proper obeisance on Qin's final assessment of the situation. *Lao-pan*s were like kings over their people: they had absolute authority of life and death over their subjects. Layne had succeeded in getting Qin to respect Matt, even if she had exaggerated a little. "I'm sure the *lao-pan* will be pleased with Hu Gang's presence, only he can negotiate. I'm nothing more than his mouth because he does not speak Haklo."

Qin rose and gave a leisurely scratch to his crotch. "Rest now, honored Shao. We must pray to the gods of wind and water that the devil winds do not devour us. Right now, we dance around the edge of their anger. Perhaps the winds will move south and bless us with calm sea gods."

Devil winds meant typhoon, and Layne raised her eyes to meet Qin's thoughtful features. "How far to Tantai?"

"Two days." And then he grimaced. He sniffed the air as if he were a dog scenting. "It smells of rain soon. The gods will decide if we reach there in that time."

Layne tried to keep the fear out of her voice. If there was one group who could possibly survive a typhoon, it would be the pirates. They knew the ocean as intimately as a lover. "Is it important we get there in two days?"

"*Heya*, the other foreign devil will arrive then and the *lao-pan* will decide who gets the men from the Golden Mountain."

"And if we don't arrive on time?"

He shrugged. "The *lao-pan* will wait. I bring him Hu Gang who carries the riches from the Golden Mountain."

Matt watched the pirate leave, the wind gusting as he opened and shut the cabin door. Moments later, Peng Li reappeared and gestured for them to follow her. Layne rose unsteadily as the junk pitched and yawed. They heard the strident voice of Qin Jun carry over the force of the wind on the deck above them. Matt's hand closed firmly on Layne's elbow, helping her toward the rear entrance. The smell of freshly cooked fish permeated the smaller cabin, which was weakly lit with a low-wattage light bulb. Layne wrinkled her nose as the wife left them. The smell of diesel from the engine that powered the junk mingled with the fishy odor. She sat down on one of the bunks built into the wall of the cabin, giving Matt a sorrowful look. "Not exactly great, but it's home for now."

Matt looked around, missing little. A light bulb swung from side to side near his head, and he had to crouch to avoid hitting the ceiling. The two bunks were built one above the other and a small head containing a toilet and wash basin stood opposite them. Matt bet that the sewage facilities were little more than a pipe leading out of the junk straight into the ocean. "At least Qin seems to be more comfortable with us," Matt commented, opening each of the drawers built into the wall and peering inside them.

Layne sat there, not realizing until now how tightly her nerves were strung. She told Matt the entire conversation she'd had with Qin.

"You make me sound like Superman or something," he said, walking carefully to the end of the cabin. There was another door, and he twisted the brass knob. It was locked. The only way out of their cabin was through the larger living quarters, which probably doubled as a dining area.

"It was important he respect you, Matt. And right now, he does. It's our ticket to Kang."

"Golden Mountain, huh?" He smiled, his face shadowed eerily by the movement of the light bulb.

"That's what they call the U.S. To them, we're all foreign devils. Or worse."

Matt came back and sat down beside her, resting his elbows on his thighs, his face cloaked in thought. "I don't care what they call us as long as we can get to Jim and Frank. The rest can go to hell in a hand basket."

"I agree. But we're on the edge of a typhoon right now, and from what Qin said, we're skirting around it in order to reach Tantai."

Matt dug out the anti-motion pills, downing one of them. He grimaced and forced himself to swallow the bitter tablets without the aid of any water. "Well, we've got enough of these tablets to last us two days, and then we'd better hit land or we're going to be in the hurt locker with severe seasickness."

Layne grinned. "Hurt locker, huh?"

"Yeah, an old navy term."

"Traitor. Can't you stick to Air Force slang?"

He twisted his head, giving her a warming smile that said how much he loved her in that one, silent caress. "Being in the service as long as I have and interfacing with all the other arms of the military, I tend to pick the best from each."

"Well, if this junk sinks, then you'd better call on your navy swim training, Matt Talbot, because we're going to need it in order to survive."

Layne swallowed hard. The ripe smell of unbathed bodies, cooked fish and constant diesel fumes were making her sicker than she'd already been. She climbed out of the swaying bunk. No stranger to the pitching motion of the deck for the past two days, she spread her hands flat against any surface, making her way out of the dingy room and going topside. Her hair had wilted beneath the rain and humidity and lay in straggles around her face no matter what she tried to do to it. Without a comb or brush, Layne decided she was beginning to look like the wives of the pirates aboard the junk.

Muttering to herself, Layne walked like a drunk up the gangway to the poop deck, sucking in deep gulps of fresh air. The gray, swollen clouds hung all around them, promising them another shower at any moment. Right now she didn't care, longing for a hot bath to cleanse her skin of the accumulated odor of the preceding day and night aboard the junk. Matt was up on the rear deck with Qin Jun, having miraculously gotten his sea legs like the pirates who took the rolling, pitching swells with agility. For a moment Layne harbored a shred of jealousy toward Matt: he seemed highly flexible in any situation, adjusting with chameleon-like ease. Well, she wasn't a chameleon, and she wasn't adjusting well; the sea never had done much for her anyway.

Several crewmen watched as she slowly made her way up to the slippery teak poop deck. As if sensing her presence, Matt turned. His face was darkly shadowed with a growth of beard, giving him an even more dangerous-looking quality, Layne thought. But the hardness in his blue eyes melted as he saw her, and she felt her heart wrench in response to his unspoken care. Layne reached out, feeling the steel grip of Matt's hand drawing her to him, to the safety of his lean body. The humid wind whipped around them as Matt steadied her against the railing.

"How long have you been up here?" she asked, turning and looking up at him.

"About two hours." His gaze caressed her features. Layne looked drawn with faint shadows beneath her topaz eyes. "Did you sleep any?"

Layne thrust out her lower lip, and Matt thrilled at the uncon-sciously provocative picture she presented. "With the smell of diesel, fish and my own stink? You've got to be kidding."

He grinned. "You were snoring away when I woke up."

"Matt Talbot, I do not snore!"

The glimmer of self-righteous fury in her eyes made him

smile broadly. Matt noted as always that the crew watched them closely whenever they were together. Perhaps it was taboo for a man to show his love for his woman in public. He had meant to ask Layne about it, but there was always too much going on. "I just wanted to see that fire leap to your eyes," he teased, leaning down and brushing her parted lips. "Actually, you looked good enough to make love with...."

A sharp ache coursed through Layne and she nodded. "It's impossible under the circumstances, that bunk is so narrow I almost fall out of it when the junk lists too much to port!"

Matt laughed deeply, sliding his arms around her, feeling the heat and promise of her body against his. Since boarding, there had been little time for privacy. The pirates were deliberately skirting the coast of China, heading in a southerly direction. Matt knew they were keeping an eye peeled for PRC cutters. The tension fairly sang through the topside crew when one of Qin's lookouts suddenly screamed and pointed toward the coast.

"Now what?" Matt growled, craning his neck to get a look in the direction that the pirate was gesturing.

Layne pushed her unruly hair away from her face, frowning. She strained to catch what was being said. "Oh, my God, Matt. They've spotted three PRC cutters coming our way!"

His grip on her arm increased and he brought her with him as they made their way across deck to get a better look. The junk had been skirting the stalled typhoon that sat north of them. Had Captain Qin unintentionally drifted into PRC territorial waters? Matt shifted his attention back to the captain, who was waving frantically at the helmsman. Almost instantly, the nimble little junk heeled drunkenly to port, the huge, throaty roar of both diesel engines pummeling their eardrums. Matt had no idea of the power of the junk or how quickly it could skim over the turbulent green ocean now littered with debris from the storm.

Layne clung to Matt, her eyes wide with terror as she watched the three sleek, gray cutters knifing their way toward them with surprising speed. The seas were moderate, with swells of eight feet, the wind twisting the tops of the whitecaps off in strangled patterns. Her heartbeat rose as she heard Matt curse.

"If they open up those guns on us, we're dead."

"What can we do?"

Matt glared around him. "Nothing. Not right now. Qin seems to know what he's doing." He squinted at the PRC ships against the late-afternoon light. "They aren't turning back. I wonder if we drifted in too far?"

Qin was screaming at his helmsman. In three quick strides, the captain pushed his man aside, taking the throttles himself, shoving them all to the firewall. The junk shuddered as it rode each wave and then slammed into the next trough. The way the swells were running, the captain couldn't head due east away from the China coast.

"All gods spit on the PRC!" he shrilled angrily.

Layne realized they had to run a southeasterly course with the swell or Qin would tear his junk apart in the violent waves created by the sea gods. Precious minutes would be wasted and they would still be in PRC waters—and prime targets for the guns now aimed at them from a distance.

Qin clenched his rotted teeth, waving a fist at the gray leaden sky. "Piss on you, weather gods! I spit upon you!" He spat, the spittle carried away by the brisk wind.

"We're in trouble," Layne confirmed, listening to the cries of the crewmen. "We're at least three miles inside PRC waters. Apparently the helmsman didn't account for the strong ocean current, and we got carried too far inland. Qin's so mad he's ready to kill."

Matt held her tightly to him, his mind spinning with options. Suddenly, the whooping sound of sirens screeched through the pandemonium up on deck. The cutters were less than a mile away and closing in fast. A helpless sense of dread crawled through Matt and he looked down at Layne. She was frightened, her eyes large and shadowed with unease. "Let's get below. If they start shooting, we're not going to be their first targets."

Layne stumbled, and if it hadn't been for Matt's steadying hand, she would have slid off the slippery deck and into the boiling ocean. It began to rain, a cloudburst that became a curtain of gray, blotting out everything and leaving no visibility within a quarter-mile radius.

As they left the deck, Layne heard Qin cry *"Aiyeee!* The weather gods have spoken! We can now run and hide in the rain. All gods be blessed! *Joss! Joss!"*

The crew took heart, cheering wildly, raising their guns that they held ready.

Matt placed himself between the hull of the junk and Layne, who sat at his feet in the living quarters. He looked out the window streaked with rain, his hand gripping her shoulder tightly, the junk bobbing and weaving drunkenly. "The sirens," he muttered. "I can still hear the sirens."

Shakily, Layne pushed the hair from her face. "He's trying to outrun them. I heard them say Tantai is only a few miles farther. I never realized it sat so close to the Chinese coast. I hope we get out of this…."

Matt heard the first round fired from the cutter toward the junk. A hollow, metallic sound whumped through the barricade of rain. Automatically, he threw Layne to the deck, covering her with his body. He heard her gasp and realized he'd knocked the wind out of her. Another shot was fired. He cringed, gathering Layne hard against him, breathing raggedly.

"They're firing at us," he gasped. "Don't move. If they hit us, we're going to have to get out of here." *If we're still alive,* he added silently.

Layne struggled to breathe. "Can they hit us? I thought they couldn't see us through the rain…."

Matt laughed mirthlessly. "Those cutters are armed with the latest in radar. They can see us, all right." His hand trembled as he touched her damp hair. "We've got to be close to the end of their territorial waters. We've been running a good fifteen minutes."

Four more rounds were fired. Matt buried his head against Layne's hair, holding her tight. He didn't want to tell her that the first few rounds would be marker rounds used to zero in on the quarry. Now that the PRC had the exact speed, direction and position of the fleeing junk, it was only a matter of time until they were hit. *Joss,* he thought. We need some *joss*....

From on deck Layne heard Qin shout foul obscenities into the wind, ordering his men to bring up the machine guns from below deck. They wouldn't be taken without a fight! She felt the junk skimming through the brackish, foul ocean.

"More power! More power!" Qin screamed. "Tantai is only ten miles away!"

Matt knew the PRC were closing in. They must be right on the boundary of territorial waters! He raised his head, watching through the window. The motley crew was now a precision fighting tool as they set up the .50-caliber machine guns on the lower deck. The Dragon Clan was not feared for nothing! Qin swung around, giving his first mate orders to prepare to fire. A few more seconds and they would be out of PRC waters! Just a few seconds!

The shower had lifted and Matt saw all three PRC cutters come abreast of one another and fire simultaneously. He saw the puffs of white smoke, the yellow-tongued flash from their cannons and—his breath lodged in his throat. Six rounds were screaming toward them. His arms tightened around Layne.

Rounds crashed into the junk, making it quiver like a great, wounded beast. One shell hit aft, tearing into the tiller and rendering the junk helpless. The second round smashed into the helm, and Qin was no more. The other two exploded amidships. The junk groaned, and hundreds of splinters of teak exploded in all directions as the main spars gave way. The ship screamed and tore apart like a wounded human ripped asunder by the grasping arms of the greedy ocean.

A hot pain ripped through Matt's left arm as he spread his body flat across Layne to protect her. A groan tore from him, and his fists clenched spasmodically. Acrid smoke belched and spewed out of the cabin behind them. The gurgling sound of water closed swiftly around them, a warning that they were sinking rapidly! He hauled Layne to her feet. Her face was ashen, her lips contorted with fear. Wordlessly, Matt pulled her along, trying to reach the outer door. The smoke became black and ominous, and Matt and Layne began coughing violently. Several main timbers had broken, barring the path. Precious seconds were lost climbing over or under them, and Layne staggered, falling to her knees.

"Come on!" Matt yelled above the panicked cries of the pirates above deck and the scream of wood tearing apart. He dropped to his knees, gagging on the suffocating smoke. Reaching out, he hunted for the door in the gloomy darkness now swallowing them whole. There! He lurched upward, the heat of fire beginning to scorch the skin on the back of his neck. Layne sagged backward and Matt jerked her up against him. She had fainted. They had to get out! Now! His shaking fingers found the brass doorknob. Opening it, he gave it a jerk and dragged Layne out of the cabin into the clean, fresh air. Layne became semiconscious as he gripped her under the arms, pulling her out of the burning cabin. Fire belched out of broken windows, and smoke wove all around them.

The junk wallowed like a dying whale as the waves carried it farther and farther away from the PRC territorial water limits where the cutters remained. Matt twisted around, searching for life vests. Nothing! Already, several pirates had leaped into the water, only to be swallowed up seconds later by the waves. Layne, her face streaked with smoky grease, coughed violently, trying to get to her knees. Matt drew her upward and steadied them on what once had been a beautiful teak and brass railing.

"We've got to jump, Layne," he shouted above the din of noise. Spotting a thick piece of severed planking, Matt dragged her to the rail. He lurched toward it, almost losing his balance as the junk heeled to starboard, a wave crashing over its broken bow. Grabbing the eight-foot-long plank, Matt dragged it back to the rail.

Layne looked up dazedly. She was in shock, sounds cartwheeling around her. Everything seemed to be happening in slow motion. She stared numbly up at Matt as he yelled at her. He snarled an epithet that was lost as another heavy deluge of rain struck them. They were going to die…die….

Matt pushed the plank off, watching it strike the water. In one unbroken motion, he jerked Layne to her feet and pulled her over-board with him.

The water was shockingly cold and Layne gasped. She went under once…twice. A scream rose in her throat and water surged into her nostrils and mouth. Then she felt Matt's arm around her as he hauled her upward until she lay half out of the water and half on the piece of teak planking. She vomited weakly. Gripping the plank with one arm, Matt used his other arm to keep her safely anchored and out of the sucking water's grasp. The waves were large and powerful. Layne blinked, realizing the junk was sinking before their eyes. But before it did, the current carried them farther away. She clung to the wood.

Layne heard muted voices but was unable to raise her head. Her black hair was in thick, tangled ropes about her face as she kept a death grip on the teak. Matt's face was grim, and she tried to speak.

"Rest," he shouted above the storm. "Just hold on to the board, Layne. I'll be here."

Darkness followed quickly on the heels of the murky dusk as she clung weakly to the wood. Her thoughts were fuzzy and dis-oriented. What had happened to the rest of the pirates? And Mai Geng? A sob rose in her throat, and Layne tried to evade the in-evitable answer: They would drown without some kind of floating support in an angry ocean like this. Layne turned her head, staring over at Matt. His face was pale, the shadow of beard making him look like a warrior in the midst of battle. A grateful thread of warmth momentarily relaxed her tense body: she was safe with Matt's help. He was a survivor. And he had just saved her life. She released her fingers one at a time from the plank, sliding them along the surface until they met and gripped Matt's hand. He jerked his head toward her, his eyes turning cobalt. In that one telling moment, Layne knew she had never loved anyone as much as Matt. Tears came to her eyes, only to be washed away by the bulletlike slash of raindrops that pounded in fury around them.

The blackness of night swallowed them up. Once Layne had

begun to revive, Matt had helped her atop the plank so that she was completely out of the water. Next, he had taken his belt and hers, buckling them together, and strapped them around the plank and his body, so he wouldn't lose his grip and be swept away, to disappear forever into the depths of the ocean. The water absorbed their body heat and Layne could only remember the roar of the wind around them, the stinging rain upon her face making it numb and the comfort of Matt's voice soothing her. Her mind gyrated to survival: what about sharks? They were famous in this part of the world. Matt's legs were easy prey for any trolling shark and the thought made her blood run icy. Layne tried repeatedly to get Matt to trade places with her, but each time he refused. And she knew why: He didn't want to see her lose a leg or her life to a hungry great white.

Each hour was a lifetime to Layne; only the grip of Matt's hand upon her arm gave her any solace. Hunger knotted her stomach. She opened her mouth, swallowing some of the rain sliding in at the corners of her lips, trying not to dehydrate. By the time morning arrived, Layne was reduced to a huddled, shivering form on the plank. Matt had systematically rubbed her back and shoulders, willing the circulation back to the surface of her chilled flesh. Layne's protests that he needed similar help went unheeded. Matt seemed indestructible compared to her own state.

"Layne?" Matt's voice was hoarse from lack of water and talking to her throughout the night. He watched her black lashes flutter against her drawn flesh. Worriedly, he touched her wan cheek. "Layne, wake up. You can't sleep. You've got to hold on to the plank. I can't hold you on anymore, honey. Please…"

She tried desperately to increase her grip, her fingers stiff with cold and cramped with fatigue. She was so tired; it would be so easy to drift off and let the ocean's sounds and movement claim her. So easy…

"Dammit, Layne! Wake up!" He gave her a sharp shake of the shoulder.

"Don't—"

"Open your eyes."

A flicker of anger came to life within Layne, and she forced her eyes open. When her gaze cleared, she saw the naked anguish on Matt's face and her anger dissolved. "I'm sorry," she rasped, "I didn't mean…to fall asleep."

Matt rubbed her briskly about the shoulders, his own joints burning with pain from overexertion. "I know you didn't, kitten. Come on, get a better grip on that board. If you slide off, I don't know if I can catch you."

Layne rallied, pushing and wriggling until she was well up on the surface again. She turned her head, her eyes focusing as another shower ended.

"Matt!" Her voice came out in a raw whisper. "Matt."

"What is it?"

Layne struggled to push her body up by her elbows. "Look, it's an island. Do you see it? There…"

Matt craned his neck to look around Layne. His heart started a slow pound in his chest. Not more than a mile away lay a long, rocky island that seemed to hover like a ghost in the grayness of the encroaching dawn. "Tantai?" he croaked.

"I—I don't know."

"It doesn't matter. We've got to reach it before the current carries us past it."

A new strength invaded Layne; excitement surged with hope as she exchanged glances with him. "If we both kick our feet, we might do it…."

Matt hesitated, his eyes bloodshot as he drank in the ocean around them. Throughout the night he had received numerous stings from jellyfish. His legs smarted and ached from continually bumping into the gelatinous creatures that swam one to two feet below the surface of the sea. There had been no sharks so far, but the closer he and Layne got to land, the more danger they could be in. Sharks were known to prowl a quarter or half mile from a beach, and kicking legs would attract them.

"No, I'll do it. You stay put."

Layne's face screwed up in sudden fury. "No! We'll either do this together or not at all, Matt! You're so tired—look at you!"

Her voice dropped to a pleading note. "Don't get mad at me. Let me help. I know we can make it if we both do it." She reached out, her hand cradling his cheek. "I love you...."

Matt relented, too exhausted to even muster an argument. The look in her eyes warmed his cold, shivering body, and he nodded. "Come on," he croaked, "let's go for broke."

Chapter 13

Layne's legs were heavy with exhaustion and cramping, but she gritted her teeth and continued to kick clumsily through the brackish ocean toward the island. Her breath came in great, tearing sobs, and her lungs burned as she pushed herself beyond all limits to try to make it to shore. Twice, her cramped fingers had slipped from the plank, and twice Matt had saved her from the grasp of the sea that would have torn her away from him— forever. Her vision started to fade. Layne tried to shake her head, then realized it would cost her too much energy.

"We're going…to make it!"

Matt's raw voice trembled with sudden emotion as the waves began to break with a resounding crash against the island only a hundred yards from them. He shot a look over at Layne. She was barely able to cling to the board, her movements jerky and un-coordinated. Despite the torturous night, the dehydration and extreme physical duress, she had been a fighter. His heart filled with love as he placed his arm around her slender waist, drawing her near. Two more swells of the heavy surf around them and they would be thrown onto the mercy of the stony island's surface. He couldn't talk; his throat was constricted with relief. Bringing Layne tightly against him, he felt her surrender to his protection as he timed the second wave that would take them to shore.

Layne heard the roar of the surf as it gurgled and boiled around them. In the next few seconds, they were hurled high as the wave crested and broke. She clung weakly to Matt, shutting her eyes, trying to prepare herself to be slammed into the rocky slope of the beach. She felt Matt twist at the last moment so that he could absorb the shock of the fall with his body and protect her. The wave smashed full force into the unforgiving island, and Layne felt the jolt as they landed on solid ground. She heard Matt groan. Water rushed and surged around them, kelp and sticky seaweed tangling about their legs, trying to draw them back into the sucking reach of the ocean. Matt had taken the full brunt of their landing, and Layne weakly rolled off him. She forced herself up, her knees cut and bruised as she crawled over the sharpened rocks beneath them. Matt lay prostrate on his back, arms thrown out from his body, his face drawn and his lips back from his teeth.

Layne helped him to his feet. Leaning heavily on each other, they staggered drunkenly out of the grasping fingers of the sea. Voices! Layne blinked, wet hair hanging limply across her eyes, blinding her. She slowly turned her head toward the excited shouts in the distance. She felt Matt sag, his arm sliding off her shoulder. Layne tried to break his fall to the rocky earth, and her knees buckled as she took Matt's full weight to save him from further injuries. A cry tore from her as he fell limply into her arms. No! Layne had no more tears as she watched Matt's face drain of color. She leaned over him, and her voice came out in ragged gasps as she cradled his head in her lap, sobbing his name. As she tried to make Matt more comfortable, she saw blood ooze over her hand when she touched his left side. A jagged laceration ran the length of his left arm where a large splinter of wood had lodged beneath his skin. Shakily, Layne pressed her fingers against her mouth in order not to scream. Her mind was spongy with fatigue, and she stared numbly at the wound, unable to think how to help Matt.

It seemed as if she were in a sluggishly moving nightmare; the only reality, Matt's chilled body, huddled next to hers. She had to keep him warm and protected from the rising and falling wind that howled off the ocean. The voices, all in Haklo, drifted in and out of earshot, at the whim of the wind. Layne shut her eyes, wearily resting her head against Matt's. Nothing mattered except that he live. Her numb fingers clutched at the soaked fabric sticking to his inert body and a whimper broke from her lips. Oh, God, please God…let him live…. Matt, I love you. You can't die…. No…I won't let you…. And then she felt herself spiraling headlong into blackness.

The sour taste of lime across her lips and the juice dribbling into the corner of her mouth brought Layne to consciousness. An old woman with shoulder-length white hair, her face wrinkled by the elements, hunched over her. Seeing that Layne had revived, she sat back on her haunches, smiling, no teeth left in her pinched mouth.

"*Aiyeee*, I told them the gods smiled upon you, honored Shao. The *lao-pan* will be pleased to hear that you live." Her brown, parchment-rough skin wrinkled even more as her smile deepened. The woman patted her shoulder. "Rest, rest. You must stay warm." She took another wool blanket and pulled it across Layne.

"Matt?" Layne croaked, her voice cracking. "Where's Matt? Is he—"

"The stranger with you?"

Layne struggled to rise and found every muscle in her body screaming in protest. As she rose, the blankets fell away and she realized in horror that she was naked. As she pulled the blankets back up to cover her breasts, impressions assailed her fatigued mind. The flicker of lamps along the cave's black walls cast deep shadows in dancing shapes all around them; the odor of kerosene mixed with the delicious scent of chicken as it wafted throughout the chamber. Layne tried to lick her cracked lips.

"The man who was with me is my husband and he's wounded."

The old woman grunted and scowled as she rose. She wore tattered black pajamas and a bright red cotton blouse, her callused feet bare. "Ahh, your husband. I must tell the *lao-pan* of this new development. You rest, Shao. I be back." She stooped down and placed a small ceramic jug in Layne's lap. "Drink this. It is lime water. Good for you, Shao."

Layne watched helplessly as the woman disappeared into the

gray shadows and through a heavy curtain drawn across the cave's entrance. Her raging thirst overwhelmed her anxiety, and Layne drained and finished the contents of the small jug. She shivered, feeling the draft across the gleaming basalt floor of the cave. Turning, Layne squinted, letting her eyes adjust to the gloom as she perused the oval room. There was a second entrance to the cave, and it, too, was protected by a heavy curtain. A small Dutch oven sat to her left, and Layne inhaled hungrily, the mouth-watering smell of a stewed chicken making her stomach growl.

Layne surveyed the rest of the meager surroundings of the cave. Several sleeping mats with a tangle of blankets upon each were scattered around. A huge cache of wood and cardboard boxes were stacked three feet deep against one wall, and Layne estimated that there must be over a hundred crates in the massive group. More than likely they were supplies stolen off some unlucky freighter. And Matt? Layne lifted her head, her chest tight with worry. The old woman reappeared, cackling like a hen who had just laid an egg. She came and hunched down by Layne.

"*Aiyeee*, the gods smile upon you, Shao. The *lao-pan*'s soldiers have dragged your husband into the first cave and left him bound and gagged instead of killing him on the beach where they found you."

"Oh, my God!"

The woman grinned, her gums gleaming in the weak light. "The *lao-pan* has given orders that he is to be brought here with you. We did not know. We thought he was an enemy washed up on the shore with you during the storm."

"Please, can I have some dry clothes? Anything? Matt's wounded. He's going to need some medical attention."

"Rest, Shao. I will have dry clothes brought for both of you."

Layne got to her feet, weak but able to stand. She pulled the blankets tightly around her, her voice high with anxiety. "I can't rest! Just get me something to wear so that I can tend my husband. He needs help!"

"Lan Ni will take care of both of you," she reassured Layne. She turned as two pirates emerged from behind the curtain, carrying Matt between them. Lan's voice rose in an imperious shrill and she gesticulated toward a sleeping pallet near Layne.

"Lumps of cow dung! Place him here! And be gentle! One cry from Shao's husband and I'll have my son put you in groaning misery! Quickly now!"

Layne blinked belatedly. This was the *lao-pan*'s feared mother, Lan Ni! She swallowed hard, recalling the abject terror of the slaves who served in the *lao-pan*'s cave fortress on Tantai for this fearsome woman. And she had just talked to Lan Ni as if she were passing the time of day with her! No one ever spoke to the matriarch of the Dragon Clan like that. But any worries over a social snafu were set aside as the pirates carefully laid Matt on the blankets at Layne's feet.

"Quickly!" Lan snarled, slapping the closest pirate on the arm. "Have the slaves bring hot water! Herbs!"

"Yes, honored Mother."

Layne sank to her knees, gripping the blankets to her body as she reached out and touched Matt's face. His flesh was cool beneath her fingertips and she bit deeply into her lower lip to stop from crying out. Pushing the damp strands of hair off his brow, she unzipped the vest and unbuttoned the shirt that clung to his body. Lan Ni hunkered over Layne, scowling.

"I'll have my slaves bring you everything you need, Shao."

"Thank you, honored Mother. Your heart is kind. We're both indebted to you."

Lan Ni grunted and straightened. "He will awaken soon, Shao. When you are finished, we want you to sleep. We are aware that Captain Qin's junk was sunk by the filth of the PRC. Rest and we will come for you much later."

Layne was stunned by the sudden, frenetic activity. Several women dressed in dark, baggy tops and trousers scurried into the cave. One carried a large bundle of clothes. Another brought a bowl of steaming water, towels and several crushed herbs in a jar and set them near Layne. They bowed and left with Lan Ni angrily scolding them.

Layne quickly rummaged through the clothes. She found a

curious ensemble consisting of a pair of baggy black wool slacks that were two sizes too large, a heavy linen blouse of pink, white socks and leather sandals for her feet. She was shaking so badly from hunger, it took her twice as long to dress. Only as she buttoned the collar of the blouse did she realize that the opal Matt had given her still hung around her neck. Surprised and grateful that the rare gem hadn't been lost to the hungry ocean, Layne thought that it truly had brought them *joss*. Bending down over Matt, she stripped him of the smelly clothes and then piled every available blanket in the cave around and on top of him to warm him.

A small teenage girl scuttled into the cave, bowed and then hurried over to the Dutch oven. Intent upon taking Matt's pulse, Layne barely noticed her. His wrist was cool to her touch, and she held her breath, waiting to feel his life pumping through his arteries beneath her fingers. There! A huge sigh of relief washed through her; his pulse was slow and strong. The slave girl came over, placing a bowl filled with chicken and rice before Layne.

"Thank you," Layne murmured, offering her a slight smile. The girl smiled shyly in return and left. Some of the worry drained from Layne as the color began to come back to Matt's pale face. Layne watched him for several more minutes before picking up the bowl. A tinge of amusement lingered in her eyes as she realized she'd have to eat with her fingers. So much for the spoons, knives and forks of the civilized world they had left far behind them. Kneeling beside Matt, Layne scooped a chunk of the succulent, spicy chicken into her mouth, almost light-headed from the experience. It was her first solid food since jumping from the junk. They were safe now. Safe.

The groan started low in his throat and the reverberation brought Matt to the edge of consciousness. Pain sharpened his hold on reality, and a gray world met his slitted eyes as he fought to rise out of the blackness. He was lying on his side, supported against someone's knees and thighs. He was warm and that didn't make sense. Again, pain lanced through his left arm and he flinched.

"Oh, God, I'm sorry."

Layne! It was her voice, but Matt was too weak to look up.

He felt her tender, loving hands move over his chilled flesh, and his emotions spiraled to the surface. Layne was alive. Alive.

"Matt?" Layne peered down at him, running her trembling fingers across his roughened cheek. "Are you awake?"

"Yeah…damn, I hurt. What happened? Where are we?"

She dragged in a deep breath. "We made it to Tantai. We're in one of the caves in the *lao-pan*'s complex. You're hurt. Your upper arm is slit open. I've been pulling splinters out from around the wound."

He blinked, allowing his senses to surface. She had been using her body to support him so that she could get to the wound. His voice was hoarse as he struggled to speak. "It happened on the junk. That third round fired by the PRC hit the cabin directly behind us. Teak splinters were flying everywhere."

Her eyes widened. The wound had been made by a sharp projectile of wood. It could have just as easily have lodged in his brain or his throat, killing him instantly. Tears sprang to her eyes as Layne realized that he had protected her from sure injury or death. "I think I got all of it. Thank God you were unconscious when I cleaned the wound. I—I don't think I could have stood trying to get out the splinters if you were awake." She took a long, shuddering breath, covering the seeping wound with a soft towel. The seawater had acted as a healing agent, cleansing the wound with brine salt. It needed to be stitched shut, but Layne didn't have the necessary instruments or the knowledge to do it. "Let me dress the wound and then I'll get you something to drink and eat."

He closed his eyes, his hand moving upward to caress her thigh. "Sounds great."

Layne frowned with worry. "The *lao-pan*'s mother, Lan Ni, has given me several medicinal herbs to pack your wound with, Matt. She says it will draw out the infection and soothe the area. This might hurt…."

His fingers splayed against her thigh and his eyes still closed, he offered her a tired smile. "It'll be okay, kitten. Do what you have to."

"I'm a lousy nurse, Matt Talbot."

"You're better than the alternative, no treatment."

Layne glanced down at his drawn face. "Masochist," she quavered and placed the herbal mixture, a dark green paste, into the wound. Anguish shot through her as she felt Matt stiffen, and she tried desperately to steady her trembling fingers. Finally, she had the wound packed, dressed and bandaged. After she'd coaxed a pair of black cotton pajamas similar to what the pirates wore over his legs, Layne helped him sit up. She eased a heavy black flannel shirt over Matt's shoulders and had trouble with the buttons, her hands were still shaking so badly.

Matt watched her, tenderness softening the hard line of his mouth. He reached out to caress her pale cheek. "You're doing fine," he soothed. He suspected her unsteadiness was a reaction to their narrow escape from death. "Here," he rasped, "let me do that." His hands closed about her own. He offered her a wan smile to shore up Layne's disintegrating composure. "I could use some water."

Layne nodded and sat back. She pushed her hair away from her face and shakily got to her feet. She barely had enough headroom to stand upright in the low-ceilinged cave. Wordlessly, she brought a jug of water and a bowl heaped with chicken and rice to Matt. She sat down opposite him, watching him drink the contents of the jug, then hungrily scoop up the food from the bowl she held close to his mouth. The flickering shadows danced across his darkly bearded face. The face she loved. Layne crossed her legs, her hands hanging limply in her lap, feeling a wave of lethargy flow through her. Her lids became heavy, and she had to force herself to fight off grogginess. It was as if she had expended the last of her strength, both emotionally and physically, and suddenly she felt too weak to cope any longer.

Matt watched her through hooded eyes, setting the bowl and jug aside. He wiped his long fingers off on a nearby towel. "Come here," he urged. "Lie next to me. I don't know about you, but I'm about ready to crash again. We need to rest, Layne."

She nodded tiredly, getting to her hands and knees and crawling next to Matt on the thin mattress. "Lan Ni told us to sleep. We aren't much good to anyone right now. Thank God you're all right," she murmured, snuggling down beside his lean, hard body.

Matt nodded and settled Layne's head on his good shoulder, drawing her near. He could smell the seawater in her hair, but it didn't matter as he nuzzled her cheek gently. She was alive. And he loved her. "Shh," he remonstrated huskily. Carefully he slid his injured arm across her body. "Let's sleep. We'll deal with everything else later."

Layne huddled closer, enjoying the heat of Matt's body. All the fears, the trauma of nearly dying, of Matt's wound, flowed out of her. Without another word, her lashes drooped closed as she felt Matt's arm pull her tightly against him. She fell into the dark abyss of sleep, knowing Matt was there, protecting her against their uncertain future at the hands of the pirates.

Matt awoke with a jerk, bathed in a sweat. Layne lay with her head beneath his jaw, one arm and leg thrown across him in sleep. He drew in a shaky breath and relaxed his tense muscles, letting his head drop back to the makeshift pillow beneath him. It had been a nightmare, just a lousy dream. He shut his eyes tightly, feeling the adrenaline coursing through him. His heart was pounding like a runaway freight train. Matt lifted his hand, feeling immediate pain run up his arm. Carefully he moved his stiff, abused muscles, his fingers resting against Layne's hair. The ebony mass was dry now as he combed his fingers through the luxuriant tangle. How long had they slept? He reopened his eyes, allowing them to adjust to the weak light of the lone kerosene lamp sputtering at the far end of the cave.

He strained to catch any sounds. It was as if they were in some kind of vacuum, unable to hear either the wind howling or the whisper of human voices. The watch he had been wearing had been torn off his wrist in their escape from the junk, and he tried to mentally count the hours between crawling up the beach and first awakening beneath Layne's gentle hands. But it was no use, it could have been a few minutes or several hours. He felt Layne stir, a softened whimper coming from her.

"Shh, kitten, it's all right. You're safe…." Matt kissed away her tears and felt her stir beneath him.

Drowsily, she regarded him in the silence. "Matt?"

"Right here," he assured her tenderly.

Layne pulled her hands free of the blankets, wrapping them around his neck and drawing him down upon her. A sob escaped her as she buried her face into the folds of his shirt. "I—I thought I'd lost you…. I couldn't hold you…. I watched you float away, screaming for me to help you…."

Matt gently cradled her, rocking her as he would a distraught child, stroking her hair. "Just a bad dream, nothing more, kitten."

"Hold me. Hold me…."

"Forever," he promised fervently, holding her as tightly as he could.

He kissed her brow. And then his voice lowered. "I love the hell out of you, lady."

Layne responded with a hard, urgent embrace. How could she put into words the tumult of feelings he aroused in her—even under these conditions? "It's funny," she said, her voice barely audible, "how a close brush with death makes you see your life very clearly."

He rubbed her arm gently. "It does," he agreed softly, kissing her hair. "What have you discovered in the past twenty-four hours?"

"That I love you. Despite my distrust of your occupation." Her lashes lifted, revealing gold in the topaz depths of her eyes as she rose up on one arm, studying Matt in the silence. "I never knew I could fall in love with someone so quickly. Is it love, Matt?"

He drowned in her liquid gaze. "Love is something you feel. It can't be logically explained." He grazed her arm with his strong fingers, his tone low and vibrating. "After we get out of here, you'll have the time you need to answer that question, kitten. No one can do it for you."

Layne raised her head, staring around the quiet cave. "I want that time with you, Matt. So many things have gone wrong. Nothing has gone according to plan."

"There were no hard, fast rules to this mission, Layne," he

reminded her gently. His mouth thinned. "I keep wondering if Jim and Frank are nearby. Are they one cave away from us and we don't know it? Or are they tied up somewhere and injured, maybe…."

"Don't torture yourself, Matt. Lan Ni said they'd come for us later. Maybe if we get up and let then know we're awake, they'll take us to the *lao-pan.*"

He rested his arm across his eyes and Layne wondered if it was to hide the anguish she heard in his voice. "I want them alive," he said in a low tone. "I don't know what I'll do if Jim's not alive…."

Layne leaned down, pressing herself against Matt, holding him. "We'll cross that bridge together," she whispered, feeling his pain. Just the fact that he would share his personal and emotional side with her sent Layne's heart soaring. The ragged edge in his voice meant he was one step away from tears, and her own eyes watered dangerously. "Jim's alive. And so is Frank. I just feel it, darling. We'll know soon."

Matt buried his face against her warm, soft breasts. She smelled sweet, and her fragrance encircled him. Matt crushed her against him, the heat of her pliant body soothing his raw emotions. Did Layne know how unselfish and loving she was? He held her until he realized he might be hurting her. Gradually, he relaxed his embrace and felt Layne shift slightly.

"Come on, let's get up," she urged in a low voice.

Matt found that his entire left shoulder and arm were stiff. After dressing, Layne fashioned a sling for his arm to keep it immobile. Matt sat on the pallet, legs crossed, and watched as Layne lit several more lamps, giving the cave new brilliance. A strange sense of peace descended upon him, and he relaxed as he watched her work over the Dutch oven. Her hair was tangled, but her face radiated an inner glow that sent his heart racing. She was happy, he realized as she returned to kneel opposite him.

"I hope you don't mind being fed," she murmured, her knees resting against his legs.

A glimmer of desire flared to life in his cobalt eyes. "I like being hand-fed."

Layne blushed and met his heated gaze. "Matt Talbot, do you turn everything into a sensual experience?"

"I try to. Life's too short not to enjoy."

Layne sobered, picking out a tender piece of spiced chicken and lifting it to his awaiting lips. She was beginning to appreciate his enthusiasm for life. He took advantage of every second, because the next second might be his last. Matt's lips closed about her fingers and tingles fled up her hand and into her arm.

"Delicious," he murmured.

"What? The food or my fingers?"

He grinned and swallowed. "I can get chicken anywhere. It's your fingers that taste so good."

Desire surged within her lower body and Layne smiled, feeding him another morsel. "I can see I have a whole new way of looking at life."

"Do you like it?" Matt prodded, watching her through his thick lashes, enjoying the rose hue staining her cheeks.

Layne refused to rise to the bait and pretended to hunt for just the right piece of meat for him. "Yes, I like it."

They were sitting in a cave on an island in the South China Sea with danger all around them. And they were dressed in clothes that hung on them, making them look like giant Raggedy Ann and Andy dolls. But none of that mattered to Layne as she lost herself in Matt's caressing gaze. She plucked another piece of chicken from the bowl and tried to give him a stern look. "I love what you do to me. And I also love pleasing you." Her smile dissolved, and she became serious. "I never knew I could make a man feel so wonderful, Matt."

His azure eyes darkened with sudden tenderness. Reaching out, he gripped Layne's hand, giving it a squeeze. "Lady, you're as hot as they come," he told her roughly. "Hot, sweet and good. Men would die for the kind of love you give in return. Loving isn't technique; it's the feeling behind your actions that makes you special, Layne. And you make me feel good in or out of bed." His fingers tightened perceptibly. "When we get out of this…when we get home…" He didn't finish, but his eyes said the rest.

Matt watched her lips part; her topaz eyes turned gold, with fire in their wide, beautiful depths, and he quivered inwardly with desire. A wry smile pulled at his mouth. "When we're in our nineties you'll still make me feel fire raging through me with just that look," he growled.

Layne gave him a startled blink. "What look?" she asked, her voice trembling.

Matt's smile widened and he lifted her hand to his lips, kissing her fingers. "Someday soon I'm going to put you in front of a mirror and show you 'what look,' lady." He released her fingers, their eyes meeting with unspoken love for each other.

Layne had just finished eating when a pirate slipped noiselessly past the curtain and into their cave. Matt became instantly alert, his eyes narrowing on the man as he padded over to where they sat.

"Honorable Shao," the pirate said, bowing, "the *lao-pan* of the Dragon Clan requests your presence. Both of you. Come, I will take you to the main chamber."

Layne motioned Matt to his feet. "Thank you," she said, returning the bow. Worriedly, she glanced up at Matt as he slipped his arm around her shoulders. Then they left the small cave and began a long, rocky walk through a series of twisting, winding tunnels. The smell of kerosene hung heavy, and the small, flickering lamps provided meager light for their progress. More and more families of the pirates were seen as they passed through larger caves. The singsong music of Haklo provided Layne a measure of comfort.

Matt missed little on their journey to meet the *lao-pan*. The amount of stolen goods in each cave was unbelievable. Expensive, hand-knotted rugs, bolts of silk of every description, crates filled with farm machinery and boxes were piled high. The families covertly stared at Matt and Layne as they walked by, and Matt recognized expensive furniture that could only have come from freighters bound for Europe or North America. Yet the pirates never used the furniture that was stacked in the corners of the caves—or the fine rugs, preferring instead the bamboo mats as floor covering.

Their guide brought them into a huge chamber brightly lit with hundreds of poorly strung light bulbs. Matt halted, bringing Layne to his side as they viewed the panorama before them. The entire area was carpeted with various shades and colors of tapestries ranging from expensive, hand-knotted ones to the cheap variety he'd seen in discount department stores in the States. Pirate guards stood at attention around the throne of Kang Ying, their swords hanging in scabbards at their hips, revolvers in holsters and bandoliers of bullets across their chests. The fierceness of their expressions and the wild, feral look in their eyes made Matt tense even more. He could sense that these men would explode like grenades at the least provocation.

Glancing down at Layne, Matt realized just how much her life had been in danger the first time she had come here to meet with Kang. Carson should have been with her. Looking at these pirates who glared back at him as they slowly walked forward toward the raised dais of Kang Ying, Matt appreciated even more Layne's special kind of courage. He would have thought no woman would dare to walk into the pirates' lair. No man in his right mind would, either. These men were little more than animals, their faces fashioned and molded by the elements of the ocean surrounding them. Their black hair was long and greasy, usually wrapped in tattered but colorful fabric. The odor surrounding them was a repugnant combination of sweaty body odor and fish.

Matt swung his attention to the dais. His heart started a slow pound, his fingers gripping Layne's shoulder a bit tighter. There, sitting like a gleaming, bronzed statue on a throne lavished with gold leaf, sat Kang Ying, *lao-pan* of the savage Dragon Clan.

Chapter 14

"The devil winds have spared you, Shao," Kang said in greeting, nodding his bald head toward her. His face was triangular, making his brown eyes large and intense beneath his straight black brows. He leaned forward tensely, studying Layne in the gathering silence. His guards stood on either side of the throne, arms across their massive chests. Kang's thin mouth pursed beneath his bushy mustache as he watched her approach the raised dais. Fine lines were etched at the corner of each of his slanted eyes and around his mouth. He wore a leopard skin across his thick shoulders and a peasant shirt of wrinkled white cotton beneath it. The red leather belt girding his sizable waist contained a scabbard with the hilt of a guerrilla knife visible. Unlike the rest of his entourage, Kang wore black leather boots with trousers of the same color bloused within them.

Layne maintained proper obeisance, head bent and gaze lowered to the carpet. Approaching the dais she knelt, placing her hands upon her thighs. "The gods have been kind to us, *lao-pan*," she began in a hushed voice.

Kang's thin mouth twitched beneath the mustache, and he made a grand gesture with his right arm. "Rise and come forward, Shao."

Layne got to her feet, and walked forward keeping her eyes focused on Kang's polished boots. Again she knelt. He extended his left hand, and she pressed her brow to it. The strong odor of fish from his fingers clung to her nostrils, and Layne held her breath until she got to her feet and took a step backward. After the ceremonial greeting, which was always accorded a *lao-pan*, Layne slowly raised her chin. Her gaze swept upward to meet Kang's curious stare. He hadn't changed much in the time since she had last seen him. At fifty-five, he appeared forty-five, and the sleek gleam of his perfectly shaped skull gave Kang an aura of undisputable authority. Layne swallowed hard, realizing that if she displeased Kang in any way, he could snap his fingers and the guards who stood on either side of him would draw their bloodied swords on her. She focused all her energies on the leader.

"It's good to see you, Lord Kang. We thank you for your help after we washed upon the beach. Without you, we would have died."

Kang's eyes lit up with pleasure. "You always bring us *joss* when you are among us. Last time we were able to board a freighter run aground by the devil winds." He smiled benevolently. "Even now, we live off the goods and trade them with Hu Ti, *lao-pan* of the Iron Tiger Clan to the south of us."

"*Joss* was not with us this time, Lord Kang. Your Captain Qin and his crew were lost. We drifted into PRC waters because of the devil winds, and their cutters began firing at us. Did anyone from Captain Qin's crew make it to Tantai?"

"The gods spit only you ashore, Shao," he answered heavily, his brows drawing downward. "My people were swallowed up by the gods of the sea. One of my best captains—*aiyeee*, let us not talk of this, Shao. We have much else to discuss."

Layne bowed her head. "Still, I'm sorry for the loss of your people. They were kind to us, *lao-pan*."

Kang raised his head, his stare suddenly fixed upon Matt, who stood with his legs slightly apart in a fighter's stance, one of perfect balance. "You have brought your husband, Shao?"

"Yes. His name is Matt Talbot. Among his people he is known as Hu Gang, Steel Tiger. He is *lao-pan* of the flying machines from Golden Mountain."

"Ahh, then he is *lao-pan* to the men we've captured?"

She suppressed a shiver of dread. "The two pilots?"

"Yes." He swung his gaze back to Layne. "I requested only

you to come, Shao. You, I trust." And then he grinned. "As much as I can trust anyone from the Golden Mountain."

Layne nodded, swallowing a small smile. "Apparently there was an error in transmission of your messge to me, *lao-pan*. I can only apologize, we did not mean to disobey your orders."

"I thought you said your husband's name was Carson?"

He didn't forget much, Layne thought. Kang had endlessly pumped, wheedled and coaxed information from her during her last visit. She compressed her lips momentarily and stalled for time. To get caught in a lie with Kang would mean instant death for all of them. Layne chose to be truthful and maintain the coverup of her marriage to Matt. "That is so, *lao-pan*. But he died nine months ago. I just married Hu Gang less than a month ago."

Kang rubbed his chin, saying nothing, his black eyes moving to Matt and then back to her. His darkly tanned face became more set. "The reason I wanted you is because I know you would not lie to me like the other foreign devils would. You are a member of our clan. You know the penalty for lying to me."

Layne clasped her hands in front of her, her brown eyes darkening with sincerity. "I'm here as an interpreter for my husband. He has the power to negotiate the release of our pilots, *lao-pan*. He does not speak Haklo or any dialect of Cantonese."

Kang grunted, eyeing Matt suspiciously. "Hu Gang is a warrior." It was a statement.

"Yes, a great warrior. If not for him, the sea gods would have swallowed me up, *lao-pan*."

"I hope Hu Gang has brought much gold with him," Kang growled ominously.

Layne nodded. "It's my understanding that we must bid higher than the others who want our pilots."

"Yes. The Soviets have sent their emissary. He is with us now."

"My lord, is it possible that my husband can see our pilots? He is understandably concerned over their condition."

Kang shrugged indolently. "Of course. The Soviet has already made sure that they are alive." A slight smile edged his mouth. "They didn't want to bid on dead men."

Layne closed her eyes, fighting back a wave of nausea. Had Kang tortured either of the pilots? She dare not ask because Kang would consider it an insult, and no one insulted the *lao-pan* and lived to tell about it. When she reopened her eyes, Kang was staring at her.

"I must know one thing, Shao."

"Yes?"

Kang lifted his head, staring blackly at Matt. "One of the men from the flying machine has a name like Hu Gang. Are they related? Or are the names of the people from Golden Mountain like our own?"

She froze. Matt hadn't instructed her on whether he wanted Kang to know the truth of the matter. But how could she lie about it? If Matt met with Jim, it would be obvious to observers that the two men were more to each other than just acquaintances. A new revelation entered her cartwheeling mind: Jim Talbot would be her brother-in-law by marriage and that might make Kang more lenient toward releasing him to Matt.

"Shao?" Kang's voice was like a whip, shattering the silence.

Layne's voice trembled slightly. "Yes, lord, Major Jim Talbot is Hu Gang's brother." She lifted her hand, pressing it against her breast. "And Jim is my brother-in-law. He is a part of my family."

Kang's brows dipped, his mouth tightening. His features grew hard as he mulled over the implications. There was distrust in his eyes as he looked pointedly at Layne. "This is not good, Shao," he warned her in a growl. "You say you are married to Hu Gang."

"Yes, a month ago. Two weeks before Jim's flying machine failed him and they landed here near Tantai."

"So you know Jim Talbot?"

"I've never met him, lord. I only know of him through my husband," and she gestured toward Matt. "They are close to one another as only family can be, even though Hu Gang does not live near Jim."

Kang's eyes were glittering as he mulled over the technicality now thrown in his lap. He turned his mounting frustration upon Layne.

"This is not good! Is this a plan of those foreign devils? How do I know you are his wife?" Kang jabbed his finger toward Matt. "Does it not seem odd that you found another man quickly after Carson's death? Did you not mourn? This marriage to Hu Gang appears rushed."

Perspiration broke out on her upper lip, and Layne felt her heart pumping hard. Should she have lied? Would Kang have been less wary as a result? Well, it was too late to regret her decision. It had been a gut decision and that had never led her wrong. Not until now. "I don't wish to recount to the *lao-pan* my unhappy first marriage," she began in a low and tortured voice. "When Brad Carson died, it was freedom that I cele-brated, not mourning." Layne turned, her eyes softening and her voice becoming stronger. "And when I met Hu Gang, he showed me what true happiness is. I fell deeply in love with him. And it did happen quickly." She turned, meeting and holding Kang's furious gaze. "But I don't regret it. I'm happy now as I've never been before. He is my life. Without him, I would cease to exist, lord."

Kang muttered a curse and straightened, gesturing to a pirate who stood near the wall of the chamber with several others. "Understand that I must make sure you are married to Hu Gang."

Layne frowned, her heart starting an erratic beat of terror as a slender pirate no more than eighteen years old came forward.

"Tang Fa," Kang barked, "take this foreign devil to another chamber and question him at length about Shao. Use your knowl-edge of the Golden Mountain tongue and speak with him. I want to know how they met, where, the place, anything that I can ask Shao to duplicate to prove they are indeed husband and wife."

"Yes, my lord," Tang Fa replied, bowing deeply. He turned swiftly on his heel and gripped Matt's arm in a vise.

Layne held her breath, watching Matt tense subtly as the pirate held him. She turned to Matt. "Go with him. Tang Fa will ask you questions in English about our marriage."

Matt's eyes narrowed worriedly upon her. She was pale and frightened. "Okay. Will you be all right here while I'm gone?"

She nodded, clasping her hands tightly in front of her. "Yes…I'll be safe."

"Come!" Tang ordered, pulling him toward the entrance.

Oh, God, Layne thought, a chill flowing through her. If their stories didn't match, Kang would—

"How did you meet, Shao? Answer me quickly, for I am not happy with the events you present me with."

She didn't have time to lie; it would have been useless, anyway. Instead she told Kang the truth, moving it back in time. That made Matt's appearance in her classroom in January and not September, with the addition of the nine-month period between Brad's death and her marriage to Matt. "He came to one of my language classes on Cantonese, hoping to learn the language, *lao-pan*. He made me very uncomfortable at first because he stared at me a lot." The story became easier as she traced their mutual development of love for one another, leaving out the fact that Matt was a Company employee. She held up her left hand toward Kang. "The wedding bands once belonged to his grandmother. And she told him that when he found a woman who lingered day and night in his mind she was the one to marry."

Kang grunted, rubbing his pointed chin as he stared at her left hand. "He is an honorable man, listening to the wisdom of his grandmother," he grunted.

"My husband is like the Chinese in regard to his family, lord. They mean everything to him."

"So, is Jim Talbot married?"

Layne felt sweat dampening her palms. God, let her remember all these facts Matt had told her about Jim and his family! "Yes. His wife, Irene, is expecting a child no more than a week from now."

Again, Kang's brows dipped unpleasantly. "Do they have other children?"

Her mouth went dry. Did Jim have other children? She didn't know. And she should. "I don't know," she said, trying to keep the tremble out of her voice. Her throat constricted even more. "They hope for a male."

"The firstborn should always be a strong son to carry on the family tradition," Kang muttered. "Females are worthless." He scowled. "Tell me more of your husband's family."

Layne faithfully repeated everything she could remember that Matt had told her about his parents on the flight over to Hong Kong. What would have happened if Matt hadn't told her about his growing-up years? There was far less danger to Matt about her background because he had studied the personnel file on her. She was the weak link that might break.

"They are of a seaborne clan such as yourself, my lord. Matt's father is a fisherman on the western coast. He fishes from the same ocean that you rule."

Kang's brows rose slightly, a pleased look coming to his face. "*Heya*, that is good."

Layne continued, telling Kang the stories that Matt had told her. By the time the inquisition was at an end, Layne felt empty and drained. Kang looked to his left as Tang Fa escorted Matt back into the chamber. The pirate made a cutting motion for him to stop at the edge of the dais. She turned, her eyes wide with fear as she looked at Matt. It was impossible to know what Matt was thinking or feeling, and Layne's heart began to hammer as she returned her attention to Tang, now leaning over the throne, speaking softly with the *lao-pan*.

After fifteen minutes of waiting she unconsciously wiped her sweaty hands on her thighs. For a second, Layne felt light-headed. Would their stories correspond? Her gaze narrowed agonizingly on Kang's stoic features.

Kang grunted heavily as Tang bowed and backed away, taking his place against the far cave wall and coming to attention once again. The pirate leader studied Layne in the thickening silence. His fists clenched on the gold-leaf arms of the throne.

"Who is Jenny?"

The question was shot like a bullet and Layne flinched. "I—"

"Why did you not mention her?"

Layne touched her brow, trying to gather her stunned thoughts. "You asked only of us, *lao-pan*. I didn't realize you wanted to know about my husband's tragic marriage to his first wife, Jenny."

"I wanted everything! Everything!"

Mouth dry, throat constricted, Layne recited what she knew of Jenny Talbot. When she finished, Kang's features hardened. He slowly rose and walked down to her. He wasn't tall, but he was powerfully built, and Layne remained anchored as Kang glared at her.

"You're nervous, Shao," he said softly, his eyes hooded and watchful. "Why?"

Layne swallowed convulsively. "I'm not a mongoose to the cobra, *lao-pan*. I have not lied to you. But I know of your power, and I'm frightened," she admitted hoarsely. "I'm not used to being treated as if I were a liar."

Kang's lips pulled away in a mirthless smile and he flicked a glance in Matt's direction. "I have not accused you of lying, Shao," he went on smoothly. "I only seek to know whether your marriage is real or false. The Soviet had warned us that they would send a spy from the Golden Mountain. And I said no, they send only Shao, and I know she will not lie to the *lao-pan*. Instead, I get you and this man who is a spy."

Layne took a deep breath. "No, he's not a spy. He is an honorable man who has been sent to represent our government to win back our pilots. Will you judge him a spy because it is his brother who is involved? Jim is a part of our family, a part of us. If there is a spy present, then it is the Soviet, not us. We come only to claim what is rightfully ours."

Kang laughed throatily. "None of you own them. I do. It was I who plucked them from the hungry mouth of the sea gods. They belong to me. But that is unimportant right now." His hand snaked out and before Layne could react, Kang captured her left wrist, jerking her hand up between them.

Matt responded a split second after Kang had made the move. Layne gasped as two pirates launched themselves at Matt, dragging him back down off the dais. Kang chortled and returned his attention to Layne.

"He is like a tiger, swift and deadly." Kang's fingers tightened around her wrist until her flesh turned white. Layne cringed against the pain, her eyes widening in terror.

"Let go of her!" Matt roared, jerking to free himself of the guards.

"No!" Layne pleaded, twisting around to Matt. "Don't move! Don't say anything!"

Kang smiled silkily, placing his palm over the butt of his guerrilla knife. He slowly withdrew the carbon steel blade from its case, holding it close to Layne's hand. "Your stories match, Shao. Either you are both telling the truth or you are both adept at lying. I don't like those who would take gold that is rightfully due me. You know that I cannot, by clan law, demand gold for Jim Talbot if he is your brother by marriage, because, as your brother, he is entitled to my protection."

"I know that," Layne quavered, her eyes large and shadowed. What was Kang going to do with the knife? A faintness swept through her.

"Shao," Kang whispered tautly, sliding the cold blade the length of her hand, "prove that Matt Talbot is your husband. Will you give me one of your fingers to prove that to me?"

Matt jerked hard, loosening his right arm. The pirate holding him slammed backward to the floor with a crash, the sound echoing throughout the chamber. Matt lunged forward, his hand outstretched within inches of touching Layne. "No!" he snarled, his lips drawing away from his teeth. "Don't touch her!"

Kang stood immobile, watching as two more guards came forward and tackled Matt. They wrestled him to the floor. One pirate yanked Matt's head back, exposed his throat and placed a knife at it.

"No!" Layne pleaded, trying to break free. "He's injured! Please…Lord Kang!" She looked back at the *lao-pan*. "Don't hurt him. God, don't!"

The icy blade of steel pressed more firmly into her index finger, and a thin ribbon of blood appeared. Kang's mouth tightened, his gaze never leaving Layne's blanched features.

Matt struggled, his breath rasping from his contorted mouth as he watched Kang. "What's he want, Layne?" he demanded. "Layne!"

Tears spilled down her cheeks. "H-he wants me to prove that you're my husband by giving him one of my fingers," she quavered. "Don't move Matt, they'll kill you. Quit fighting! It won't do any good."

Her finger? Matt gritted his teeth, loathing sweeping through him. His nostrils flared, his breath hard and sharp. "Tell him to take mine, then, dammit! Tell him to leave you alone!"

Layne's vision blurred and she bit down hard on her lower lip. Matt needed his hands in order to fly the planes he loved so much. He'd never be able to test aircraft again if he lost one of his fingers. A huge sob rose from her chest and threatened to cut off her breathing. She felt the continued coldness of the steel blade against her flesh as she tried to mentally prepare herself to lose her finger. She had seen others among the Dragon Clan who had lost one, two or three fingers. And she had seen men's hands wrapped in bloody rags shortly afterward. Her insides became queasy, and she shut her eyes, dragging in a deep, shaky breath.

"What does he say?" Kang demanded.

Miserably, Layne translated. Kang removed the knife from her hand and released her bruised wrist. He took the knife and slapped the butt of it into her opened palm. His voice was graveled. "Kneel down before me and give me one of your fingers. Now."

Layne stared down at the knife in her opened palm. Cut off one of her own extremities? And if she didn't? She cast a wild look in Matt's direction. Kang would have them killed after he got what he wanted in the way of gold payment for the pilots. He would never allow her or Matt to leave Tantai alive. And two other pilots' lives were at stake. She tried to reason with herself as she slowly knelt down before the chill dais of polished pink marble.

Matt's voice carried hoarsely throughout the complex. "Layne? What are you doing?" He struggled futilely, the guards tightening their hold on him. "Answer me, dammit!"

All color drained from Layne's face as she knelt at Kang's booted feet. Her heart was pounding like thunder in her ears, and she blocked out all of Matt's wrenching protests as she spread her left hand flat on the marble floor in front of the *lao-pan*. So she'd better get on with it, she thought dispassionately, wielding the knife awkwardly in her right hand. The long blade gleamed as she slowly brought it down and rested it against the little finger of her left hand. How was it done? Did chilled steel cut through bone? Those questions spun through Layne's head as she contemplated how to do it as quickly and mercifully as possible. There would be pain. Oh, God, the pain… Layne bit down hard on her lower lip, tasting the blood, taking a firmer grip on the knife.

"Layne, no!" Matt's strangled cry caromed off the walls, and he fought like an animal to break the guards' hold on him.

Kang leaned over in one lithe motion and gripped her wrist. His strong, browned fingers wrapped around her flesh. "That's enough, Shao," he rasped. "You've shown your loyalty." Kang flicked a glance at Matt. "And so has he. Rise."

Sheathing the knife, Kang ordered the guards to release Matt. The *lao-pan* turned to Layne. "He must love you or he would not have volunteered to change places with you, Shao. If he was a spy, he would have stood there and let you lose your finger instead. Nor would he have fought like a tiger to free himself to get to you before you took your finger. And you were going to give me your finger."

She shakily touched her brow, overwhelmed with a rush of tightly leashed emotions held at bay until that moment. "Y-yes, *lao-pan*."

Kang's voice was tired. "Go to him. I will require no more proof that you are husband and wife. Jim Talbot is free to leave with you. I will not make him a part of the ransom."

She felt faintness sweep through her, but she kept her back ramrod straight or she would have fallen. Matt slowly got to his feet, and it was obvious that his wound had been greatly aggravated; blood stained through the fabric of the shirt he wore. Layne turned, walking numbly toward Matt, her face ashen. A sob tore from her lips as she found protection within Matt's embrace. He crushed her to his sweat-soaked body, and Layne buried her head against his shoulder, trembling badly, trying to control the urge to cry.

Matt's blue eyes were shards of ice as he glared up at the pirate leader, who had sat back down on his throne. He didn't know what had been said between Layne and Kang, but it appeared that the pirate believed them to be married. His stomach turned as he vividly remembered Kang's knife cutting into Layne's finger. Whispering words of reassurance to Layne, he felt her gradually begin to relax.

"I'm all right," she quavered, stepping away from Matt. With a brush of her hand, she wiped her cheeks dry of the few tears she had shed.

"Shao, I'll have Tang escort you to the cave where we are holding the men of the flying machine. You tell Jim Talbot he is free to go."

Layne bowed her head. "I will, *lao-pan*. And thank you for your mercy."

Kang grimaced and waved his hand. "Tomorrow morning you and the Soviet shall bid on who is to get the other pilot."

"Very well, my lord. Tomorrow morning, then."

Kang sat slouched on the throne, staring moodily after them as they left, obviously discouraged at the turn of events that meant the loss of Jim Talbot as merchandise to be bartered with.

"Where are we being taken?" Matt demanded grimly, keeping his arm around Layne's shoulder to steady her. Hatred toward Kang and what he had almost had Layne do made Matt tremble.

"To see the pilots."

He looked down, assessing her worriedly. "Layne?" She was almost waxen, her eyes a dark brown. The rocky corridor widened, and it made walking easier as they moved along, one pirate marching in front and another in back of them.

"I'll be okay in a minute."

Leaning over, Matt kissed her temple. Her face was glistening with a sheen of perspiration and he knew Layne was in mild shock. Wouldn't he be, if Kang had asked for one of his fingers? "I love you," he whispered hoarsely. "You're one hell of a brave lady."

Her lashes fanned her cheeks, and wordlessly Layne leaned

against Matt, dissolving in the aura of his love. "And I love you," she said in a trembling voice.

They walked another five minutes before the pirates gave them a signal to halt. In front of them a cave was being guarded by two other pirates bearing submachine guns. Matt recognized them as AK-47s, hardware carried by the North Vietnamese during the Vietnam War. They were ugly weapons.

"In there," Tang Fa instructed, pulling the heavy wool curtain aside and gesturing them to move forward. "You will stay until dark and then we take you back to your cave."

"Please, Tang, can you bring some medical supplies?" Layne asked. The sleeve of Matt's shirt was stained with bright red blood. "Hot water? More bandages?"

Tang glowered for a moment and then gave a curt nod of his head. "Very well. Go!"

Matt stood with Layne just inside the curtain, allowing his eyes to adjust to the dimly lit cave. His gaze swept across the barren and shadowed area; the basalt gleamed dully beneath the kerosene lamps that sat on the floor near the left wall. Two men were lying inert on thin mattresses at the other end.

"Jim? Frank?" His voice carried hollowly through the maw.

Layne gripped Matt's hand as she saw both pilots stir. The metallic sound of chains being moved broke the stilted silence. Had they been asleep? Drugged?

"Yeah?" a voice thick with sleep answered. "Who's there?"

Matt glanced at Layne, his face suddenly softened with relief. "Jim, it's me, Matt." And in ten strides he was at the pilots' sides.

Layne's vision blurred as Matt knelt down beside his younger brother and threw his good arm around him, holding him tightly for a long, poignant moment. Jim was stockier than Matt, his face square, with those same penetrating blue eyes. His hair was short, like Matt's, but had a reddish tone to it beneath the lamplight. The copilot, Frank Walters, sat up stiffly, his gray eyes widening in relief and surprise. Both pilots were bound with heavy chains around their wrists and ankles to prevent their escape.

Matt's knuckles whitened as he gripped Jim's shoulder, and

their heads bowed against each other. Taking a long, unsteady breath, Matt released him, his hand resting on his brother's arm. "We got here as soon as we could. We're here to get you released, Jim." And then he looked over at the copilot. "I'm Major Matt Talbot, Jim's brother."

A disbelieving smile broke out on Walters's full face, and he shook Matt's hand. "Are we ever glad to see you!"

"But how?" Jim asked, glancing first at Matt and then up at Layne. She stood in the semidarkness and Jim searched her strained, shadowed features. "And who—"

"Meet my wife, Layne," Matt said, giving Jim a warning look that spoke volumes. Matt pulled her down beside him. "Layne, you finally get to meet my brother, Jim."

Layne knew Matt was going through the charade for good reason. She wouldn't put it past Tang Fa to be eavesdropping outside the curtain, since he spoke and understood English. She forced a wan smile and leaned forward, kissing Jim on his darkly bearded cheek. Kang had done little in the way of social amenities for either of the pilots; they were in dire need of a shave and worse, a bath. Their one-piece khaki pressure suits smelled of the ocean and their own body odor. She met Jim's perplexed blue gaze.

"I've heard so much about you, Jim," she began, keeping her hand on his arm, "but everything has been in such a state of mass confusion since we were married a month ago, that we haven't had a chance to fly out and visit you and Irene." And then she gave a slight, strained laugh. "And these certainly aren't the circumstances I had expected to meet you under. But I'm glad you're safe. Both of you."

Jim's square face became contemplative as his gaze moved from Matt to Layne. "Yeah," he murmured. "Irene and I have been meaning to give you guys a call and congratulate you and all…."

Matt took a relieved breath, his shoulders slumping. "Layne's come along to act as our interpreter since she teaches Cantonese in D.C. The pirate leader knows her from two years ago when she first visited Tantai and wrote a series of three articles about them."

For the next fifteen minutes the tenuous atmosphere continued between them. Layne was amazed at the astuteness of the pilots. It was as if they needed only the barest shred of a hint to catch the underlying meaning and go along with the charade. Tang Fa reappeared, scolding two women slaves as they brought Layne the medical supplies she had requested.

Layne smiled up at Tang. "Tang, since Jim is my brother-in-law, will you take these shackles off him? The *lao-pan* has given him back to us."

Tang nodded, giving orders to one of the guards who came and quickly dispensed with Jim's manacles.

"And for the other pilot's comfort?" Layne hedged. "Could we take—"

"*Aiyeee*, the *lao-pan* would have both our heads! I'm not an empty-headed female. He stays in chains!" Tang glared at Frank and did an about-face, marching off in a huff.

"What was that all about?" Jim muttered, looking over at Layne as he tenderly rubbed his raw and bleeding wrists.

"I asked him to take the chains off Frank, too. But he wouldn't do it." She managed a wry smile. "And he made a few chauvinistic comments to boot."

Frank shrugged his broad shoulders. "Thanks for trying, Layne."

"Well, if things go as planned, we'll have them off you tomorrow morning," Matt apologized.

Jim scratched his jaw, giving Matt an odd look. "Hey, how about filling us in on what's going on? Ever since we bailed out right on top of these crazy bastards, our whole world's been turned upside down. And we've got some Soviet emissary snooping around here, politely trying to interrogate us."

Layne said nothing and allowed Matt do the explaining. She eased the shirt from Matt's left arm, and her stomach became queasy as she peeled back the blood-soaked dressing. The wound needed to be stitched closed. Layne bit down on her lip, trying not to hurt Matt as she cleansed the ugly laceration with warm water and soap. Occasionally, he would wince or his voice would grow strained, but he never told her to stop. Finally, she had the new dressing in place, and with his help, bandaged it back up, the clean white cotton cloth stark against his tanned arm.

Moving between the brothers, Layne tended Jim's lacerated wrists, wrapping each of them in a protective dressing and bandage. Jim gave her a grateful look that said everything. Frank Walters had sustained a deep cut on his left hand and he was next to be taken care of. Matt gave each of the pilots the antibiotics he carried in his vest to combat any potential infection.

Two Chinese women silently entered the cave, bearing trays laden with freshly cooked pork, rice and fragrant steamed vegetables. They set the items down, then brought a bottle of plum wine with dainty teacups. After they left, Layne shared a smile with Matt, dishing up the hearty meal in the wooden bowls that were provided.

"This isn't exactly what I'd call a Miss Manners dinner, but it will have to do." She handed them each a set of chopsticks.

Jim eagerly took the bowl, gazing down at the food with hungry intent. "Are you kidding me? Man, the past week we've had nothing but rice and water! This is a feast in comparison!"

"Amen," Frank muttered fervently. "I must have lost ten pounds. They've barely fed us anything."

Layne felt Matt's hand on her thigh momentarily, and she stole a look over at him as he settled next to her on the pallet. His azure eyes were tender with unspoken thanks for her help. She leaned over, kissing his cheek, before she handed him his bowl of food.

Jim glanced up, a wicked look dancing in his blue eyes. "Now you're making me jealous. I miss the hell out of Irene. How is she? Has she had the baby yet?"

Matt cradled the bowl in his left hand against the sling and picked up the chopsticks with his right hand. "No, not yet. We're hoping to get you back in time for that."

"If you can get Frank released."

Matt's face became grim. "We will, don't worry."

Layne poured them each a cup of the plum wine and settled back, a sense of peace cloaking her. Both pilots were starved, and she refilled their bowls twice before their hunger was sated. The dampness in the cave worried her: Kang wasn't going out of his way to keep the pilots warm. On the other hand, the *lao-pan* hadn't tortured or killed them, either. There was much to be grateful for.

After the meal, the Chinese women again appeared briefly to take the trays away, then left. Layne was chilled and pulled her knees close to her body, wrapping her arms about them. Matt moved closer, putting his arm around her shoulders and drawing her against him. Jim's confused expression made her smile. To Jim, it was only an act, a coverup for the real reason she was on Tantai. He probably thought she was a government agent. And there was nothing that could be said to tell him that they were truly in love with each other. That would have to wait until they could get off the island.

"Tell me what happened with the B-2," Matt said, directing his attention to his brother.

Jim grimaced. "You know that the bird rides on a shock wave when it's up to speed?"

Matt nodded. "Then you were over target and taking photos?"

"Right. I had switched the automatic pilot on to fly the bird while we devoted our time to filming." Jim looked over at Layne. "I don't know how much you know about the flyability of the B-2."

"Not much, Jim," she admitted, feeling warmer now that she was huddled against Matt's lean body.

Jim pursed his lips. "Okay, then I'll break down and explain what happened so we don't go talking over your head."

She smiled. "As long as it's unclassified, I'd like to hear what happened."

"It's unclassified," he assured her, giving Matt a quick smile. Crossing his legs, Jim leaned forward and began speaking in a lowered tone that wouldn't carry outside the foursome. "The bomber is unstable as hell at supersonic speeds. If we're subsonic, the bird handles like a well-behaved fighter. But anything over Mach I and she's a bitch to fly. We've got onboard computers and backup system to help us keep her stable. Any aircraft flying supersonic creates a shock wave behind the engines, Layne. You can't allow that wave to pass through the jet engine or it will do what we call 'flame out' and stop burning."

"And then we're in trouble," Frank added grimly.

Jim nodded, his eyes darkening. "As I said, the B-2 rides on that shock wave, Layne. And you can see the wave move back along the bird. The 'spikes' or cones in the engine-intake cuts provide a way to manage the shock wave if it moves up to the threshold of the intakes. If the wave moves back toward the engine, the computer will move the spike forward and shut the intake. It won't reopen until the air has been expelled through the ducts."

"Yeah, and when an intake closes, it will cause the bird to yaw to the right or left." Frank grinned. "It's so violent, Layne, that it will slam your helmeted head against the side of the cockpit. And in our lingo, it's known as an 'unstart' or an AD—an aero-dynamic disturbance."

"Which," Jim continued, "we like to avoid. No one likes getting knocked in the head in that cockpit; we've got too much going on to have that added to the list."

"So, did you have an AD?" Layne surmised.

Jim glanced at Matt. "This wife of yours is pretty savvy," he congratulated him.

Matt squeezed Layne. "I think so, too," he murmured, giving her a caressing look.

"Come on, I was just adding up what you've told me so far. Genius, I'm not," Layne protested, smiling. "Just practical."

Jim looked impressed nevertheless. "I like practical women. Anyway, an experienced pilot can avoid ADs. You can hear what we call a 'duct rumble.' And when we hear that, we know we have to intercede because the shock wave is moving too far back. When we're over target, we put the bird on automatic pilot and the computers on board are supposed to prevent AD." His features became sober. "But this time it didn't happen. Some-thing went wrong with the main computer and the backup. We experienced AD in both engines of the bird simultaneously."

Matt's eyes narrowed as he realized the implications. The B-2 would have yawed violently from side to side in wild, uncontrolled motions. "How the hell did you get back under control? Did you hit restart on the engines?"

Jim nodded. "We tried everything. As it was, I managed to get the bird stabilized at twenty-thousand, but neither engine would restart. We had total computer failure and I can't figure out why."

"As it was," Frank said, "we bailed out at eight thousand, right over a bunch of Chinese junks. The bird is lost about ten miles east of Tantai. She went in with a series of explosions. If there's anything left, it isn't much."

"Yeah, so this Kang picked us up out of the water and brought us here. The rest is history," Jim growled.

Chapter 15

Layne wondered if a typhoon raged around the island of Tantai or if it had slid off in a southwesterly direction and the oceans were relatively calm with sunlight dancing off the waves. Hidden in the complex of interconnected caves there was only darkness illuminated by kerosene lamps, with no hint of weather conditions. It was depressing, she decided, walking wearily back with Matt as Tang Fa escorted them to their own quarters. She missed the fresh air and potential warmth of the sun. The precious hours spent with the pilots had revived both of them. She peered up at Matt's shadowed features and realized that a great load had been lifted from him after discovering Jim was alive and safe. As if sensing her inspection, Matt turned his head and gave her a slight smile. His arm tightened momentarily around her waist.

"Hanging in there?" he asked softly, his voice carrying hollowly down the passageway.

"Always. I'm like a cat, I may dangle by one claw, but I fight to survive."

His eyes glinted appreciatively. "Lady, you are a cat, there's no doubt about it. Nine lives, too."

Her lips pulled in a line resembling a grimace. "I feel like I've used up eight of them already on this adventure." Becoming more serious, she asked, "How's your arm, Matt?"

"It hurts like hell."

Her eyes grew shadowed. So far, the wound hadn't bled since she had last cleansed and dressed it. "I worry about infection. It looked like it was getting red and angry around the edges."

"I'm taking those antibiotics I brought along," he soothed, "and I'm sure they're working, or I'd be running a fever and laid flat on my back."

Tang Fa halted and pulled the curtain aside, motioning them into their quarters. "I come for you at eight tomorrow morning," he told them in fractured English.

Layne bowed her head. "Thank you, Tang. Good night."

The young pirate exited without a word. Matt led her over to their pallets and then systematically went around turning out the kerosene lamps with the exception of one that sat in the far reach of the cave. His face was drawn and pale as he came back and wearily sat down on his mattress.

"Here, let me help," Layne insisted, and knelt between his legs. She began to unbutton his shirt, all her attention focused on the task.

Matt watched the light flicker across her black hair, noting the bluish highlights. Several thick strands slid from her shoulders and tumbled down across her breasts as she leaned slightly forward. He released a sigh, cupping her chin with his hand. "Do you realize there isn't anything that you do that isn't sensuous?" he told her in a gritty voice. He caressed the smooth velvet slope of her cheek and his breath lodged in his throat as he watched Layne's lashes slowly lift to reveal a dreamy gaze that melted his soul. "God," he said thickly, "a man could lose himself forever in those golden eyes of yours…." He eased his hand downward, capturing the slender nape of her neck, and drew her forward to meet his descending mouth.

A low groan of pleasure reverberated throughout his entire body as he felt Layne's lips, tasting of the sweet, tart plum wine, mold and blossom beneath the hungry pressure of his mouth. She leaned forward, her arms carefully encircling his neck, her breasts lightly brushing against the wall of his chest. It was the first time Layne had willingly come to him without hesitation, obeying the natural instinct of her body. There was a bond of trust between them, he realized hazily. The onslaught of her pliant lips jolted him as Layne returned his passion with equal ardor. Re-

luctantly Matt released her, and saw the dazed pleasure lingering in her tawny eyes. A wry smile crossed his mouth as she
settled back down on her heels, slender hands coming to rest on
the curves of her long thighs.

"I like what you do to me, kitten," Matt whispered, grazing
her parted, glistening lips tenderly. "You're warm and feminine
and honest."

Layne drowned in his cobalt gaze. His kisses always tore at
her senses, and she slid her hands over his, bringing his palm to
her cheek. "You make me fly…. I feel like an eagle sailing
through the sky where there are no limits."

Matt's mouth drew into a tender smile as he watched her eyes
close, vulnerability written in every nuance of her relaxed features.
"Love gives you that kind of freedom," he confided huskily. "Love
sets you free, it should never bind or imprison you."

Layne roused herself and opened her eyes, basking in the
light of his love encompassing her in that molten moment. Her
vision blurred. "I've never known love until now, Matt. I wake
up happy when I'm with you. You make me ache inside with a
kind of joy I've never experienced before."

Matt cupped her face, his voice ragged with emotion. "No less
an ache than within me, kitten."

"Really, Matt? I know how much you loved Jenny. I heard it
in your voice; I saw the love in your eyes." She hung her head,
afraid to see his reaction as she whispered, "I envied your love
of her, wishing it was my own. I never knew a man could feel so
strongly about his woman—with a love so powerful that it would
take your breath away."

"Come here, kitten," Matt coaxed thickly. "Lie down here with
me." He knew what it had cost Layne to admit her feelings to him.
She had exposed herself to him, and he realized he was seeing
another facet of that same sure, blind courage he had seen time after
time on the mission—her willingness to put everything on the line.
Now Layne had entrusted him with the core of her self, knowing
he had the power to destroy her with it if he chose. As she came into
his arms, fitting her body next to his, Matt felt a pang of frustration.

"I wish we were home right now," Matt said quietly, his lips near her ear. "We'd pack up a couple of suitcases, tell our bosses to go fly a kite and take a week off at the Oregon coast."

Layne nuzzled him, placing small kisses the length of his firm jawline. "Tell me more," she urged throatily. "I love to talk of dreams."

Matt closed his eyes, content as Layne fitted herself next to him, and drew up the covers to protect them from the constant chill. Her black hair spilled across his chest as she rested her head in the hollow of his good shoulder. "Speaking of dreams," he continued, "I had always fantasized that one day I would have a cedar cabin just inside the woods, but close enough to the beach so that I could hear, smell and see the ocean. I made that dream come true. I have a small cabin near Brookings. It's a seacoast town of golden beaches, plenty of fishing and some of the most beautiful scenery in the world. The cabin sits up in the foothills, surrounded with rare myrtle trees and all kinds of pine and fir. I go in the summer and again in the late fall when the leaves are beginning to turn. It's my time to enjoy nature and bring myself back into a simpler way of life. It helps me put everything that's going on around me into proper perspective." Matt lightly traced a pattern across her shoulder, feeling Layne relax against him.

"It sounds wonderful," she whispered, her voice drugged with exhaustion.

"I've never taken anyone to that cabin since I built it, Layne. But I want you to come. I want to share it with you."

"I'll come," she quavered.

"Promise?"

"Promise."

"As soon as we get back, Layne. I don't give a damn what anyone else thinks, we need time together when we get Stateside."

Layne lay awake for a long time after Matt had surrendered to a deep, healing sleep. Her eyes were dark as she tried to sort through her emotions. She loved Matt. And she couldn't conceive of life without him.

Snuggling down beneath the covers, her arm protectively

thrown across his chest, Layne gave in to exhaustion. Tomorrow morning, they would square off with the Soviet in a bid to win back Frank Walters. She had no idea how something of this magnitude was conducted. Thank God, Matt was there and in charge, because she had been pushed too far beyond her own limits to think clearly.

At precisely 8:00 a.m., the auction involving Major Frank Walters began. At one end of the cave the pilot stood in manacles between two pirate guards whose fierce expressions mirrored the tension. Layne sat cross-legged beside Matt, her hands clenched in her lap. Opposite them at a low teak table sat the Soviet emissary, Colonel Viktor Surin. He was in his mid-fifties, a frail-looking man Layne had thought at first. But upon closer inspection, Surin radiated authority, and his face was lean, like a wolf's, with an air of cruelty. His dark brown hair was cut short, with strands coaxed across the top of his head to disguise baldness. She had never seen a Soviet soldier before, and Layne had to remind herself to not stare at Surin as a child would. The olive-green uniform trimmed in red made him appear pale, as if he never saw the sun.

Kang stood at the other end of the table, one booted foot resting languidly against the other. Layne licked her lips, stealing a glance at Matt. She wasn't sure who possessed a more expressionless demeanor: Matt or Surin. She could feel the iciness strung between the men.

"Well?" Kang demanded briskly with a gesture of his right hand toward the captured pilot. "What is your opening bid, Colonel Surin? What will you pay me to release this prisoner to you?"

"Half a million," Surin rapped out, first in Haklo and then in English.

Kang laughed uproariously, holding his sides. "In rubles? *Aiyeee*, you take me for a softheaded female."

Layne suppressed the start of a smile. She had told Matt earlier that morning about the Chinese and their love of bargaining. Nowhere else on earth were there better traders. There wasn't a

Chinese in Hong Kong or among the pirates who wasn't aware of currency and its present international value. Rubles weren't strong against the American dollar and Kang knew that. But then, so did Surin. The Soviet wasn't going to give away the barn with the horses, either. She rubbed her damp palms against her thighs.

Surin snapped his head to the left. "Rubles? Why not rubles, comrade?"

"Bah! The devil winds whisper in your ear, Colonel. And don't call me comrade. I'm no friend of yours. Rubles are weak."

Surin's face remained implacable. "A half million in…U.S. dollars?"

Layne's eyes sparkled and she caught Matt's glance. It had almost made Surin choke to say: *U.S. dollars*.

Kang's eyes glittered with feral interest. "That's slightly better. But not enough. Paper money can be destroyed by fire, swallowed by the gods of the ocean or rotted by the gods of the earth." With a shake of his bald head, Kang fastened his attention on Matt. "All right, what do you have to say? What will the lords of the Golden Mountain pay me to release this man back to them instead?"

Matt raised his head, his gaze locking with Surin's. "A half million in gold bullion, *lao-pan*. Delivered today. You can have it in your hands in less than three hours."

Layne's eyes widened. Three hours? How? She translated, and it was obvious that Kang was pleased. Unlike paper money, which was held in contempt, gold was a true measure of wealth to any self-respecting Chinese businessman. She gave Matt a worried look. He had a plan, and typical of Company policy, he hadn't told her anything about it beforehand.

"Ahh," Kang murmured, "for a foreign devil, you know how to bargain." He raised his thick, black eyebrows, looking archly over at the Soviet.

"You heard him. He offers me gold instead of useless paper. What is your counteroffer?"

Layne held her breath, her fingers clenched beneath the table. She saw the Russian's pale white features begin to glisten with

222

Heart of the Tiger

a sheen of sweat. Surin's unblinking eyes reminded her of the cobras in their hotel room. The Soviet met Matt's steady gaze. "You'll give him gold today?" he sneered.

"In three hours," Matt promised, every muscle in his face tight as he glared across the table at Surin.

Surin's paper-thin nostrils flared. "No doubt the gold's aboard that destroyer waiting off Tantai."

Matt's voice lowered. "Not to mention a carrier and a couple of missile frigates, too, Colonel."

"We are tracking their movements," Surin countered stiffly.

Layne felt the razor's edge of tension thrum between the two men. The explosive atmosphere sharpened as they stared at each other like a mongoose and cobra circling to do battle.

"And we're tracking yours," Matt returned easily.

Layne shivered, suddenly realizing that more than likely, both Soviet and American ships were standing by close to Tantai. What if Soviet ships started firing at American ones? And a U.S. carrier was present. That meant air superiority and helicopters. Rapidly Layne began to piece together Matt's plan. A helicopter would bring the gold bullion to Tantai and pick them up for return to the safety of a U.S. ship. Unconsciously Layne chewed on her lower lip, watching Kang pace back and forth.

"I am waiting, Colonel! I don't want your worthless rubles. And I don't want Golden Mountain paper, either! Gold," he rapped out, "you must pay me in gold!"

Surin's mouth tightened in the slightest of movements. He flicked a glance at Kang, who now stood before them, his thick, short fingers resting imperiously upon his hips. "Very well, a half million in gold bullion."

"*Aiyeee!* You take me for a monkey? The foreigner from the Golden Mountain has already offered that much! You must offer more if you want Walters."

"Six hundred thousand, then."

"Am I an ox without brains?" Kang roared, his face turning livid. "That man is worth more than that! He has the secrets of his flying machine in his head! You come to me on bended knee begging to let you have him." Kang's eyes screwed up with fury. "Hu Gang?"

Matt lifted his chin, staring up at the pirate. "Three-quarters of a million in gold bullion."

Surin's mouth dropped open, gasping. "Seven hundred and fifty thousand!"

"That's right."

Kang grinned, running his short fingers across his black mustache, obviously placated with the offer.

"Eight hundred thousand," the Russian growled.

The tension did not lessen in the room. Layne found herself sweating, the cloth beneath her armpits becoming damp. Beads of sweat stood out across Surin's brow as the price escalated. Had it been the KGB who had tried to kill them back in Hong Kong by having the cobras placed in the room? Layne swiftly put more missing pieces of the puzzle together: The Soviets were probably behind the cobra fiasco, thinking that they could get rid of the U.S. emissaries before they reached Tantai. Then, they could pay Kang a paltry sum and walk away with both U.S. pilots. Instead, Layne and Matt had made it to Tantai, and it was obvious that the Russians hadn't counted on bargaining for only one pilot at such a high price in gold. Gold for any country was its foundation of financial worth. And if she was any judge of Surin's reaction, he didn't want to part with much of the precious metal.

Surin's stiff upper lip whitened, and he glared at Kang, who stood nonchalantly stroking his mustache. "What about the avionics?" he rapped out.

"Avionics?" Kang asked lazily. "What is that?"

"Black boxes! You said that besides the pilots, there were boxes retrieved from the aircraft. I want to see them. We are interested in both the pilot and those boxes!"

"Did I say black boxes?" Kang murmured innocently, his dark eyes wide and solemn.

Surin clenched his teeth and glared first at Matt and then at Kang. "If you don't have them, then I see no reason to continue this ridiculous bartering over one miserable pilot!"

Kang's innocent expression disappeared like a black cloud covering the sun, his face suddenly hard. "There are no, as you call them, black boxes, Colonel. You bid on this prisoner or on nothing at all."

Surin uncrossed his booted legs, getting up with some difficulty from his position on the floor, his face splotchy. "Then we are not interested!" The Soviet glared at Talbot. "Let these capitalist whoremongers from the West pay you one million in gold!" With that, he made an about-face on the heels of his highly polished boots and stalked out of the cave.

Layne turned to Matt, rapidly translating the last exchange. There was a brief flicker of victory in Matt's eyes, but otherwise, he betrayed no other emotion on his closed features.

Kang came swaggering over, grinning fully. "He is yours, Shao! Now, ask Hu Gang when the gold shall arrive!"

Layne didn't breathe a sigh of relief until the four of them had been transported safely to the carrier, USS *Enterprise*. The small radio disguised as a pack of cigarettes that Matt carried in his vest had been their lifeline to the carrier sitting fifteen miles off Tantai. Matt's message had been brief and in typical military code: "Red rover, red rover, throw the ball over. Seven five zero." Layne smiled as Kang demanded to know what Matt had said into the powerful little radio. And even after Layne had repeated the cryptic words, Kang still seemed baffled. Well, that made two of them! She had no idea what Matt was talking about, and he wasn't bothering to explain it to either of them.

The sunlight offered a blinding but warm welcome as they emerged from the cave complex on Tantai. Layne felt like Persephone emerging from the dark grip of Hades. Kang was pleased, as seen by the grin on his face, when the U.S. Navy helicopter landed on a flat, rocky area near the beach where they had washed ashore. She had remained at Matt's side as the gold bars, crated in wooden boxes, had been lifted out of the aircraft and placed at Kang's feet. The pirate and his chosen men had opened each crate, taking out their deadly-looking knives and cutting into each bar to make sure it wasn't lead posing as gold.

As soon as the transaction had been completed, Kang had ordered his men to release Frank Walters from his chains. The two B-2 pilots had then climbed aboard the helicopter along with the other three naval personnel. Kang had approached Matt and Layne, his brown eyes narrowed.

"Tell Hu Gang he is a man of honor. I would never trust a foreigner, especially from the Golden Mountain, but he has earned my respect." Kang pointed to the southern tip of Tantai. "Tell him that the flying machine is over there. I will have one of my captains take his junk and float over the area where the machine went down."

As Layne translated the message to Matt, he nodded. Unzipping the canvas vest, Matt handed it to Kang.

"Tell him this is a gift from me to him." Matt pulled open a secret compartment inside the vest, exposing a knife that he had been carrying all along.

Kang's eyes glimmered with interest as he took the gift, carefully examining the weapon resting in the scabbard between the layers of cloth. The *lao-pan* looked up at Matt, a glint of amusement evident. Both men knew that Matt could have used that weapon against Kang at any time. A slow grin tugged at Kang's mouth.

"Hu Gang is a worthy warrior, Shao. Thank him for this." Kang put on the vest, shrugging it over his meaty shoulders and smiling like a fox.

Layne bowed her head in respect. "We are honored with your help, *lao-pan*. Getting our pilots back was most important. We thank you for your assistance in trying to locate our flying machine."

Kang snorted. "*Aiyeee*, there won't be much left! I saw it skip once, explode and then tunnel into the sea gods' home with a vengeance." He lifted his arms. "There was much metal tearing through the air."

"I'm sure that our navy will be needing your help for the next few days in trying to locate the flying machine."

Kang looked significantly at the crates of gold bars. "We will help the seaborne devils, Shao."

"Then Matt and I must leave, *lao-pan*. May all the gods be kind to you."

"*Joss*, Shao."

Joss, Layne thought as they stepped onto the deck of the carrier. The blades of the helicopter whipped furious spates of wind all around them. They were met by a contingent of officers and guided below. Only then did Layne begin to relax and realize that the nightmare mission was over.

But there was little time to analyze the backlog of feelings that she had pushed out of her mind while they were on Tantai. After taking a hot shower and washing her hair, Layne was surprised to find the clothes she'd left at the Princeton Hotel laid out in her room. She slipped into a pair of beige slacks and a cool green blouse with long, puffy sleeves. She had barely dried her hair when a knock came at the door. Opening it, Layne felt her eyes widen.

"Matt…"

He gave her a devastating smile. "How are you?"

For no discernible reason, Layne blushed, feeling the warmth steal into her face. Her pulse accelerated beneath his heated in-spection. And he looked no less appealing to her dressed in his Air Force summer uniform of light blue short-sleeved shirt and dark blue pants. The silver wings denoting his status as pilot rested above his left breast pocket. How handsome he is, she thought—even with his arm in a sling.

"Fine. Come in."

Matt slipped into the cabin and glanced around. As he turned toward her, he put his right hand on his hip in the characteristic pilot's gesture. He was clean shaven, his carefully combed hair dark from a recent shower. Before she could say anything, Matt stepped toward her and reached out, combing his fingers through her silky hair. The caress sent an ache of longing through Layne. The dream isn't over, she exulted. He does care for me!

"You clean up pretty well, lady," Matt teased with a wry smile. His fingers grazed her temple, moving across the slant of her cheekbone and brushing her parted lips. "And you look ravishing, on top of it," he murmured, leaning over.

A jolt of raw pleasure sizzled through her as his strong mouth grazed her unprepared lips, then pressed more surely, molding masterfully against hers as his fingers slid across the nape of her neck, buried in the ebony mass of her sweet-smelling hair.

Reluctantly, Matt drew inches away, brushing her lips once more for good measure. Layne rocked unsteadily within his embrace and he smiled to himself: he felt a little shaky, too. His need for her was almost overwhelming…. But first things first. Keeping his arm around her shoulder, he gave Layne a quick embrace.

"We're going to grab a bite to eat over in the officers' mess, and then we've got to deliver our report to a team that's just been flown aboard."

Layne nodded and tried to extract herself from the heady euphoria Matt's branding kiss had caught her up in. Her heart sang with a giddy happiness. Her mind's doubts had been silenced by his continued caring. "It's tempting to stay right here," she said, her voice low with emotion.

Matt laughed softly. "Believe me, I agree, lady. But I don't think the Company team would be very understanding if I locked this cabin door and kept you in here for the next couple of hours."

"I don't think they would, either," she agreed, picking up her purse. Layne met Matt's smoldering gaze, her body responding to the unspoken invitation that lay in his eyes. She looked at his arm in the sling. "What did the doctors say about your shoulder wound?"

He opened the door and they stepped across the raised entrance and into the gleaming passageway. "Twenty-five stitches, two shots of second-generation antibiotics, a tetanus shot and a stiff warning not to get the wound wet for the next two weeks."

Layne closed the door and Matt slipped his arm around her waist as they made their way down the maze of passageways. She leaned up on her tiptoes momentarily, inhaling his wonderful male fragrance. "I'd say you showered."

He grinned boyishly. "Wound or no wound, I wasn't going to

stink. What the doctors don't know won't hurt them." His eyes softened with affection. "And I can tell you that your touch was a hell of a lot gentler than theirs."

Some of the mirth in his eyes disappeared, and he gently pulled her to a halt. "Listen to me," he began, his voice intimate, "we aren't going to have the time to share much while we're on board, kitten." He touched her chin, his thumb caressing her full lower lip. "If I can get my way, I'm going to try and persuade the head honcho to drop us back off in Hong Kong. Then we can take a flight home on a civilian airline. How does that sound?"

Her pulse fluttered beneath his cajoling touch. "Fine."

Matt's eyes grew intense as he stared down at her. "Just trust me, Layne. The next few days are going to be unsettling. But remember what I told you. We're going to make it to my cabin by the coast. Okay?"

"I'm with you all the way, Matt."

"That's my brave lady. God, how I love you for your courage. You simply amaze me," he growled, leaning down and gently pressing a kiss to her lips. But as Matt raised his head, Layne watched him become more military in bearing, more distant and on guard.

Chapter 16

From the moment they landed at the airport in Washington, D.C., Layne had little time with Matt. Chuck Lowell was there with several of his men, all of them in natty three-piece suits, looking more like successful businessmen than spies. Why did she still resent them? If it hadn't been for the Company, Matt's brother and Frank Walters would have ended up with a very different fate. Layne tried to choke down the bitterness she was feeling and allowed herself to be escorted out of the airport and into the gathering dusk to a waiting limousine. The September evening had a sharp chill to it, and Layne shivered.

Chuck sat opposite them. After they broke free of the airport traffic, he gave them a genuine smile. "Layne, you did an outstanding job. We owe you a great deal."

Layne shrugged tiredly. "I'm just glad everything turned out so well."

Matt gave Layne a worried glance. She had slept off and on throughout the flight from Hong Kong, and right now, she looked pale and washed-out. The stress of the past few days was stalking her in earnest, and Matt didn't want Lowell or anyone else bothering her. "Chuck, I hope you're planning on dropping Layne off at her apartment."

Lowell gave him a cursory nod. "That's our first stop. I imagine you're pretty tired. We'll have someone bring your luggage by later, Layne. Your mother has been contacted, and she's expecting a visit from you sometime tomorrow. We've reassured her you're safe."

"Thank you," Layne said, finding comfort by simply resting against Matt. She was grateful that Matt had stayed a bit distant from her after landing: it was none of the Company's business that she loved him. And despite everything, Layne couldn't halt the ache in her chest that was becoming more and more painful by the minute. Why did she feel so lost? Abandoned? One look at Chuck Lowell and Layne knew why: they intended to interrogate Matt extensively about the mission. He wouldn't get any rest until he had given them every nuance of information. Layne rubbed her face tiredly. Maybe it was necessary.

"Well, you get a good eight hours under your belt and then you call us tomorrow." Lowell gave Layne an apologetic look. "We'll need to debrief you, Layne. It's standard procedure. When you're up to it, I'll have a car come and pick you up and bring you over to our offices."

"All right," she muttered, leaning back and closing her eyes. Tears formed hotly behind her closed lids and an utter sense of futility overwhelmed her. What was wrong with her? Too many time-zone changes? The stress of the mission? Why did she feel so alone? Matt was beside her, giving her occasional looks that told her he was worried about her present state. Sleep finally soothed the raw edges of her unaccountable anxiety, and Layne remembered nothing else until Matt shook her awake and then led her into her apartment.

Matt opened the door and checked out the apartment thoroughly. Satisfied, he came padding back to the living room where Layne stood. The silence was awesome as he lightly rested his hands on her shoulders, drawing her back against him. He pressed his face into her thick silky hair, and his low, gritty voice sent an ache of longing through Layne as he spoke to her in an intimate tone.

"Get a hot bath and hit the sack, kitten."

"What about you?"

"I'll go through the twenty-questions routine with Lowell before they release me."

Worriedly, Layne reached up, caressing his stubbled cheek. "And then?"

Matt gave her a tender look. "Then I'm coming back over here—if you don't have any objections."

She whispered his name and slid her arms around his neck, pressing her length against him. "I love you so much," Layne said brokenly.

"Hey, tears?" Matt kissed her temple, then forced Layne to meet his blue gaze. "What's going on inside that head of yours?"

Layne dashed the tears away. "I—I just feel as if Chuck is going to tear us apart, that something is going to happen to—to take you away from me."

Matt shook his head. "No way, lady, no way," he soothed, caressing her hair. "Listen, you're exhausted, and your emotions have been stretched to the limit by this mission. Come on, I want you to get that bath," he coaxed. "I'll get your bed turned down for you."

Embarrassed by her display of emotion, Layne mustered a smile. "I'll be okay. You'd better get going or Chuck's going to wonder what happened to you."

"Let him," Matt growled, pressing a long, tender kiss upon her lips. "I'm keeping your apartment key. I'll let myself in whenever I get done with this marathon with Lowell," he promised.

Layne stood in the middle of her apartment, arms wrapped around her body, unable to shake the feelings that haunted her weary state. After Matt left, she trudged to the bathroom, intent upon a fragrant bath to help chase away her depression. In a few hours Matt would be back, Layne hoped. Back and sharing her bed. Sharing the love they had discovered with each other.

The first rosy fingers of dawn were nudging the cape of night down from the shoulders of the sky as Matt quietly entered Layne's apartment. The peacefulness cloaked him immediately, and he hesitated in the living room, absorbing this part of Layne. Slipping the key back into the pocket of his dark blue slacks, he padded soundlessly to her bedroom, taking off his flight cap. A pale wash of pink on the horizon gave the lavender-wallpapered bedroom a decidedly feminine look. Matt hesitated at the door, all his exhaustion melting away as he looked at Layne.

Sometime during the night she had pushed off the eyelet lace spread, revealing a clinging apricot satin gown. Matt dragged in a deep, unsteady breath as his gaze lingered on Layne's features. No longer were there shadows beneath her eyes or tension about her delicious, parted lips. In sleep the true depth of Layne's vulnerability was apparent, and it drew out all of his protective mechanisms. Sitting gently on the edge of the bed, he hungrily memorized her: the low-cut gown revealed the swell of her breasts covered with the thin apricot satin, enhancing their curved roundness.

Matt wanted to pass his hand gently across those beautifully formed breasts; but now wasn't the time or place. He only had ten minutes before he had to leave. Either that or the sergeant in the official Air Force vehicle waiting for him would get tense. Reaching out, Matt lightly caressed Layne's cheek.

Layne stirred beneath his touch. Thick lashes heavy with sleep barely lifted to reveal cloudy topaz.

"Matt…why are you in uniform?" Layne's voice was unusually husky as she wrestled with the drowsiness.

He rested his hand on her shoulder, the pliancy of her flesh a reminder of her femininity. "I've got some bad news, kitten. I've got to leave for Nellis Air Force Base right away. It seems they've encountered a problem with the bird we're testing, and they need all three test pilots who have flown it to sit down with the design engineers and try to figure out a better mousetrap." He saw her eyes widen with shock, quickly replaced by fear. Matt knew what she was thinking: he was like any other Company agent; he had lied and would walk out of her life just as Brad had done all the time. "Listen, there's a car waiting downstairs to take me over to Bolling Air Force Base. I'll be hopping a flight back with one of the Pentagon generals from Research and Development. This is something serious or they wouldn't have ordered me back like this, Layne."

Layne struggled into a sitting position, her black hair cascading across her shoulders and down to her breasts. Worriedly she slid her hand across his. "Will you be all right? I mean, have you gotten any sleep yet? What about your arm? How can you fly with that?"

Matt's mouth curved into a tender smile and he framed her serious face with his fingers. "That's what I love so much about you," he whispered, his eyes locking with hers. "You could have asked 'When will you be back?' But you didn't. You were more worried about me."

Layne fought the sudden rush of tears. "I—I have no right asking when you'll be back," she forced out.

"Sure you do," Matt countered.

He combed his fingers through her hair, aware of the suffering in Layne's eyes. "I love you, kitten. And I'll prove that to you. I'm sorry that I've got to leave now, but I'll be back. I promise you that." He forced her chin up. "Look at me," he ordered. "Thanksgiving, Layne. You hear me? I want you to meet me out in Oregon and we'll spend the holiday there at the cabin. By that time this problem with the bird should be straightened out, and I can get the time I promised you we'd have." His eyes feverishly searched hers. "Tell me yes. Tell me you'll meet me out in Brookings at the end of November."

She shut her eyes tightly. "A-all right. November."

Matt's voice lowered to a frustrated growl. "No, dammit! Say it like you mean it, Layne."

A soft sob broke from her and she blindly fell into Matt's arms. "Hold me, Matt. Just hold me…."

The trees were brilliant in their colorful autumn reds, oranges and yellows. Layne lifted her chin from her pensive thoughts. Two days—two of the most tortured days of her life—lay behind her. After Matt had left, she'd gotten up, unable to sleep any longer. She had paced the confines of her apartment, at a loss to properly identify her real feelings. The opal that rested in the hollow of her throat was a continual reminder of the love she'd thought they shared. She raised a hand to touch it, trying to reassure herself. If their farewell kiss was any proof of Matt's love for her, then he would be back. But now… She stared down at the wedding rings she held in the damp coldness of her palm: his grandmother's rings. She slowly closed her fingers over them, pressing them against her aching heart.

It was best this way, Layne told herself, moving mechanically to the desk. She had no right to keep them. Matt had made no commitment to her, and to her the rings symbolized exactly that. Carefully she deposited the rings in heavy cotton and wrapped them securely. Two days, and no word from Matt. Well, what did she expect? He was a test pilot, and chances were he was in a marathon of meetings with designers. All she needed to hear was his voice, his reassurance. But Layne knew differently as she forced herself to pick up her purse and head for the post office to mail the wedding rings back to Matt.

Layne drove to her mother's house after mailing the rings, and Millie welcomed her with a warm hug.

"This is a nice surprise. A visit two days in a row." Her mother paused and studied her briefly. "You look terrible, honey. What's wrong?" she asked then, leading her into the Oriental living room.

Layne sat down on the blue couch. "I need to talk to you, Mom."

"Sure, honey," Millie soothed. "How about some tea? Jasmine? Your favorite."

"Sounds wonderful, Mom." She was so close to tears, so close to breaking apart all over again.

Millie brought in the tea service and placed it on the coffee table between them, then sat down opposite Layne. "Why are you feeling so badly?"

Layne sipped the fragrant jasmine tea. "Physically, I'm exhausted, Mom. Emotionally… Well, it concerns Matt Talbot."

"How is Major Talbot? Did you get along with him?"

She winced. "Mom, this is going to sound absolutely stupid," Layne muttered, setting the teacup down on the coffee table. "I fell in love with him. Do you believe that? I swore I'd never get mixed up with another agent as long as I lived and yet—" Her voice cracked and she buried her face in her hands.

Millie rose and moved over to Layne, sliding her arm around her shoulders. "There's nothing awful about falling in love, honey. Are you sure it isn't just an infatuation? Since Brad's death you've avoided other men. You're coming out of your grief over your marriage, and it's natural to want to be with a man." She held Layne tightly, feeling her daughter tremble.

"This is much more than that… I love him, Mom. He—he's so different from Brad. Matt's warm and sensitive…."

"The kind of man you've always needed," her mother murmured, stroking Layne's hair. "So why are you looking as if you've lost him, honey?"

"I'm so torn up inside, Mom. One part of me wants to believe Matt will be back. He had to go back to Nellis on short notice. There's a problem out there that he's got to work on. The other part of me thinks he's used me just like Brad did. He hasn't called me. There's been no word from him in two days. Nothing."

Millie nodded her head sagely. "I see. And because he left so soon, you think he's running out on you?"

"Yes. And that isn't fair to him." Layne pressed her hand to her breast. "I know that here, Mom. Here. Matt was just as torn up over his having to leave as I was."

"You know what I think?"

"Right now I could use some wisdom, Mom. What do you think?"

Millie's eyes sparkled and she patted Layne's hand. "I think you ought to make a point of writing that wonderful young man a letter telling him of all your fears, your hopes and your love. I know when I first met your father, he was in and out of my life without a moment's notice. And it was the lifesaving letters that we took the time to write to each other that helped us through those tough times. That and phone calls."

Layne's spirits rose as she absorbed her mother's warmth. Wiping her eyes free of the last of the tears, she gave a small laugh. "I've been behaving like an immature teenager, haven't I?"

"I'm sure he doesn't think that of you, Layne. You'll make him understand your fears, honey."

"Matt's aware of my less-than-glorious past, Mom. He knows I never dated anyone before Brad. Or after…"

"Your lack of experience doesn't detract from you, Layne. If Matt knows all about that, then I've got to think he'll know how to proceed from here. He couldn't help it if he got ordered back to Nellis right away. As for calling you, he's probably hamstrung in the kind of never-ending meetings your dad had to endure! I'm sure he wants to spend time with you."

"He does. He wants me to fly out to Oregon and meet him at his cabin for Thanksgiving—"

"Well, there you go! Now put that sad face away, honey. Go back to the apartment and write to him. Both of you will benefit from that letter."

Layne gave her mother a tremulous smile and stood. "That's the best idea I've heard in the past two days." She hugged Millie tightly. "I love you, Mom."

"And I love you, honey. Now, go on. There's a young man who's waiting to hear from you."

Matt let the phone slip from his fingers and drop back into its cradle. His office was flooded with bright Nevada sunlight poking through the slats of the venetian blinds. A scowl formed on his brow. Where was Layne? Tiredly rubbing his face, Matt could no longer fight off the exhaustion. Two lousy days trapped in a small room with panicky design engineers and a total of six hours of sleep had worn him down to nothing more than a snarling animal. He stared over at the black phone on his desk. Should he try calling Layne one more time? He'd tried five times already today. Was she all right? He knew he wasn't thinking clearly. He'd better drive off base to his home, in a suburb of Las Vegas, and get some badly needed sleep. When he woke up, he'd try calling again. That way, he'd be in full charge of his senses. Right now, he was worthless to everyone, including himself.

The continued chime of the doorbell brought Matt out of sleep. Blearily he rose up on his elbow. What time was it? Strands of dark hair dipped across his forehead as he looked down at the watch on his wrist: 4:00 p.m. He had slept almost ten hours. The doorbell sounded again.

"All right, all right," he muttered, throwing back the covers.

Who the hell could it be? Matt shrugged into a blue terry-cloth robe and padded through his small home to the front door. He jerked it open to find the postman standing there.

"Yes?" Matt growled, shoving the wayward strands of hair off his brow.

The postman gave him an apologetic look. "Sorry, sir, but there's a registered package here that you have to sign for."

Matt took the small box, placing it under his arm and signed the form. "Thanks," he muttered as he shut the door. He looked at the return address, and his heart hammered briefly with joy: it was from Layne. Some of his grouchiness dissolved as he held the package between his lean, strong fingers. He went to the kitchen where the light was better and set the package down on the table. His mood improved markedly as he made himself some fresh coffee. Maybe he was going to live, he thought, as he sat down with the steaming cup.

It was like Layne to send a gift, Matt acknowledged, carefully setting the brown paper aside. He pried off the tape. Inside, in a bed of foam chips, was another, smaller box. Frowning, Matt took it out and worked the lid free. His heart wrenched as he stared disbelievingly down at his grandmother's wedding rings. His mouth compressed in a line of unremitting pain, Matt searched through the rest of the box for some note explaining Layne's actions. There was none.

He sat for a long time with the box resting in the palm of his hand, his blue eyes awash with unshed tears. He'd tried to call her without success since coming back to Nellis. And he poignantly remembered the fear in Layne's eyes as he'd left her that morning in her apartment. She must have thought he was walking out of her life forever. He cursed the Air Force and then the Company. He'd been a puppet to their whims, when every instinct had screamed to stay with her and prove he truly loved her and wasn't going to use her as Carson had done.

Finally Matt roused himself. He took a shower and reached for clean clothes. The terror in the pit of his stomach never left him. As he shrugged on a bright red polo shirt, Matt went into

238 *Heart of the Tiger*

the small but comfortable living room. Sitting down on his favorite rocking chair, he reached for the phone and dialed Layne's number. She had to be home. She just had to be….

"Hello?"

Matt released a held breath. "Layne?"

The silence shattered between them. And then Layne's quavering voice came back on the line.

"Matt? Are you all right? My God, I've—"

He gripped the phone until his knuckles whitened, his voice tortured. "I love you, lady. You've got to know that…." Matt heard Layne's sharp intake of breath and then a small, choking sob.

"And I love you. So much that I hurt. The rings, Matt…"

"I just got them."

"Oh."

"Nothing's changed, Layne. I know you were hurt by Brad. And you have every right to question my sudden disappearance out of your life. I guess I don't blame you for sending the rings back. I think I know why you did it."

"I haven't heard from you for three days. Not even a phone call. I—I didn't know what to think. I've made such a mess of things. I'm sorry, Matt. I never meant to hurt you."

"Shh, it's going to be okay, kitten. Come on, you're crying so hard I can't understand you."

"But—the rings—"

"I wanted you to keep them, kitten."

Matt waited patiently, wishing they weren't separated by the distance. Right now all he wanted to do was hold Layne and soothe away all the misery he heard in her voice. "With time," he told her huskily, "you won't be so wary or distrustful, kitten. Don't be hard on yourself. I won't be. When people get hurt like you have, it takes a long time to heal, much less begin to reach out and try again. You've come a long way in a short time, Layne. I'm proud of you. Just hang in there with me. We'll get past the next month and a half together. You aren't alone anymore, Layne. You have me. And I want you. We're an unbeatable team, you and I."

Layne sniffed and managed a broken laugh. "We are a good team, aren't we?"

Matt closed his eyes, his grip relaxing on the phone. "The best, kitten."

"I love you so much, Matt."

"I know. I can hear it in your voice. Do you know how good that makes me feel? My heart feels like it's going to explode."

"Don't die of happiness."

His mouth curved upward into a smile—one he wanted to share with her. "Don't worry, I'm going to live for our happiness. Feel better?"

"Much better."

"Good. Me, too."

"I—I just finished a ten-page letter to you…."

"You did?"

"Mom said I should write to you. She said it had helped her and Dad when they were going together." She laughed, relieved beyond belief. "Has anyone ever told you that you're the most wonderful man in the world?"

"No, but it's nice to hear. I'm afraid my reputation for being patient and easygoing is shot all to hell here at the base. The past two days a starved cougar would have made me look good. Everyone's giving me a wide berth over at Design."

Layne's uninhibited laughter flowed over Matt like warm honey and he relaxed completely. Everything was going to be all right.

He laughed freely, deeply. "Late November," he warned Layne in a gritty tone. "And lady, I won't keep my hands off you. Expect to spend our first few days together in a tangle of sheets."

Layne's voice was breathless. "Late November, darling…"

Chapter 17

Matt spotted her first. He drew to a halt, mesmerized by the picture Layne made, standing on the Oregon beach. He had arrived on a later flight, anxious to see her. Weeks earlier, he'd mailed Layne the key to his cottage. When he'd arrived in his rental car, he'd seen that she'd made herself at home. Her footprints led from the back door through the sand and he'd followed them to where he stood now. Layne's black hair lay in silky abandon, moving restlessly beneath the cajoling, inconstant sea breeze as she hunched down over a tidal pool. The simple grace of Layne reaching out, dipping her slender, artistic fingers into the water to retrieve a brown and white shell shattered his immobility. Matt smoothly descended the last few feet from the path onto the golden sand. The crash of surf mingled with the cry of the white gulls circling above him as he walked slowly toward her.

All his exhaustion disappeared as he hungrily drank in each of her graceful movements. In that split second, Layne was a child investigating one of the many pools, retrieving shells or starfish from their watery depths to study them and then gently return them back to their homes. Her cheeks were flushed to a beautiful shade of rose. She'd grown excruciatingly lovely since he'd last seen her. How? Her lips were the color of ripe pomegranate, parted in awe as she discovered and lifted a half-destroyed abalone shell upward, the pearl-gray and silver color capturing her attention as the noontime light glanced off its polished surface.

Matt drew to a halt only a few feet away from her. Layne

couldn't see him; her back was to him now. Matt smiled. She was a creature of nature right now, absorbed within the roar of the pounding surf frothing and boiling up on the sloped beach. They were embraced by the mournful cry of the gulls and terns overhead and cloaked with the perfume of salt air. Matt didn't want to break the spell—those moments out of time as she raised her fingers, sliding them in a caressing motion across the pearly interior of the abalone shell, sending a hot shaft of longing through him. He trembled and imagined her fingers sliding across his flesh with the same reverent movement, and his body hardened with the desire to absorb Layne into him. And this was part of his discovery of her: watching her worship the wild, untamed beauty unfolding around them on that deserted Oregon beach.

"Layne?" He had whispered her name, his voice drowned out by the roar of the surf and the cry of the seabirds. But she heard his call, as if by some telepathic communication with him.

She gasped, dropping the shell as she twisted around. Black hair swirled around her face, framing it, emphasizing her widening topaz eyes. "Matt!" She rose like a gazelle in one heart-stopping motion.

Layne flew to him, throwing herself into his waiting arms. Her body was yielding, melting against his own as Matt crushed her in an embrace that forced the air from her lungs.

"God, how I love you," he rasped, showering her with small kisses across her cheek and temple.

"Matt…Matt…" And Layne tilted her chin upward. His mouth slanted hotly across her lips, searing them with the raw power of his hunger for her, goaded beyond all his normal controls. Six weeks…six lonely weeks with the memory of her in his arms. Hungrily, Matt parted her lips, seeking her sweet, liquid depths. A groan reverberated through him as he felt Layne eagerly press against him, her arms tightening around his neck, her breasts taut against his jacket. He devoured her like a starving man, unable to get enough of the taste, smell and touch of her.

His fingers trembled as he caressed the outer curve of her breasts, reeling with the pleasure of her flesh molding beneath

his hands. She had gained back those needed pounds; her ribs
were no longer prominent. The familiar scent of lilac welcomed
Matt and he slid his arms around her waist, holding her tightly
to him, their hearts beating in thundering unison.

Layne's eyes shimmered with tears as she framed Matt's face.
"I've missed you...missed you so much," she whispered
brokenly, placing warm, wet kisses all over his face.

"I'm here now," Matt soothed, kissing the corners of her trembling mouth. "You look so good, Layne." His voice shook with
powerful emotion as he held her at arm's length.

Layne managed a startled laugh, her cheeks flushed. "Me?
What about you?" And then she launched herself back into his
arms. "Hold me, Matt. Just hold me," she pleaded, burying her
head against his shoulder.

"Forever," he promised hoarsely. They stood locked in an
embrace that healed the loneliness each had experienced. Matt
blinked back his own tears, raising his face to the suddenly
stormy sky. "Come on, let's get back to the cabin. It's going to
start raining any second now."

They broke into a trot along the beach and sprinted up the path
to make it to the porch of the cabin before the shower broke
around them. Layne gasped, falling into the safety of Matt's
steadying arms as they halted on the porch. Wordlessly, Matt
swept Layne up, pushed the door of the cabin open and carried
her into the warmth of the living room. Pushing the door closed,
he took her up the stairs to the master bedroom.

Layne closed her eyes, content to be in his arms. The master
bedroom was large and roomy, with a hand-carved cedar four-
poster bed. A rainbow-colored quilt covered its king-size
expanse. The bed faced the cathedral windows that reminded her
so much of a magic castle made of glittering glass. Matt gently
set her down on the bed, continuing to hold her. Their breaths
mingled, his mouth resting against her cheek. Layne slid her
hands up the expanse of his powerful, sinewy chest. Even beneath
the cotton of his dark blue shirt, she could feel the taut muscles,
and she yearned to savor his body once again.

She lifted her chin, meeting his tender blue eyes. "I want to undress you," she breathed softly. She saw his mouth curve in silent answer, and he leaned over, pressing a kiss to her temple.

"Go ahead..." he invited throatily.

"I've never undressed a man before."

Matt placed his hands over hers as they rested against his chest. The simmering desire in his eyes urged her on, and wordlessly Layne nudged the denim jacket off his broad, capable shoulders. Each grazing touch, each tremor of her hands as she unbuttoned his shirt, sent an unbidden shock of fire dancing through her fingertips. She licked her lips nervously, after taking off his shirt and shoes, as she asked him to lie down on the bed. The jeans proved more difficult and Matt helped her with the snap, giving her a look of silent praise that made her feel warm and confident. It wasn't until she ran her hand across the rough texture of the denim on his hips and felt the hardness of his desire for her that she began to tremble with need.

Layne, barefoot, straddled Matt's legs, tugging and pulling until his jeans finally came off. Her fingers slid along the thickly corded power of his long thighs. He was beautiful, with the gray light of a midafternoon rain shower softening the tightly angular planes of his body. She was locked in his heated gaze as he watched her as a cougar would his next prey. She felt the danger—the explosiveness—that throbbed rawly between them as she shyly reached out, running her hand up his leg.

Matt closed his eyes, his hands knotting at his sides as Layne gently caressed him. He gripped the bedding with his fists, groaning as he allowed Layne to undress him completely. Her touch was provocative, naively sensual, as she continued her hesitant exploration of him, sending a river of molten longing exploding through him.

Layne knelt at Matt's side, drinking in the expression on his face. She offered him a small, tremulous smile as she drew the apricot sweater over her head. And she was shaken by his intake of breath. She had worn no bra, and her breasts, softly shadowed in the half-light as Matt reached for her, were taut with anticipation. Layne was unprepared for the contact of his roughened hands against her sensitized flesh as he cupped her breasts, his thumbs brushing the nipples that hardened beneath his experienced onslaught. A moan of pleasure broke from her lips and Layne swayed into his hands, wanting, needing the pleasure he showered on her.

Matt's hand slid down over her torso, hot fire igniting wherever he grazed her tightening flesh. She threw her head back, a startled cry torn from her as he eased his hands between her thighs. Just the pressure of his palm against the texture of her slacks shook the last vestiges of sanity from her, and she would have lost her balance if Matt hadn't taken quick action. Dizzy with need, overwhelmed by her response, Layne found herself being laid down on the bed. Matt moved next to her, his hand cupping her face. She was trembling, her breath coming in shallow gasps.

"It's all right," he soothed, caressing her cheek. "Here, let me help you out of those slacks."

Each time Matt touched her as he divested her of the slacks and then her lacy panties she felt herself reduced to a state of devouring need. And yet, he seemed to realize what was happening to her. Tears glimmered in her eyes as Matt turned and gazed down at her.

"Matt?" It was a plea, a cry from deep inside her to be completed by him.

He skimmed his hand down her long torso, across the flat of her belly. "Trust me, kitten. Give yourself to me," he said in a low, gritty voice. "I'll help you. Just hold on to me. Hold tight." He eased his hand between her dampened thighs, pressing his palm against her swollen core.

A ragged cry tore from Layne as she gripped Matt, arching against his hand, the pressure mingling with the aching pain that threatened to tear her apart. Her body convulsed and her cries became anguished as he pressed against her straining, feverish body. Suddenly she stiffened and her entire body spasmed, released from the agony of need, the ache miraculously transformed into an explosion of pleasure. Gradually, her clenched hands released him and she sank languidly back into his cradling arms.

Matt removed his hand, gathering Layne back to him, feeling her sweat-slick body tremble in the aftermath of the powerful climax. He pressed her against him, gently caressing away the dampness on her limbs. "You needed that," he whispered, nuzzling into the silk of her ebony hair. "My hot little thoroughbred. My woman who is more woman than she knows…. It's all right, kitten. Just rest…."

His dark words slowed her beating heart and cartwheeling confusion. What had happened? Layne weakly lifted her lashes, bewilderment written in the depths of her gold-flecked eyes. A tender smile lingered on Matt's mouth as he leaned down, kissing her gently. "Matt," she began, thinking her voice sounded very far away, still buoyed on that golden cloud of fulfillment, "what—"

"Six weeks is a long time for some people to wait for good loving," he told her in a gritty voice. "You were hungry and it got the best of you, kitten."

"I—I've never felt like that. I had no control. I was shaking, I needed you so badly…." And Layne gazed up into Matt's strong face.

"It's a special gift two people who really love each other can share. You wanted me so badly that you were coming loose at the hinges." Matt gave her a reassuring smile. "And that's one hell of a compliment to me. When you want me like that, well, it's a priceless gift to both of us."

Layne raised her hand, feeling the tensile strength of his chest and wiry hair beneath her fingertips. "But that isn't fair…. What about you?"

Matt gave her a heated look as he brushed her nipples to hard life beneath his hand. He saw the languor in her expression melt back into smoldering desire once again. "Remember what I said about a tangle of sheets?" he growled, taking small nips down the length of her slender neck. "We have all day, all night. Forever. I'm in no hurry, kitten. All I want to do is share you, make you a part of me, make you mine…."

His words fell over her like liquid fire, and Layne arched shamelessly toward him, pulling his head down upon her aching breasts. She wanted Matt all over again, without even trying to understand what her body was doing that her head didn't know about. None of it mattered. She wanted to satiate herself in the smell, taste and texture of Matt. Nothing more. Nothing less. As he drew her swollen nipple into the heated moisture of his mouth, she gasped, her fingers digging deeply into his shoulders. A shuddering flame exploded through her as he pulled her on top of him.

Layne straddled Matt and felt his strong hands settle on her waist, lifting her, guiding her. The instant he slid into her fiery depths, she arched again, her back like a drawn bow. Her head was thrown back, a murmur of utter pleasure sliding from her parted lips. He was hers; she felt his hardness fill her, thrusting deeply into her, giving, taking until she realized for the first time that heaven surely existed on earth.

Matt's fingers tightened convulsively on Layne's hips and he groaned, thrusting upward, burying himself deeply into her sweet, moist depths. A gurgling sound of joy bubbled from her and he felt himself moving beyond his massive control. He wanted her, how his body screamed for her! Her thighs gripped him tightly and he pushed farther into her as she moved with added sureness against him. Sweat gleamed against his flesh and a fierce growl tore from deep within him as he gave himself to her completely. Seconds later, he felt her tense, and he brought her to another shattering climax. Then Layne swayed and he cushioned her fall forward, bringing her into the safety of his arms, her black hair spilling across his chest as she lay gasping for breath.

"Beautiful," he growled, caressing her damp shoulder, "so beautiful…"

Layne had no idea how long she slept in that position on top of Matt. The physical release had drained her, and she snuggled against the soft hair on his chest, his strong arms wrapped protectively around her, the male scent of him a trigger to her memories.

Later, she woke as he gently moved her and tucked her in

beside him. Only the rainbow quilt being drawn across her made her smile languorously—because that was the way Matt made her feel: like a shimmering rainbow of utter happiness.

Layne stirred sleepily as Matt nudged the tendrils away from her black lashes. Her brown eyes were flecked with drowsiness as she opened them. She raised her hand and touched his jaw with her fingertips. "I didn't mean to sleep."

"Pretty normal reaction under the circumstances. I did, too."

Layne blinked, realizing that the bedroom was bathed in gold. Lifting her head, she gasped. "Oh, Matt…look…" she said with awe as she struggled into a sitting position, her black hair tumbling in wild abandon.

"I've been lying here watching you and the sunset," he confided quietly, running his hand lightly down her arm. The quilt had fallen away, revealing the sculptured beauty of her breasts, torso and waist. Matt glanced up at her, reveling in her discovery. "It's like this all the time here."

Layne had never seen such an incredible sunset. The gray clouds had disappeared, taking the rain with them. Instead, the light blue sky was dotted with a few clouds along the horizon, lined with the blinding brilliance of the setting sun. Joy suffused her heart, and Layne surrendered herself to the power and texture of Matt's returning ardor, the flame of longing igniting easily between them.

Matt finally rolled over on his back and urged Layne to rest on top of him. He smiled up at her, his heated gaze moving downward as he felt her nipples hardening against his chest. "I think you want me again," he teased, caressing the curve of her breast.

Layne purred, closing her eyes, allowing the full measure of his touch to arouse her. She pressed her hips daringly against his. "I think the feeling's mutual," she whispered, nuzzling his cheek and kissing him hotly.

Matt sobered. "But it's a hell of a lot more than physical need we're talking about. It's love. And with love, all the gates fly open and all the walls we've hidden behind come tumbling down. Because we trust each other."

She stretched forward, kissing the tip of Matt's nose. "I do trust you."

"You were willing to risk your life for me. I'd say that's the ultimate proof of trust."

"I would have," Layne responded gravely, remembering Kang, then the night she and Matt had drifted on that wooden plank in the South China Sea. "You saved *my* life."

He patted her rear. "We're even. Hungry?"

"Starved!"

Matt grinned and gently deposited Layne beside him. The bedroom was flooded with the dying rays of the sun, the warmth of the reddish cedar coming alive all around them. It was bliss. Utter bliss, he thought, drowning in Layne's loving gaze. And she was perfection to him. Sheer perfection. The opal gleamed softly at her throat, reflecting the joy in her eyes. He touched the stone gently. "Michael was right—the opal has brought us luck...and happiness." He saw Layne nod in agreement, her topaz eyes velvet with love. "Come on," he urged, "let's take a shower together and then I'll fix you a 'Welcome home to Oregon' meal."

Except for the dancing firelight from the huge stone fireplace in the living room, there was no other light in the cabin. Layne curled her fingers around the stem of the crystal glass, watching the bubbles from the champagne rise to burst at the surface of the golden liquid. The meal of freshly caught sea bass, steamed broccoli and a garden salad had been delicious. And it had been fun sharing the cooking duties in the kitchen. Matt remained in his dark blue terry-cloth robe and she in her apricot one as they relaxed before the fire. He lay on the sheepskin rug, stretched out like a big cat, his blue eyes hooded as he looked upon her, resting his head on one hand. He took a sip of the champagne.

"I used to sit in front of this fireplace, Layne, and dream."

Layne sat cross-legged, her hips nestled against his thighs. As she looked down at Matt, her heart ached with love. "What kind of dreams?" she probed gently.

"Future dreams. I used to wonder if this cabin would ever ring with the laughter of two people. Or if another woman would ever share my life." Matt's voice softened. "I tried to imagine who she might be—what she'd look like. Would she cry with joy over the beauty of a splendid sunrise or a dying sunset? Would she find life in the simplest things like a broken abalone shell washed up on the beach after a storm…." His eyes moved to meet hers. "My future is here. Now. It's with you, Layne."

Tears glimmered in her eyes. Her fingers knotted around the stem of the crystal. "I'm not perfect, Matt. You've seen that. I feel like a little girl in some ways."

"I don't want a perfect woman, kitten. And your awareness of yourself is something that any man in his right mind would die to share with you." He ran his hand across her arm. "I'm looking forward to making love with you on the mountain, down on the beach, sharing all those firsts with you. Things that we can press between the pages of our hearts." His fingers sought hers and he squeezed them. "Marry me, Layne. Not because of what you aren't, but because of what you are—a sweet, sensitive woman who carries a faith in the world around in her heart. A woman whose courage is breathtaking and whose ability to love brings me to tears."

Her fingers tightened on his forearm. "What about your Company job?"

Matt brushed her temple with his lips. "I turned in my resignation the day we got back from that mission."

Layne twisted around, disbelief etched in her widening eyes. "You did?"

"Yes."

"Why?"

"I figured if I was going to marry you, one dangerous job was enough. I didn't need to compound your worry by having two of them." He allowed the hint of a grin to leak through his serious expression. "And testing is infinitely safer than being with the Company." He saw Layne's entire face glow with joy. "Can I get a more enthusiastic yes from you now, soon-to-be Mrs. Layne Talbot?"

With a cry of happiness, Layne threw her arms around Matt. Their shared laughter danced through the cedar cabin, making it vibrate with joy. Gently, Matt lowered her to the rug. His smile overwhelmed her, and she could do nothing but drink in huge draughts of their shared time in each other's arms. The firelight danced across the planes of his face—a face molded by experiences both harsh and kind. He had been through so much; and so had she. Layne's smile dissolved as she caressed his cheek.

"We were like two wounded animals, you and I. You had lost Jenny and I'd been nearly destroyed by Brad. We were both hurting so much, Matt. It's a miracle we've survived to love again. To love each other."

He agreed and took a small box from the pocket of his robe. "But we did it. We're living proof that if you just hang on long enough and do what feels right, things will straighten out." Matt lifted his head, and his voice was strained as he spoke: "I never thought I'd love again, Layne. I had already prepared myself to be alone for the rest of my life." His blue eyes glimmered with a caressing warmth as he met her gaze. "And then you came into my life." He opened the box and his grandmother's rings sparkled in the firelight. "I knew these belonged to you even if we never did get married, Layne," he said, slipping the engagement ring on her left hand. "You're the only woman who lingers in my mind." Matt shared a tender smile with her. "You know, I think my grandmother was a pretty wise old lady."

Layne stared down at the engagement ring. This time it was for real; this time it was for the rest of their lives. "I remember thinking the first time you slipped the rings on my hand, that I wished I really could be your wife."

Matt drew her back into his arms so that she could rest her head on his shoulder. "And I'll be a real husband to you, kitten. I'm going to enjoy watching you make those discoveries…."

Layne cupped his chin and drew his mouth down to hers. She molded her lips against his, the sweetness of the kiss lingering between them as she drew inches away from him. "Discover me…" she murmured.

"Every day of our lives," Matt promised.

* * * * *

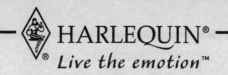

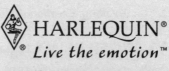

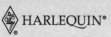

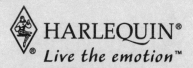

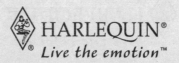